ECLIPSE
THE
SKIES

ECLIPSE THE SKIES

MAURA MILAN

ALBERT WHITMAN AND COMPANY
CHICAGO, ILLINOIS

Library of Congress Cataloging-in-Publication
data is on file with the publisher.

Text copyright © 2019 by Maura Milan
First published in the United States of America
in 2019 by Albert Whitman & Company
ISBN 978-0-8075-3638-4 (hardcover)
ISBN 978-0-8075-3640-7 (ebook)

Printed in the United States of America
10 9 8 7 6 5 4 3 2 1 LB 24 23 22 21 20 19

Cover artwork copyright © 2019 by Craig White
Cover model: Jessika Van
Design by Ellen Kokontis and Aphee Messer

For more information about Albert Whitman & Company,
visit our website at www.albertwhitman.com.

100 Years of Albert Whitman & Company
Celebrate with us in 2019!

For my mom, the toughest
and most caring person I know

CHAPTER 1
KNIVES

KNIVES ADAMS drummed his fingers against the top of the brushed-steel counter, tapping at a ring-shaped circle of dried archnol. He scanned the room. It was filled with travelers from across the All Black, their faces weary from drifting and their eyes drooped from drink.

His father had just left Aphelion after appointing Knives as headmaster, filling the hole that Bastian had left. Knives had endured a grueling week of following the general's footsteps down the halls, and he knew he had to get out as well, to cleanse himself of everything that was his father. A trip to Myth was an obvious choice. Once he returned, Aphelion would be as it was. Crumbling. A mess. But without his father's orders echoing down the halls.

Knives liked it on Myth. It was so different from Aphelion and from the Commonwealth's capital star system, Rigel Kentaurus, where he grew up. The ventilation on the space station was cheap and shoddy, perfume mixed in to mask the suffocating odor of recycled air, but there wasn't enough freshener in the universe to hide that distinct smell. He breathed in the chemical potpourri of uranium vapors and burned-up engine grease. It was the smell of Dead Spacers, of Drifters, of anyone who spent more time on a ship than on land.

The last time he was on Myth, he had almost gotten his ass kicked, but this time he would be more careful, especially with all the white hearts pinned on people's suits. Einn's supporters were clearly patrons of this place. No matter what he heard in the shuffle around him, even if it bothered him, he would absolutely, definitely not get involved. He was here for one thing.

A girl.

"Look who's back." The bartender sashayed over and rested her elbows on the countertop. She leaned in so that his whole world became her.

Knives angled his head, his eyes flicking from the curl of her dark eyelashes to the part of her lips. She was as beautiful as he remembered.

"What brings you all the way out here, pretty Bug?" The bartender took a sip from her vapor stick and blew the trail of smoke out so that it spiraled all around him.

Through the haze, his eyes locked onto hers. "I've been wondering what your name is."

"All this time?" She leaned in, flipping her head to the side so that he could get a view of her neck. Her light-brown skin looked soft, smooth. "If you want to know my name, you're going to have to try harder than that."

He angled his head so that he could get a glimpse of the sapphire in her eyes. "Should we go somewhere more private?"

* * *

Her fingers slipped through his, and he ran his thumb against her buttery-soft wrist up to the calluses on her palm. She led him through back galleys, shooting him coquettish looks after every other step, and he felt heat rush into his face at the way she made him feel. There was a part of him that wanted to stop her, to pull his arm around her waist and feel the warmth of her cheek against his.

They passed a group of breakers, still dressed in their mining armor, leaning against the wall. They were a loud lot, yammering about the increase in uranium costs and the current market for scrap. One of them, a heavyset man with a thick beard, made eye contact with them as they passed. Knives heard his voice, scratchy through the everlasting hum of the refurbished space station. "Where you going? Can we join?"

"No," the bartender snapped without looking back. "Not allowed."

The breakers chuckled, hooting to each other about what Knives was in for, but their words barely registered. His mind was singularly focused on what would happen at the end of their journey through the back halls of Myth. Knives reached up to let his fingers fly through the waves of her hair. She guided him to a door at the end of a long stretch of hallway, then turned to face him, her back resting gently against the doorframe.

"These are my quarters," she said, a breath of nervousness rising in her voice.

"So are you going to tell me your name?" Knives asked.

Her gaze met his, her eyes open with a strange vulnerability that didn't match the metal and steel of Myth. With quickened breath, she smoothed her hands up his chest until they circled around the back of his neck. Her chin tilted, and her lips parted in invitation. "My name's Eve," she said.

He smiled at her, and she went up on her tip-toes and kissed him, her lip lacquer sweet upon his tongue.

From past experiences, he knew every kiss had its own unique flavor. His first kiss had reminded him of hot chocolate at nighttime. While this kiss—this kiss was of smoke, and salt, and need. Very different from another girl's.

He broke their embrace, trying to hide the confusion in his eyes. She nodded back to her room. "You want to come in?"

He faltered. Despite the grime on her cheeks, there was something innocent in the way she stood before him. A part of him felt guilty for what he was about to do.

He placed a hand on the wall so she had nowhere else to turn but to him. As he leaned in, his mouth came to her ear. "Yes," he breathed, and he felt her body stiffen. He could see her pulse quicken underneath the skin along her neck.

Eve rolled her body to the side, her elbow pressing against a sensor on the wall. With the screech of metal grinding along unoiled rails, the door behind them inched open, and she pulled him into the darkness.

But he could feel her, and he could hear her. And his ears perked at another sound. Of the doors shutting behind them.

That was his cue. Knives stiffened, detaching himself gently from Eve's embrace.

With a click, a light came on, blooming like nightshade

in the corner of the room. Someone else was there, waiting for them.

Eve's eyes pulsed from him to the figure sitting on her desk, her lithe fingers curled upon the switch of the rusting table lamp.

Eve immediately reached for the pistol at her side. His fingers clamped around her wrist, stopping her. Her expression shifted as the realization settled upon her: she'd been had.

Knives pulled his gaze away so that it rested on the person sitting on top of the desk in the corner, one leg propped on the plastic tabletop. He took in the curves of her familiar face and the mischief twisted behind her grin. His eyes locked upon hers, and she nodded, satisfied by his trickery. He was here for one thing.

A girl. *This* girl.

He'd done his part, and now it was all up to her.

Ia Cōcha leaned forward out of the shadows. "Hello, Eve."

CHAPTER 2
IA

IA DODGED THE FIRST BLOW, missing the swipe of Eve's nails by only a few centimeters.

Eve snarled, then centered a punch. Ia grabbed her wrist, misdirecting her movement so that Eve stumbled to the side.

"You're not a fighter," Ia said. "Stay down."

Eve bared her teeth. "I should have known that he was yours."

Ia's gaze snapped to Knives, who raised his eyebrows in response. She rolled her eyes and jerked her chin to the door. "Keep watch outside."

Knives nodded, giving Eve one last look, and for a long moment, Ia wondered what really had happened between them.

Once Knives left, Ia crouched before Eve.

"What do you want, Cōcha?" Eve hissed.

"Information," Ia said. She reached out, wiping a trail of blood falling from a split in Eve's lip. "I need to know what's happening in my territories. I noticed there are a lot more White Hearts around this entire hub."

Shoving Ia off her, Eve sat up. "Go back and cuddle with your Bug," she said, nodding to the door. "We all know you joined them. Dead Space is no longer yours."

Ia looked down, cheeks red with rage and embarrassment. She was Ia Cōcha. Sovereign of Dead Space, Blood Wolf of the Skies.

Traitor to her own people.

After everything that had happened this month, Ia had known they would desert her. But she didn't realize how much it would sting.

Eve took a puff off her vaporizer. A plume of smoke curled upward, hanging in the heavy air. Her eyes flashed in the low light as she looked Ia up and down. "After you left, there was a hole. An absence of hope in the already-vacuous All Black. But Einn came, and people had something to believe in again. A fight. A purpose. They wanted something to hold onto. It just happened to be him."

Ia sat on the couch, balancing the tip of her chin on her knees, surveying Eve's lean legs sprawled across the dusty floor. "And what about you?"

"I've never taken sides, Ia. You know that."

"Yes, but why do I have a feeling that you'll at least play favorites." Ia had heard all about the women and men that Eve had been romantically involved with. Einn and Eve were together on and off for a few years. Eve was even part of their crew for a time, but not after the breakup. Starships had more space than the average fighter jet, but no matter where you were, you could still hear every joke, every moan, every insult thrown behind closed doors.

Ia's lips curled upward in a smirk. "You hate me, but I know you hate my brother more."

Eve rolled her eyes. "What do you want?"

Ever since Ia had agreed to a truce with Aphelion, her days had been nothing but meetings with that damn general. Ia Cōcha was once her own entity, feared and unknown. A dangerous, devouring mystery that no one dared to seek out. Now she was nothing more than the pieces of information the Olympus Commonwealth wanted to carve out of her head. They wanted to understand. They wanted to strategize. They wanted to win.

But it wasn't about victory for Ia, about setting in motion a change of events or protecting what had already been built. For her, it was very, very simple. She wanted to beat her brother. The brother she'd once loved, once trusted more than anyone.

Until he tried to kill her.

After session after session of sitting through the general's endless barrage of questions and getting no useful information in return, she'd quickly realized she needed *more* than meetings. She needed outside help.

Ia looked at Eve, her eyes catching the light. "I want you to send a message for me."

CHAPTER 3

BRINN

BRINN STEPPED OUT of the bathroom, the brisk air from the bedroom chilling the damp skin on her cheeks. Since the Armada slaver attack over two weeks ago, the temperature controls had been on the fritz. That included both the water and room settings. For the time being, her showers were very cold and very quick.

She grabbed a few sweatshirts and pulled them on over her base layer. Ia was on a mission with Knives somewhere, but she hadn't said what it was. She rarely talked about what Olympus wanted from her and what her plans were, but Brinn could tell there was always something going on behind those sharp, black eyes. She wished her friend would tell her what it was more often.

As she walked around the empty room, Brinn heard the soft buzzing of her holowatch, which she had taken off before her shower. She scurried about, tossing everything to the side until eventually finding her holo underneath her messy bedsheets.

The ID read Mom. She answered.

A holoscreen floated in front of her, displaying her mother's face, elegant yet softened with wrinkles around the eyes and lips. Her navy-blue hair was tied in a neat, tight bun.

Her mother nodded stiffly. It was her way of saying hello. "Your hair's growing out nicely."

Brinn dragged her fingers self-consciously through her fine, downy hair, shaved short right before she and Ia fought the Armada. It was an undercoat that was never seen, but now there it was. For almost her entire life, she had dyed her hair brown to fit in, to be seen as a Citizen and hide from her Tawny heritage. But now her natural navy-blue hair was growing out. And it would keep growing, until the navy strands hit her chin, her shoulders, the middle of her back. There was no way she would return to that life. To hiding who she was.

Dying her hair had been a source of contention between Brinn and her mom for so long.

It was so strange to speak with her like this. Because now they were the same.

"How are things going at home?" she asked.

"There are more protests on the street," her mom said. "That's actually why I called. I need you to talk to your brother."

Since Brinn had last spoken to him, her brother's eyes had been opened to a movement taking over the refugee communities back home. With the Sanctuary Act on the chopping block and refugees of the Uranium War in danger of losing their homes, Tawnies, Dvvinn, and other integrated communities raised their voices in protest. At the same time, Commonwealth Citizens rose up like a wall that refused to move. They wanted the refugees out. And while Brinn and her family weren't technically refugees, the political left was crumbling, and it was possible that their Citizenship could be revoked. Who knew how long they would actually be safe? Brinn understood why her brother wanted to stand with those crowds, to raise his fist and scream.

Because things weren't right.

And what about her? She was training to work for a government who was standing idly by, whose values, she realized, were a sham. *Of Progress. Of Prosperity. Of Proficiency.* She had seen none of that, not since she stepped foot on Aphelion.

Yet she was still here. She shook her head, trying to stop her thoughts.

She glanced back at her mother and took a deep breath. "I can't stop him from doing what he wants to do, Mom."

"You've always been good at looking out for him."

"Fine." Brinn scratched the fuzz at the back of her head. "Let me see him."

She watched the screen as her mom walked throughout their house, and warm feelings of home came flooding back to her.

Finally, her brother's face was on the display. His hair, like hers, had been cut to show off its true color. His lips were pulled tight as if he knew what she wanted to talk about.

"I'm going," he said.

"Are you sure that's a good idea?" Brinn asked. "The news says they're gonna start using pulse cannons."

"Let them. You know that what's happening is wrong, Brinn."

She knew. She didn't even want to hide it on her face, and that was enough to bring light to his eyes.

"You should be back home, marching with me. With us," he whispered.

"I can't fly back like that, Faren. I have my studies. I have responsibilities."

Faren's expression narrowed. "Why? Why are you still there? After everything that's happened..."

Brinn couldn't give him an answer because she didn't have one. Those were the same questions that ran through her head when her eyes fluttered open every morning. She looked at the walls of her dorm room, which had been smooth and pristine when she first arrived and were now warped and damaged from all that had transpired since then. Would she wait until they were fully cracked open before she finally left?

She wasn't ready to leave Aphelion. Not quite yet. So she could only offer her brother a few words. She hoped that would be enough.

"Please, Faren," Brinn said. "Be careful."

Faren looked at her, his eyes the same shade of gray but somehow clearer than her own. "I will," he said, and they said their goodbyes.

Brinn sank onto her bed, resting her face in her palms. She hadn't told him to stop. She hadn't told him to stay home. Because she was proud of her brother. That was true.

But she also wanted him to be safe. And the only real way to ensure that was for the government to keep the Sanctuary Act in place.

She decided to put her trust in her government one last time.

Right at that moment, the lights cut out.

CHAPTER 4
KNIVES

KNIVES SAT IN THE PILOT SEAT of his 504 Kaiken, staring out into the expanse, the stars in the distance blinking at him. They only made the silence more obvious. Even without looking back, he knew Ia was slumped in her seat. She was sulking. It emanated off her like a dry heat.

"You got what you needed?"

"Keep this under wraps, Knives," she reminded him. "You can't go reporting that we ran off to Myth."

"Of course. You think I want to hear the general screaming into my ear?"

Ia quieted at the mention of General Adams. Ever since she'd found out the true identity of Knives's father, things between them had been strained. But was that really why she was giving him the cold shoulder right now?

"It was nice getting off campus," Knives said, trying to lighten the mood. "We should do it again."

"I'll make sure to invite Eve," snapped Ia.

He stabbed his finger down on the autopilot button and swiveled his chair around to face her. "What does that mean?"

Ia shrugged. "You seemed comfortable with her."

"You told me to get her into her room. I wasn't going to lead her at gunpoint in a space station filled with—"

"With what? Dead Space murk?"

"No. That's not what I meant. Dead Spacers don't like Citizens. You would know."

Her eyes narrowed. "And I still do."

"Fine," Knives muttered to himself. He turned his chair back around and gripped his steering wheel. She was trying to start a fight. About anything. Everything. There was no point talking to her, not until she cooled down.

He flew the rest of the way in silence, pretending to pilot when in actuality the navigation systems were still set to auto. He took the time to think, to seethe, to simmer. All he wanted was for things to be calm between them, to have her stand beside him and smile, but since the attack on Aphelion, it sometimes felt like they were still on opposite sides of a chasm.

They spoke all the time, but they weren't actually talking. Any mention of the fact that his father was the general was always a conversation killer.

And they never brought up *that kiss*.

Yet it was all he ever thought about. The taste of her lips, the brush of her hair against his cheek, the pull of her fingers, closer and closer.

He shook his head.

The problems were on the table, and they were still there,

looming like big, clunky wultakus in the room.

The Kaiken cleared the Birra Gate, and Knives's eyes focused on a white planet, its atmosphere swirling with angry gray clouds. He disengaged the autopilot system and grabbed the steering wheel, bringing the Kaiken into its descent.

They were home.

The Kaiken rumbled from the chaos of the atmosphere until finally it broke through the clouds. Below them was the Piro Range, a string of mountains formed in AG-9's northern hemisphere. He spotted a curve in the lengthy chasm underneath. A flurry of snow ripped right through. He needed to find the right lull, or the Kaiken would be smashed into the side of the rock.

"Are you sure you don't want me to do it?" Ia piped up.

He gritted his teeth and refrained from answering her. Instead, he focused on the snow, whipping back and forth on the current of wind. He saw an opening. He cut all the thrusters, and the Kaiken dove through. As it cleared, they felt the force of wind against metal, and he heard Ia groan in annoyance. He knew what she was thinking. *I would have done better.*

He pulled the steering wheel toward his chest, leveling the Kaiken out before reigniting the mid thrusters built into the wings. They crested around the curve of the ravine to where the flight deck opened up, but instead of seeing the flare of the entrance force field and the lights inlaid along the tarmac, there was nothing. Just darkness.

"What on Ancient Earth?" Knives's heart rate spiked within his chest, and memories of their recent visit from the Armada burned into his mind. Was it another attack? So soon?

He tapped on his holowatch and brought up a stream to Comms. No answer. He disconnected and redialed, but after several tries, there was still no response.

Ia leaned over his shoulder to get a better view. Her breathing was shallow, edged with panic. "If something's happened, we need to get in there."

But it was impossible that something would have happened. Not with all the new security measures in place. Since the slaver attack, RSF had placed motion detectors and mine bombs—cloaked with jamming transmissions and painted so black they were undetectable to the human eye—around the perimeter of the entire system. The Birra Gate itself was under heavy lock and key. Only high-level Star Force personnel could get in and out. Now that Knives was temporary headmaster of Aphelion, he was one of the few people who actually had access.

No one would ever be able to get in, he told himself. But he flew a little faster.

As he landed on the tarmac, lights from the wings of the Kaiken probed the darkness, spilling over the line of training jets parked along the flight deck's wall. He powered down the engines and waited for the hatch of the cockpit to slide open. Before he could hop out, he peered down the ladder.

Professor Meneva Patel, one of the youngest faculty members at Aphelion, was already waiting for him, her arms crossed, annoyance written across her face. Her white lab coat was wrinkled from a full day's wear, but in no way had it been ripped, burned, or shredded by an incoming enemy force.

"Everything okay?" he asked, to be sure.

Her expression remained the same. Aggravated.

"The power's out," Meneva said. "Again."

CHAPTER 5
BRINN

BRINN TARVER SAT in the corner of the canteen. It was so dark that she could detect only the silhouettes of the cadets around her. They were sequestered there during the power outage to keep everyone safe.

Most of the mess left by the Armada attack had been long cleaned up, but signs of it remained. Blast marks still scorched the surface of some of the tables, and the metal floors were dinged from the fallen debris.

The other cadets were seated around the tables in small clusters. After what happened with the Armada, a lot of them had transferred out. Including Angie. It wasn't her choice, Angie had explained to Brinn the day she was scheduled to leave. Her father had ordered her transfer to another academy. He could barely deal with Ia also attending Aphelion, so the slaver attack was the last straw.

Sitting there, Brinn suddenly missed Angie's relentless string of observations, about how stiflingly boring the lectures were, about some dashing boy she was paired with in comms classes that day. Brinn had tried to tune them all out before, too busy reading over materials for her next class or worrying about Ia, but now that Angie was gone, Aphelion felt a bit more empty.

She knew everyone else noticed it, too. The usual chatter in the canteen had been replaced by a tension that clung silently to the air. The slaver attack had changed *everything*. Before, they lived behind a glossy sheen. It tricked their eyes from seeing what was really out there. All that danger, all that destruction and loss. And now that the sheen had dissipated, none of the parades and fanfare could persuade Brinn otherwise: their world wasn't as perfect as they thought.

Angie had told her that together they would fix all of the problems of the Commonwealth from the ground up, starting with Aphelion. But in the end, the promise they made to each other was just words. She didn't blame Angie. Maybe it wouldn't have been worth it anyway.

"Cadet Tarver," a voice called from behind her.

Brinn turned to see Professor Patel coming toward her, using a light screen to illuminate her path. Her long, black hair was swept into a tight knot at the top of her head. Brinn stood and tipped her head in acknowledgment. Professor Patel wasn't a ranking officer, but she still deserved respect.

The professor looked her up and down, her eyes weary from endless hours of work and lack of sleep.

"Follow me," Professor Patel said. "It's going to be another one of those nights."

"And what kind is that?"

The professor sighed. "Long."

* * *

Brinn looked up at the uranium core, its burning blue luminescence almost hot enough to sear the skin off her forehead. The ventilation pipes latticed across the ceiling groaned noisily. The Armada's attack had laid waste to most of the academy grounds. Fortunately, the structure of the core room remained intact, but the wiring and computer systems were a bit more fragile—nearly the entire system had shorted out. Only about 15 percent of the available circuitry was still usable. The core had an immense amount of power, but now there was no way to direct it. Hence, the rolling blackouts.

Because of the power issues, the protecting force fields that surrounded the core were barely at full capacity. Brinn studied the shimmering edges where the holes were located. She'd return to the surface with slight radiation burns on her cheek, but with enough rest, she would heal quickly due to her Tawny ability to regenerate.

Since security was tight, supply routes were also limited, and they didn't have enough radiation pills to go around. So Professor Patel had sent Brinn down there alone while she handled the generator units above the surface.

Well, not exactly alone.

"Is this what people consider idling?" Aaron stood a few meters away, observing her. He was a borg, constructed of metal alloys, durable synthetic plastic, and fiber wires, so the radiation had no effect on him. His facial structure had been completely repaired after the attack, as had his other malfunctioning operating systems, but his grumbling attitude was pretty much the same as it'd always been.

"I'm not idling," she answered as she walked the lines of panels tiling the ground. "I'm searching."

She edged around the core reactor, following it in a circle all the way to the back, and then stopped. The toes of her boots met a yellow square stenciled along the edges of one particular panel.

Aaron peeked over her shoulder. "That looks sealed shut."

"It isn't." Her eyes scanned the panel until she located a notch at one of the edges. Even with a lever in place, she wasn't strong enough to lift 40-centimeter thick vinnidium steel. Brinn turned and held out the crowbar for Aaron to take. "That's why you're here."

Aaron rolled his eyes, and Brinn wondered why Professor Patel had programmed him to react like that in this type of situation. He grabbed the bar and slotted the angled end into the notch. With no difficulty, he hoisted the heavy sheet of metal paneling off to the side.

Brinn crouched and gazed at the web of wires crisscrossing from one end of the panel to the other. It looked like a mess, but there was order in that madness. Half of the wires dead-ended at fried circuits, so she unplugged them, quickly rerouting everything so that the power could be redirected.

Her fingers were on the last wire when she paused. The cable was frayed almost all the way through.

Brinn unplugged the severed wire, swapping it out with a brand-new one and closing the circuit. A few bulbs lit up above, their sterile white glow casting an eerie sheen across the room. She had managed to patch part of the grid, but there was still damage elsewhere.

She looked at the frayed piece of wire in her hand.

"What do you think could have done this?" she asked Aaron.

He stared at the damaged cable. "Rats."

She raised an eyebrow. "Rats found their way through nearly half a meter of vinnidium steel?"

"Those pests can get into anything," Aaron said. "There's a reason why they survived past Ancient Earth. Not even cockroaches could do that."

He was right. Rats had evolved to the point where they could survive space travel. They planet-hopped from system to system, making their own colonies among the stars. She felt the jagged edges of the exposed fiber, pressing the sharp points against the pad of her thumb. Well, if there were rats in here, that meant there was a bigger problem to deal with. The core room wasn't as secure as everyone thought. Somewhere in this room, there was a weakness, an opening for mysterious things to come in and out. And take. She made note to tell the headmaster. It was better to be safe than sorry, and she already knew what "sorry" was like.

"Are we done?" Aaron asked, interrupting her train of thought.

Brinn glanced back at the bright uranium core, her eyes narrowing at the sight. "Yeah," she said. "For now."

* * *

She walked back to her dorm room and found Ia hunched over and drying her hair, a tangle of thick, wet black. Brinn couldn't help but notice the tattooed feathers inked dark on Ia's forearms, like smoldering ash on golden skin.

"How was the water?" Brinn asked.

Ia glanced up through the folds of the light-gray towel. "Tepid."

Brinn's lips quirked, remembering her own shower earlier. "At least tepid is better than freezing."

Ia tossed the towel to the floor and then sat on her bed. She nodded at an empty spot next to her, and Brinn sat comfortably on Ia's ruffled blankets. There used to be a clear division between their sides of the room, but now they moved into each other's halves freely.

Ia's muscular arms fished through her pack. "I got us something," she said.

She pulled out an amber bottle, a dark liquid sloshing within the curve of its walls. Ia popped the stopper at its mouth and handed the bottle over for Brinn to drink.

"What is it?"

Ia smirked. "The worst drink you will ever taste in your life."

"Then why drink it?"

"Because I think we deserve to relax," Ia said. "Just for a little bit."

Brinn sniffed at the contents of the bottle, sweetness wafting to her nose, but when she took a gulp, it was like acid in her throat.

"It burns," she gasped.

Ia laughed. "It's supposed to." She grabbed the bottle and took a swig, sticking her tongue out after she swallowed.

Brinn howled in giddy laughter. It was something that she couldn't control. Sometimes, she felt the old Brinn rearing her head, holding herself back from her emotions, but not now. It was strange that the most dangerous girl in the known galaxies could do this to her. Even though the room was dark. And the universe out there was grim. At least they could still smile.

They spent the next hour talking, about this and that, catching up but never really. Ia rarely spoke about her meetings with the general, and Brinn didn't mention her worries about her brother. It was a time to talk about things that could make them giggle, and to ignore the dark stains in their hearts.

As the drink started to dig its claws into her emotions, the merriment turned to silence, and Brinn's thoughts overtook her. She was faced with the slight shifts inside her that had taken place over time. Most of all, there was this strange sense of disappointment. In herself. In the Commonwealth. In her place in life. It emptied her out completely, and the archnol wasn't enough to help her forget. She was alone with these thoughts. More than anything, she wanted Ia to ask her how she felt about these things, but she never did.

Ia stood and adjusted the blankets so that Brinn would be warm. Brinn squinted at her, Ia's face hazy in her eyes from all the drink.

"You should get some rest," Ia said. "We have to prepare. Tomorrow, we train."

Brinn raised her eyebrows, barely comprehending. She fell asleep to the sight of Ia sitting at the center table, her eyes focused in the distance. As if she was trying desperately hard to see what was coming for them.

CHAPTER 6

IA

IA GRABBED BRINN'S WRIST, and with a quick shift of her weight, she threw her friend's body across the training ring. "You're so bad at defending yourself. Remember your angles." They had been training for almost three weeks now, and Tarver still hadn't improved.

The gym was empty except for the two of them. There wasn't enough power to light the whole space, just the spotlights flaring hot over their ring. There wasn't even enough power to run a fighting simulation. They were forced to train fist to fist, without the protection of impact gloves. Around them, the light trailed off quickly into the darkness so it looked as if they existed only in this little circle of the world.

Right now, it wasn't a safe place to be.

Brinn rolled onto her knees. She rubbed at her side, casting Ia the most vicious of glares. But Ia was immune. She could survive those insufferable looks, steeped with annoyance and aggravation. They were easy to deflect, but a knife to the throat or a pistol pointed right at the head—those were not. Those left you dead. She needed Brinn to understand that.

"I'm not always going to be there to protect you," Ia said.

Brinn stood, stretching the ache away from her limbs. "I can't win against your brother. There's no contest."

She pointed a finger at Brinn. "You need to get that type of thinking out of your head. You might be smaller than he is, but that doesn't mean you can't beat him." Even from this distance, Ia had to lift her chin to look at Tarver. For the most part, Ia's height kept her at a disadvantage, but in small, close spaces, she was capable of a wealth of damage.

"If you haven't noticed"—Brinn motioned to the oppressive darkness around them—"the power system is on the fritz. We've got a rat infestation in the core room. Not to mention what's going on out there, outside the academy. There's strife in the territories. My brother is out protesting in the streets."

It was the first that Ia had heard of Faren in a while, but not the first time she'd heard that heaviness in Brinn's voice. It had been there when Faren went to the hospital for defending a refugee student several months ago. That worry.

"Civil unrest, protests—none of that matters," Ia said. Brinn's eyes flashed in quiet anger.

But Ia ignored it, because there was something larger going on in the universe. After Einn infiltrated the Fugue testing grounds, the Olympus Commonwealth had decided to turn everything there into scrap—including GodsEye, the structure that Headmaster Bastian Weathers had been developing. The general was keeping quiet about what exactly this structure did. The only thing Ia had gathered was that it was a unique gate system of some kind. Unique enough for her brother to find interest in it. Einn had taken the knowledge he'd acquired at Fugue to build his own model. Ia knew there were holes in his research; otherwise she would have seen his replica's power by now. Einn needed someone to finish it.

Her eyes focused on the friend she had to protect.

"My brother is coming for you, Tarver. You've seen Knives. He still has scars from their last encounter. Not to mention what happened to the previous headmaster, who, I don't know if you've forgotten, is very much dead in the ground right now."

Brinn's face twisted. "Stop lecturing me," she said sharply. "I'm not you. I don't have the same type of survival training you have from being out in the All Black for so many years."

Ia's gaze seared through the gap. There were times they got along, but there were tense moments like this that she couldn't explain. She thought that after what had happened with the Armada, they would understand each other more, but that wasn't the case. Ia massaged her temples and stepped back.

"You don't have to be me," Ia said. "You just have to be clever. And I already know you're good at that. I'm just giving you more tools to survive."

Across the room, someone cleared his throat. Ia squinted her eyes, trying to pick out a face in the darkness. She saw him. The Nema wannabe. He even looked like the famed captain with dark brown skin and hair buzzed neatly against his head.

"Good. You're here," she said. Liam Vyking stepped to the

red line that marked the edge of the ring. He was as broad-shouldered as ever and had maybe even grown a few more centimeters in the past month.

"What is he doing here?" Brinn asked.

Ia waved for Liam to join them and tried to ignore the growing blush on Brinn's face. "You both need the training."

Liam flashed a quick smile at Brinn before turning his attention back to Ia. Ia had sparred against Liam before, so she knew he was an adequate fighter, although he still had to work on his stance, his technique. But it wouldn't hurt to have more muscle when it came to protecting Brinn. Ia knew Einn's fighting style, so she could teach people how to defend themselves against his tactics.

She pointed to the two of them. "Square off."

Brinn shot Ia a mortified look, her mouth open as if she wanted to say something, but Liam had already taken his place in the ring.

"Now what?" he asked, waiting for Ia's instruction.

"Attack," her voice rose out, ringing over the hum of the spotlight above. Liam threw a hesitant glance over at Brinn.

Brinn quickly shook her head. "Let's get it over with."

Liam lunged, his arms spread open, the length nearly inescapable from each broad palm to the next. Brinn hopped back, which made Ia frown.

"You need to be within striking distance to take him down." Ia's voice came out cold, stern.

"I'm trying," Brinn gasped between hurried breaths.

Liam lunged again. Tarver brought her forearm up in an attempt to keep Vyking at bay, but his weight was too much.

"Watch your angles," Ia screamed. "Keep your elbow up. Don't lift your shoulder."

But it was already too late. Tarver's arm collapsed inward, and soon Liam had Brinn in a stronghold.

Ia shook her head in disappointment and then clapped her hands to stop the fight.

Liam loosened his arms and stepped back sheepishly. Brinn avoided his gaze, her face flushed redder than even the core radiation burns left on her cheeks.

That wasn't good enough, Ia wanted to scream at her. She shook her head. They really had no idea. Of course they wouldn't. Only a handful people knew that the crimes on her record were all planned by Einn, minus the ambush at K-5 Neptune. That gruesome death count was all on her shoulders. Not to mention he'd almost killed her. It was hard to acknowledge defeat, but it was there, staring right at her. If she fought her brother again...

Ia shuddered.

Taking Liam's place in the ring, she lowered herself into a fighting stance. "I'm not going to hold back," Ia said, her eyes narrowing at Brinn. "Now, are you ready?"

CHAPTER 7
KNIVES

KNIVES WAS HUNGRY. Why was he always on the verge of starvation every time one of these faculty meetings was called to session?

He pressed his lips together, trying not to conjure thoughts of semicrunchy ramen cooking in a pot of aromatic broth. The best bowl of ramen he'd ever had was from a street vendor in the Mio system. He made a mental note to make a stop there as soon as he had time in his schedule. Which was never.

"Headmaster?" a stuffy voice called out from across the room. But Knives was still umami deep in his ramen fantasy.

"Headmaster Adams!" This time two voices called at him at once.

And Knives rocked forward in his chair, his head shooting up to see stern eyes staring back at him. Marik and Meneva were two of the smartest people he had ever met. One of them should have been given the role of headmaster. But, alas, the Star Force favored their officers, and he was the highest-ranking officer on the grounds, so the responsibility went to him.

Headmaster. Every time someone said that word, he still expected to hear Bastian's voice, even just the hmms and hums that took up the spaces between his old friend's answers. Those sounds were ones he truly missed.

Having finally caught his attention, Meneva leaned forward and tapped her finger on the tabletop. "What are we going to do about the core? The electrical structure keeps failing, and don't tell me to fix it, because I've already tried."

Marik's voice edged in. "It's impossible to get through a lecture without a power failure. How do you expect me to teach without my holomaps?"

Knives tapped his index finger hard against the table's surface. "Use pen and paper. Draw on the walls if you have to."

Marik grimaced as though Knives was some ancient earthworm. No one used ink and parchment these days. No one except for Bastian. So yes, no one.

"What do you all suggest we do?" Knives asked.

"I left you there to make decisions, not ask questions." A voice boomed out from the speakers, crackling with the static of far-off audio waves, but even through the hiss, Knives knew who was on the other end of that line.

"General," Knives said. "I didn't know you had joined us."

"I've been listening in since the beginning," the general said through the speaker.

Knives cringed at the thought of his father sitting in his office at HQ, judging every word—or lack of words—he said.

Aphelion was in complete disarray. Once a bastion of

strength and prestige, Aphelion was the oldest and most respected academy in Commonwealth history. But in its current state, it was no longer fit for that title.

Knives sifted through all the possible choices he could make.

"So what is your decision?" his father asked.

Aphelion had been his home for three years. Knives had followed his sister here, found his purpose, lost his way, and then discovered a new one. Whether he liked it or not, Aphelion had made him the person he was today. Rough and clever and aware.

He stared at the clear plastic speaker orb positioned in the middle of the conference table. Even through the silence, he knew his father was waiting for the right words to come out of his mouth. Knives was headmaster of Aphelion, and he had to make a choice.

"Well then"—Knives sighed—"we leave."

* * *

Once the general had signed off on the decision, Knives was the first to stand, and thus the first to leave.

The door to the conference hall slid open. Cadet Tarver was waiting for him outside, her eyes tired and her body favoring one side as if she were nursing an injury. But at the sight of him, her body straightened, and she held her fist to her heart in salute.

Knives waved a hand lazily to dismiss her salutation.

"Sir," she said, "there's something I need to tell you."

He started toward the canteen, too focused on checking the time to pay attention. It was well past lights out, which meant one very tragic thing: the kitchen was closed. He rubbed the bridge of his nose and glanced over at Tarver, his eyes painfully dry and tired.

"Do you have any food on you?"

Tarver's eyebrows squiggled together like cursive. She patted down her pockets, which took a while since a regulation uniform contained no less than ten, of various shapes and sizes. Finally, she pulled out a twist of chocofluff buried at the bottom of her hip bag. "It's a bit smushed."

But Knives didn't care. He snatched the piece of chocofluff from her fingers, twisted off the plastic wrapping, and popped it in his mouth. The chocolate on the outside melted immediately, exposing the light puff of sugar hidden inside. It was exquisite.

He hadn't even swallowed when Tarver began to speak. "Sir—"

And Knives suddenly remembered that Cadet Tarver was not there just to give him a piece of old chocofluff.

"I think there are weaknesses in the core room security," she said.

By this point, the temporary happiness from all the sugar had dissipated, and he was faced once again with the realities of his role. "And?"

Brinn cleared her throat, clearly surprised by his response. "Well, I thought you should know."

If she had told him this months ago, even a day earlier, he would have cared. But now...

Cadet Tarver stared at him in expectation, but he merely turned away. "It's against the rules to be out past curfew."

Cadet Tarver raised her voice, and it carried sharply on

scissored wings to his ears. "Headmaster Weathers would have addressed this. He would have—"

Knives was quick to interrupt her. "Well, Bastian's not here, is he?" It wasn't really a question, so he required no response. He turned and made his leave down the hallway toward the instructors' wing.

He was ready for a long night of sleep to buffer him from his thoughts and worries, to shield him from these comparisons. Bastian had been in a league entirely different from his own. Knives was used to being compared to powerful people, skilled beyond their years. There were expectations that maybe, just maybe, he would come close to his father's greatness. His sister, Marnie, had been under the same pressure when she was at Aphelion. But she was an actual prodigy, a master at flight. And Knives, well, he was just an average flyer with a photographic memory.

But this thing that people were now doing, comparing the new headmaster to the old, often made him sigh. The type of sigh that was summoned from the blood deep within his bones.

There was something tragic about photographic memories. You remembered every single detail, every single second. They were wounds that could never fully scab. Always fresh, always painful, and always there.

He wished more than anything that he could turn back time, knowing what he knew now. Maybe then he could be quicker, faster, and more clever than that monster called Einn. Maybe then he would have saved his dear friend's life.

But he was no magician, he told himself.

On his way to his quarters, he stopped in front of a metal door with a large bronze nameplate screwed tight by the doorframe, familiar letters etched into it. He hadn't been inside, not since Bastian was killed.

After Marnie's death, Knives held on to their treasured places. He visited the Nest when he needed to fill his heart, to stoke the flames of his sister's memory alive.

But when Bastian died, Knives stayed away from the familiar spaces, especially the one that reminded him of his old mentor the most. There were days he would stand there, his fingertips resting on this metal door without going in.

But tonight would be one of his last at Aphelion, so he pressed his fist against the entry sensor. The door slid open smoothly with a *whoosh*, just as he remembered it.

He took a breath and stepped inside.

Bastian's office was large and airy, with minimalist wooden furniture breaking up the open space. Tiny cleaner units were still scheduled to attend to this room, and it was as spotless as ever. The aesthetic of the space had always been clean lines and greenery—a bit of nature on a planet where nothing grew. But now, the plants that had decorated the corners of the room were limp and brown in their ceramic pots, starved like forgotten prisoners.

Death lingered in the air, that suffocating smell of old soil and decay. It wasn't a strong smell, but it reminded him that things were not as they used to be.

Knives walked around the headmaster's desk, his fingers trailing against the smooth wood as if each crack and swirl was a message from Bastian himself.

He slumped into Bastian's chair, then adjusted his posture, sitting as straight as he could. He clasped his hands on the wooden tabletop, absent of any clutter, so different from all the times he had visited Bastian's office in the past.

Usually, there were papers—sometimes in neat piles, but oftentimes in scattered chaos all across the desk so you couldn't see a patch of wood underneath.

What had happened to all of Bastian's work? The headmaster was the type who never saved anything on his holodevices. Knives knew this because the Commonwealth was required to catalog an officer's entries after death, but they had reported none of his personal work on those devices. Bastian had used them only for access to student files and for communication with Commonwealth HQ, while he kept his most important work analog, in a nondigital form. Einn had taken Bastian's journal, the one Knives had memorized during the mission in Fugue. But what about everything else? All the scratchings, sketches, unproven theorems—where were they?

There were two main drawers on each side of the desk, big enough to hold Bastian's files. Knives opened the drawer on the right. There was nothing inside but a bag of once-fresh bokhi beans from the Nakiv jungle, hand plucked by Jaspek finches and fermented from nesting.

The other drawers appeared to have been cleaned out and emptied. He stopped at the bottom drawer on the left, giving it a sharp tug, but it remained closed. Knives examined the handle and noticed a lock underneath, one that didn't require fingerprints or pulse scans. It needed a key. Metal keys, like pen and paper, were barely used these days. But Bastian had always considered himself a traditionalist.

There had to be one somewhere. But there was nothing else in the other drawers and nothing remotely key-shaped on the desk.

"You always thought I was so talented," Knives muttered, "but look at me, I can't even open a miffing drawer."

Well, perhaps it was meant to stay that way. Locked and forgotten. Buried like a corpse.

Knives stretched, feeling the weariness of sleep start to crawl over him. He walked to the wall of class photos, taken each year since Aphelion's beginnings. There were hundreds of them, but if he was going to leave this place, he only needed to take one.

He went to the bottom row and grabbed the third-to-last frame, angling it in his hands so he could take a better a look. There was Marnie, standing in the last row with the second-year flyers.

"Better days and bigger dreams," he said as he looked at Marnie's face, forever strong and captured in time. He liked to think she wore the same expression in her last moments, but that was something he would never know.

Knives's eyes flicked to the bottom portion of the photo and found himself in the second row with the First Years. In the picture, he was smiling. He barely recognized himself. This was a kid who thought a bright future was right in front of him, who was excited for the man he would become.

That version of him was much different from the man he'd grown up to be.

He shook his head and wedged the frame underneath his arm. He pressed the door sensor with his elbow and inched backward through the doorframe to take a final look at Bastian's office.

A satisfying goodbye would have been a real handshake and well-wishes muttered underneath a hug. But this, this was another one of his snapshots, a memory to carry with him forever. So in a way, it would never be a true goodbye.

Because he would see it again, even if he didn't want to.

CHAPTER 8
BRINN

THERE WAS ANOTHER late-night blackout, and the safest place for Brinn to be was in bed. Toes were less likely to get stubbed when they were underneath blankets. Her holowatch buzzed lightly on her wrist. Brinn swiped the display, and a small glowing screen appeared before her. A triangle with bold lines flashed in its center, a sign that there was a new message. She tapped on the icon to open it. It was from Faren.

There was nothing written in the body of the message. The only thing displayed was an article from the front page of her home planet's readstream, highlighting Nova Grae's main news stories.

She didn't have time to read the headline; she was too focused on the photo that was right underneath. It was a protest in front of Commonwealth Hall, the one located in the center of her hometown. There were hundreds of faces filling the space of the image, and her brother was in the center of it all. He was standing on the hood of a Roader and holding up a sign.

This IS my home.

At the end of the month, the Council would meet to repeal the Sanctuary Act. Refugees who had been living in Olympus since the Armistice were banding together, ready to speak up for their right to stay within the Commonwealth, to keep their homes. For many of the children, the Olympus territories was where they had grown up. And for the elders, this wouldn't be the first time a home was taken from them.

She rubbed her palm against her scalp, her short navy tresses as natural a color as the day she was born. Everyone on campus knew who she was now. That she was Tawny, a people who had been hated since the Uranium War broke out. Mungbringers, Citizens called them. That was why she had hidden it. She was scared of the disdainful looks that everyone would throw her way once they found out. Faren was better than her in many ways. He fought for people beyond himself, while she was only looking out for herself and her family.

And that was why she was *so* worried. She looked across the room to see if Ia had stirred, but her figure remained still in the other bed. Brinn could have woken her so that she could talk about all the anxiety she was feeling. Then she remembered how Ia had brushed it off when she mentioned Faren was out there protesting, standing up to the Commonwealth in those crowded streets. Ia had ignored it, as though he wasn't important. As if Brinn shouldn't be worrying every night because of it. But that was impossible. To Brinn, there was nothing more important than her brother's safety. She would rather take a dagger to the throat than see anything awful happen to him.

No. *It's okay. He's safe.* That was her mantra every night before she went to bed.

And so she chanted it again tonight, murmuring it over and over like a prayer before sleep could take her.

* * *

Brinn woke up a few hours later, her holowatch buzzing around her wrist again. Under the cover of blankets, she looked at the notification icon on the screen. Another message. What was Faren up to now?

Before she clicked on the icon, she examined the sender address at the bottom of the screen. The letters were garbled, shifting and changing so that she couldn't read the name. The last time she had received a message from an unknown sender, her identity had almost been exposed to the whole school.

She rubbed the sleep out of her eyes and stared at the triangle icon for a long moment. Finally, she tapped it.

She scrolled to the side to see if there was a subject line.

There was.

A bristle of alarm crept up her spine.

Tell the Blood Wolf I'm here.

CHAPTER 9
IA

IA DREAMED about another home—one that floated on a bed of rocks, nestled in the abyss of the All Black. She was surrounded by familiar faces—Vetty, Eve, and even her brother, Einn—and somehow she felt safe. They called her. *Ia, Ia, Ia.* Their voices merged together to a unified whisper.

"Ia." It was Brinn's voice.

Ia groaned and turned in her bed. In her dream, the images of familiar faces rolled with her, swirling and swirling into the pit of a black hole.

She blinked into the sterile darkness. The smooth panels of the ceiling joined together in a grid. Six of them. She had counted them over and over so that now they were almost as familiar as the place in her dream.

"Ia, wake up," Brinn said.

Ia turned, propping herself up on her elbow. Brinn stood in the middle of the room, the light of her holoscreen dim upon her pale-white skin.

"I think we're in danger."

Ia squinted into the corners of their dorm room, but no one and nothing else was there except for some dirty academy flight suits that she had discarded and never dropped off for laundry service.

"What are you talking about?" Ia grumbled to Brinn before dipping her head back down to go back to sleep. But before she could close her eyes again, a holoscreen zoomed across the room and hovered in front of her face above her pillow.

"This message came for you just now," Brinn pointed out.

She squinted to get used to the screen's brightness. Her eyes read the subject line, and she saw the title that had replaced her own name for years. One that inspired fear across the deep reaches of the All Black.

Ia sat up, studying the screen. So this person was looking for the Blood Wolf of the Skies. Only a madman would seek her out. Her viciousness was what had gotten her on the Commonwealth's Most Wanted list for four consecutive years. Not as the third or the second. But numero uno. *Go hard, or go home,* she always said. And she didn't have a home, so she didn't have an option.

Brinn was already on her way toward the door. "We should warn someone."

"No, if it was another one of my brother's attacks, you'd already be snatched up and gone by now," Ia said as she grabbed a flight suit from the floor and zipped it on, touching the fit buttons on her shoulders so the material would conform to her body.

Besides, she had an idea who it was, and if it was indeed him, he was already here.

"Come on," she said as she walked to the door and tapped the sensor on the wall.

The door opened, and her eyes landed on the empty chairs in front of their room, the ones usually occupied by her tedious guards. Aaron was in the borg development department receiving his full system update, and Geoff—poor Geoff—had already been shipped offworld to recover from a broken clavicle. The med bay, in its current state, was in no condition to tend to critical injuries.

Fortunately for her, Aphelion Academy was in shambles and understaffed so there was no replacement to supervise her. Besides, her agreement to work with the general had given her some leeway.

"Where are we going?" Brinn asked behind her.

She thought of the infestation in the core room that Brinn had mentioned. If one pest could get in, so could another. Ia stepped out into the dark and empty hallway. "We're going to find ourselves a rat."

* * *

Ia stopped in front of the elevator to the core room. She looked back at Brinn, who stood at a distance.

Ia nodded at the security panel. "I need access."

Brinn stared at her carefully, her eyes filled with questions the shape of needles. "This doesn't seem right."

Ia bristled with annoyance. "Nothing is ever right."

Brinn crossed her arms. "What does that mean?"

"You question every single thing I do and say," Ia snapped. This had become a pattern. Ia would tell her to do something, and Brinn's immediate response was to refuse. And complain.

And make things *difficult*. Ia just didn't understand.

"This is *so* like you," Brinn said. Even in the darkness, Ia could see Brinn's temper flash across her face. "Sometimes it's impossible to talk to you because you don't bother to listen to me. It takes two people to have a discussion, Ia. If you can't understand that, you can do everything yourself."

Ia took a deep breath and reached out to hold Brinn's hand, something she hadn't done since the night they went after the Armada. The night they survived, the night she gained a friend, a confidante. But even now, there was a distance between them. There was always a storm, and no calm. Maybe it was all her own doing. With Einn out there waiting to make his move, it was hard for Ia to act lightly and accept help when she was responsible for her friend's life.

"You have to trust me." Ia's eyes searched Brinn's for some sort of recognition, some spark of faith. "Please."

Brinn stared at her, and her eyes softened a tiny bit. She moved toward the elevator and placed her hand against the scanner. The lights on the panel illuminated, reading the grooves and patterns of Tarver's palm print.

Ia clapped her friend on the shoulder. It was the only way she could express her thanks. If she actually said it, she'd have to punch herself in the face for being such a sap.

The doors to the elevator slid open, but there was no elevator. Ia looked down the empty, dark shaft.

The lift was stuck at the bottom. *Deus. The blackout.* The security systems must be on backup generators, while the elevators were on the main grid. Without the power on, there was no way this one was coming back up.

As Ia's eyes adjusted to the dark, she spotted the rungs to a ladder that led to the ground floor. Well then, she'd have to climb.

Ia turned to Brinn. "If I'm not back in thirty minutes, shut these doors and don't open them."

Brinn's eyes widened as if she finally understood the danger of the situation. "If that happens, I'm going for the headmaster."

Ia nodded, even though she knew Knives wouldn't be able to do anything. The rat that was down there was a big pain in her ass. He was strong and resilient, and no matter how many times she beat him down, he always survived.

She hopped down the ladder, skipping two or three rungs at a time. Once her feet touched even ground, she turned, following the bright-blue glow of the uranium core. A dry and dangerous heat filled the space. Beads of sweat rolled down her forehead, and she wiped them away, keeping her eyes alert, sweeping through all corners of the room. This rat, in particular, had a tendency to hide.

"You got here quick," she called out, knowing that he was lurking somewhere, watching.

In her periphery, a shadow slipped closer. She turned, catching a glint of light mold over a seemingly transparent shape. Camouflage, through a layer of specialized cells built onto the skin, eyes, and hair's surface.

If he had stayed still, he would be impossible to pick out from her surroundings, but she knew he wanted to be found. She knew he wanted to see the look on her face when she discovered it was him.

"Well, it's not every day you get a message from your archnemesis." His voice was small, a whisper, almost gone but not quite.

Archnemesis. She wanted to laugh in his face, but she kept it down for the sake of bargaining for his favor.

She crossed her arms. "Show yourself already, Goner."

Slowly, she started to see the outline of a figure merging not quite completely with its surroundings, like an image under flowing water. All at once, the strange surface rippled like puzzle pieces being rearranged before her, each skin cell of his body shifting to a new shade until she could distinguish his sharp eyes, the lavender irises so large that there was very little white. The skin around his eyes was black, and so were his nose and the flesh of his bottom lip all the way down to the chin. The rest of his skin was a stark white. From a distance, it looked like a skull. And that was the face that everyone recognized.

Goner, that perpetual parasite in her backside and *second* on the Commonwealth's Most Wanted list.

His abilities were unique; she had never seen anyone like him. Someone who could completely disappear. Goner's skin was similar to that of a scuttlesquix, a marine creature with the ability to create millions of shades and patterns upon the surface of its skin. It allowed him to blend into any environment.

His armored flight suit was also somewhat of a rare commodity, made with iridescent metal that could absorb and reflect the same light waves as its surroundings. With his natural abilities and his armor, he was destined to be an expert thief, and an even more capable spy. Too bad he had a habit of destroying everything in his path.

She didn't know much about his past. Dead Spacers usually liked to keep their previous lives secret since anything and anyone could be used against them. Goner had shown up a year after she had landed on the scene. Ia had already started to make a name for herself, though not as the Blood Wolf. At that point, she had been called the Hunter of the Wastelands, known for picking up Commonwealth convoy ships that hovered near the Fringe Planets.

But there were whisperings of someone new. Someone who loved blowing things up.

She'd witnessed this firsthand when she and Einn had taken control of a supply train at the edge of the territories. They were about to reroute it when an explosion ripped the coupling connecting the front ship from the rest of haul.

Ia had scrubbed through the security footage to see what happened. She had to blink twice the moment she saw it. At first, she thought it was a trick of the eyes. But then a very person-like shape slipped across the shadows, its colors changing uniformly to the surrounding patterns, and for a split second, she saw that skull. She wore her helmet; this was *his* mask. A pattern on his skin, so no one else would see his true self underneath.

That same ghastly skull stared back at her now.

"So, this is the famous Aphelion Academy," Goner said as he stood in front of the core, staying close to it because he knew that Ia couldn't. His skin had built-in defensive measures, thick enough to withstand extreme temperature, radiation, and high-impact attacks. She had found that out when she tried to shoot him in the face, but the blast bounced off him, smoldering a little bit on his skin but not leaving a mark. It annoyed her. He was so hard to get rid of.

"Wasn't too hard for you to get here?" Ia asked.

"You know more than anyone—there's always a way in."

He stared at her, and she glared back at him. "What?"

"It's funny. Seeing you face-to-face." He waved his hand between them. "Without that red feather in the way."

She rolled her eyes.

"Rumor has it that you've found yourself a Bug to bed with, and that's why you're here."

"Careful," she hissed. "The last person who said that to me almost got all his fingers broken off."

"The key word there is 'almost.'"

She wanted to tear at his eyes until the lavender flecks turned to red.

"So why did you call me here?" A smile danced on his lips, and he leaned his ear an inch closer, almost close enough for her to knock her knuckles right into it. "Please tell me you want to fight."

She arched an eyebrow. "There's a reason why I was always number one on the list. You never came close to winning."

He snorted. "But now that you're off the list and working with the Bugs, I wonder where that puts me?"

He swiped the holowatch on his wrist and a screen materialized in between his fingers. A series of names appeared on the screen, all people she knew from her Dead Space days. Terrorists. Assassins. Superhackers. And on the top of the list was Goner.

"You're such a child," she said. Goner was only a little older than she was, but most eighteen-year-old boys she knew often acted like children.

"Am I?" He leaned in, a wild sneer striped across his face.

This time he was closer, and she lunged forward, wincing at the momentary heat of the uranium core. She grabbed him—one hand at the back of his head and the other hand on his shoulder—and yanked, tipping his balance forward. He stumbled away from the protection of the core's heat.

He threw a punch to her sternum. She blocked it, then grabbed his wrist, pulling him off-balance. He stumbled to the ground, rolling into his shoulder to avoid the crack of the floor to his forehead. He was up on his feet in no time, glaring at her.

"I could do this all day long," Ia said, "but that's not why I called you."

"What are we doing, then? Grabbing a cup of bokhi and catching up?"

She pointed between them. "This is all the catching up that we need." She took a deep breath, knowing she was going to hate herself after she said her next words. "But I do have a request."

Goner angled his head. The color receptors on his skin brightened a shade before settling into their natural tone. Which meant he was either very surprised or very pleased. "I don't think I heard you correctly."

Ia clenched her jaw. "I need your help."

A smile drew across his face like a knife slicing through frail skin.

"Why aren't you asking your crew? What about Vetty?"

That wasn't a completely foolish question. She trusted her

crew more than anyone, but she didn't want to drag them into this. Plus there were other reasons. It would be awkward to see Vetty again, even though they had ended their relationship on good terms. She wasn't sure how keen he'd be to see her once he found out she was now allies with Olympus, the Commonwealth that he had so eagerly escaped from.

But calling Goner in for this favor was more of a strategic choice.

"If I ask Vetty and the rest of the crew to do this, Einn will know I sent them," she answered. "But you? He knows I hate you."

"So what is it that you want me to do?"

"I want you to track down my brother," Ia said. She had some ideas where he'd be. The word *Nirvana* rang clearly above the rest, but she needed to be sure. "I need to know where he's positioning his base."

"And why would I ever do anything for you? I could burn this place to the ground if I wanted to."

"I'm pretty sure you're going to help me."

Ia looked him in the eyes, long enough that it made him flinch, a ripple of colorful patterns flaring across his face like endless stains of ink. There was something that she had never told him until now, interesting information she'd found out on her trip to the Kope system over a year ago.

"Because," Ia said, "I know where to find your twin."

Goner pressed his lips together.

"All right then," she said as she turned her back. "I guess I was wrong. You can burn this place to the ground and be on your merry way."

"Fine." His voice reached across the gap between them, softer and less wild.

She glanced over her shoulder. She never knew if she could trust him, but when she looked at him, his shoulders were hunched, and his eyes studied the floor. It was a side of Goner that she had never seen before. Vulnerable. But it was only a moment before he had activated his camouflage again and began to fade. He was invisible. A ghost. Gone.

"We'll be in touch," she said to the empty space, and she made her way up the ladder.

Once she was at the top rung, she looked up to see Brinn, wide-eyed and holding a spare pipe in her hand, her arm arched to strike.

"It's me," Ia said.

Brinn's arm relaxed, and she extended a hand to help Ia up. She didn't need the help, but she took it anyway.

"Who was down there?" Brinn asked.

Ia pinched the bridge of her nose. "Just a rat." She moved out of the elevator corridor and into the hallway. "Let's get back to the room before Knives catches us."

"No, Ia," Brinn said sharply. "Tell me what happened. I heard someone else's voice down there."

Ia stopped in her place, weighing her options. She knew Brinn was going to be upset if she told her and more upset if she didn't. "It was Goner."

"He's here?" she hissed. The horrified look on her face perfectly matched the tone of her voice.

"Was," Ia corrected her.

"We should tell the headmaster about this."

"Don't." Ia shook her head. This was getting unnecessarily complicated. That's why she never liked telling anyone about her plans, and when she had to, her crew had learned never to question her. Because when she talked to them, she gave orders. It wasn't like what was happening now, now that she had so many *friends*. Whom she had to explain everything to, in detail, at all times. "I don't want Knives to find out that I wanted to meet with him."

"You planned this? You brought the most wanted criminal in the Commonwealth *here*. Just so you could meet?"

"I guess technically he's now the most wanted criminal on that list," Ia started to explain, "but seriously, if I was still on there…"

Brinn didn't even give Ia a chance to finish her sentence.

"I can't believe you. Don't you realize you're putting all of us in jeopardy?"

"I need allies, Brinn. I can't fight my brother alone."

"You're the one who was blabbering about trust earlier," Brinn said. "So use *us*. Trust us."

Ia said nothing.

"Fine. I'm not going to be there if this blows up in your face." Brinn stormed off.

This was only one of several of their fights, and Ia was tired. At this point, she had no choice but to watch as Brinn disappeared into the dark.

CHAPTER 10
KNIVES

KNIVES THREW HIS TRAVEL PACK on his bed and unzipped it. They were scheduled to relocate in two days. He had no time to discern what he actually needed from the pile of regulated flight suits that he'd hoarded throughout the years. They all looked exactly the same, but some of them were worn in at the limbs a little worse than others. He decided to pack them all. He'd figure out what to do with them later.

His brown leather jacket was something he'd wear on the flight to HQ. He had other trinkets, too. His desk was cluttered with medals he had won for time-trial events over the years, a busted simulation visor that he had been trying to fix for months, and the photograph he'd taken from Bastian's office.

He picked up the class photo framed with painted black wood. He looked at the image of Marnie, and realized there was one last place they needed to visit together.

* * *

The Nest was cold this time of year. It was a circular space, the walls reaching several meters above him. They tapered at the top where there was a large metal hatch, which had lain open since the Armada attack.

Ropes hung like vines from the top of the shaft, fastened there by the slavers so they could find their way down. The ground was now marked with the scuttle of loose rocks and cracked lines, the telltale signs of their enemy's footsteps.

Even this sacred place was defiled.

He lit a candle on the cold floor and stared up at what stars peeked through the clouds, gray against the midnight sky.

"This is it, Marn," Knives murmured. "We're finally leaving this place for good."

The Nest was an Adams sanctuary, one for both him and Marnie to retreat to whenever the stress of the academy got to them.

He remembered the time they tried to climb the walls without ropes or hooks. He hadn't gotten very far and fell when he was only a third of the way. But Marnie had reached the top. She'd hung onto the grating like a Nonoko ape and yelled into the open sky. She had no fear. None at all.

He studied his fingers, the skin cracked and thick from years added to his life since then. Perhaps if he tried today, he'd reach the top.

Even though he was currently Aphelion's headmaster, the general was still adamant about Knives's return to the field. Make use of that officer's title, his father had told him during his last visit.

These walls were not going to protect Knives any longer.

This was something he had to face in the coming months. It was time for him to grow up.

He positioned the frame upon a small rock ledge at the back wall of the Nest.

"I'm going to move forward, Marn," he said.

Marnie would always be with him, no matter what, but where he was going, he didn't need to bring his cadet days with him. He took one last look at his sister, her brow set and her eyes ready. This was the Marnie he would always remember, the one who would inspire him to keep going, keep going.

As Knives turned back to the entrance, the wind whistled through the open grate and down the cavern. A crash of glass echoed against the walls, and he looked over his shoulder knowing that the picture frame wasn't where he left it.

It was on the floor, the glass shattered and the frame broken into pieces. Among the debris, something glinted in the moonlight.

It was small and silver.

And it was shaped like a key.

* * *

Knives rushed through the hallways passing clusters of cadets, each of them swiveling their heads as they watched him go. The mystery key lay in the safety of his fist until he was back in Bastian's old office.

He went straight to the locked drawer. He uncurled his fingers, exposing it to the light. It was flat with a square head that extended to a small sliver of metal with grooves and jagged teeth.

He stared at it. Could this be the key he was looking for?

And why did Bastian put it in the frame for that particular photo? Could it be that he wanted Knives to find it?

With anxious fingers, Knives inserted the key into the keyhole. It fit in easily like a sword to its scabbard. He took a deep breath and turned it. It rotated smoothly until finally he heard something click within the locking mechanism.

The drawer hitched loose, sliding forward from its rails.

Knives peeked inside, expecting to see stacks of Bastian's journals waiting to be opened and read.

But there were no books, no loose papers, not even a torn-off corner from a page.

All he saw was a fountain pen. Smooth black with golden trim.

This was it? This was what Bastian wanted him to find?

He had seen this pen before, always either in Bastian's chest pocket or in his hand, making inky scratches in his journals. It was strange that he hadn't taken it on his final trip to Fugue.

He had left it there for Knives to find. A memento. Maybe that was all there was to it. He could leave it behind, like Marnie's photo. But he had a feeling he'd be needing more of Bastian's guidance in the days ahead.

"All right, Bastian," he muttered as he picked up the pen and placed it in the chest pocket of his leather jacket. "All right."

* * *

Hanging halfway out of his Kaiken, Knives rearranged his duffel bags on the floor of his cockpit. A RSF battleship was scheduled to land the next morning, so that the engineers could move all of the flight vehicles onto the vehicle bay for transport to headquarters.

They were packing up the labs and shipping over all the armaments in development, as well as every single one of the available Borg models, both assembled and disassembled.

They'd have to leave the uranium core, but Professor Patel had spent the past two weeks with Cadet Tarver securing the space so no one without proper access would be able to find their way in.

"You planning an escape?"

The sound of Ia's voice made him smile, but he forced his grin away before he turned to face her.

"You want to come with?" he said as he stepped down to the tarmac to meet her.

She smirked at him. "I know you. You would never run away."

Aaron stood behind her, still programmed to keep a close eye. Knives remembered the days when Ia was always scheming to escape, always trying to figure out different ways she could pinch that heart tracker from his cold, dead body. The heart tracker was long gone, yet somehow she was still there, studying him, smirking.

"You excited to go home?" she asked.

HQ was located in Rigel Kentaurus, the capital star system of the Olympus Commonwealth, specifically on the planet Calvinal, orbiting four planets away from a yellow dwarf star. Aphelion had been his home for the past three years, but Calvinal was where he grew up. He'd lived a wonderful life there, but he did not miss it.

To deflect her question, Knives nodded over at Aaron. "You know once we get there, he's going to have to start doing his job again. In fact, it'll be worse. My father will be there."

Ia shrugged. "At least this time, I can outrun him without falling to the ground from a heart attack. Escape isn't off the table yet, Adams."

"Yeah, but where would you even go?" he joked.

She glared at him, clearly annoyed by his quip.

Yes, he had given Ia her freedom. It was the right thing to do, but he also knew that the fact that she had come back meant her loyalties with her brother were no longer something she could fall back on. As odd as it sounded, she was better protected allying herself to the Commonwealth, and her decision to stay was obviously a strategic one. Could she go rogue? Of course she could. Maybe she was even plotting something as they spoke.

"Why are you here, Ia?" he asked her.

Suddenly, the troubled lines on her face softened, and she stepped up to him, her black eyes looking up into his. "Wanna grab some food?"

He bit his lip, stopping the grin from growing on his face. "Sure."

She smiled at him, and somewhere in the universe, the sun was shining.

It was moments like this that he thought there was another reason why she stayed.

CHAPTER 11
BRINN

BRINN TOOK ONE LAST LOOK at Aphelion. Even though the flight deck was busy with activity, it was still so much emptier than it used to be. The parked starjets on the track above were all gone, in a storage bay of another Star Force battleship that would follow them to the new academy. Some that had been in the middle of repair were left splayed across the ground as scrap.

"That's the Olympus Commonwealth for you," Liam said as he stepped beside her. "Take what they want, and leave behind what's broken."

She raised her eyebrows, noting the displeasure in his voice.

But he was right. That was the way the Commonwealth approached everything. Like when they colonized her own planet, Tawnus.

Was that how they would treat her, too? Throw her away when she wasn't useful anymore?

"You know they never presented a soldier's medal to

Cammo's family after he died?" Liam's voice grew tense. "A son of Olympus so quickly forgotten."

She stilled at his words. Something had been different about Liam since the attack on Aphelion. That day was full of screams, and blood, and death. His eyes no longer had the spark that she remembered seeing when she first met him, but they were still painfully bright and kind. It was all forced, a counterfeit expression that he wore every day. Because it was expected of him, to be strong as a shield.

Together, they walked toward the shuttle that would take them and the rest of the cadets to Nauticanne, an academy in the heart of the Olympus Commonwealth, where the walls were stronger, more fortified. Where Einn would not be able to get her, and she would be even more closed off from her family, from everything.

And where she would become an officer of the Royal Star Force.

Half a year ago, this was the path that *she* chose, but now she could clearly see the end of it, an image of her future self waving back at her. It made her pause, wishing for left turns, U-turns, a detour. There was something inside her screaming for her to stop. But she got into the shuttle anyway.

Brinn and Liam wandered through the aisles, spiraling around the center of the cabin until they found empty seats in the corner.

She caught sight of Ia entering the shuttle, her guard Aaron in tow, but when Ia glanced in her direction, Brinn did her best to look away. They hadn't spoken since their fight by the elevator. Their argument bothered her, but it bothered her more that Ia didn't care. Maybe that was the type of friend Ia was—if she was even still a friend at all.

A notification popped up on her holowatch. A news alert from back home. Her heart stopped when she read the words.

Protest in Nova Grae Disrupted by Large-Scale Bombing. Hundreds Dead.

Her thoughts narrowed. *Faren.*

What if he was there?

Oh Deus, no.

NO.

The air in her lungs grew thick. Her body slowly curled into itself, so all she could see were her knees. Because she knew her brother. She knew he was at that protest.

A voice came onto the speakers. "Ready for takeoff. Please turn off all holos for the remainder of the flight."

"Brinn," Liam said. "Are you okay?"

Brinn turned off her holowatch, unable to look Liam in the eye. She placed a hand at her heart, feeling it race inside her chest. She remembered the words she recited before she went to sleep. *It's okay. He's safe.* She repeated them again now as she willed her heart to slow and slow until finally it was at a normal pace.

Her heart was easy to control, but the tears blurring her vision—all she could really do was blink them away.

CHAPTER 12

IA

IA WATCHED AS THEY ASCENDED above the clouds. She saw just a glimpse of AG-9's white, harsh terrain before the windows blacked out entirely for solar protection. Ia had wished for this more times than she could count, to escape Aphelion, her prison for the past few months. Yet there was a part of her that didn't want to leave. Aphelion was one of the oldest academies of Olympus. Its location was remote and harder to visit, which meant fewer Bugs came to check on her. The relocation to Nauticanne meant all the high officials would be there, keeping a close eye.

She glanced across the aisle and then, reminded of who she was sitting with, quickly turned her eyes away. Nero's dark glare followed her, his loathsome face symmetrical all the way down to that dimple in the center of his chin. There had been no other seats left, so she had no choice but to endure him for the duration of the flight. Most of his cronies had been ordered home by their parents, but for some reason, Nero

Sinoblancas, the heir to the most powerful corporation in all the known galaxies, had chosen to stay.

"Why aren't you with the mungbringer?" he asked, his tone a little less acidic than usual, as if it was normal to speak through slurs and insults.

She sneered at him for his use of that word, but something within her felt compelled to answer. Maybe because she was so alone in her frustration. "We had a fight," she said.

Nero shrugged. "That *is* what you do best."

Ia could have said something, but she didn't. Because he was right.

She leaned back in her chair and crossed her legs in messy oblong angles so that she would take up more space and feel a little less small. "Why are you still here?" she grumbled to Nero. "I thought you'd already left this place."

"Because," he said. "Going back home would mean I'd have to start working for Sino Corp."

Sino Corp was at the forefront of technological change, sponsoring labs and research that greatly improved the lives of the Citizens of the Olympus Commonwealth. "Are you telling me you chose the Star Force over Sino Corp?"

"Trust me. There are things we do that I wished I never knew."

And she wanted more than ever to find out exactly what he meant by that. But then she thought about the other Sinoblancas she knew.

"Is that why Vetty left?" Vetty was Nero's cousin. He had taken his leave from Commonwealth life to be a part of her crew.

Nero nodded. "As much as I hate how he ended up

working for you, Vetty was smart for getting out of it while he had the chance."

She looked him straight in the eye, something she never did because he was hardly worth it. But there was something very odd about what he had said to her. "Why are you telling me this?"

"If you haven't already noticed, the Commonwealth is falling apart. I thought you should know that there are more players in this game than you realize."

Ia furrowed her brow at his warning and looked away. She hoped to Deus that he wasn't right.

* * *

Nauticanne Academy wasn't how it looked in the action streams. There was a Kinna Downton one that came out last year in which she played a tough and go-get-'em flyer. All the training montages were supposedly filmed at Nauticanne. But apparently those were all lies.

Because Nauticanne was bigger than it appeared in the stream story. Way bigger. The campus on the ground was a facade, made to look like an old museum from Ancient Earth. The bulk of the academy was stationed in the clouds. All the classes and training took place on a line of older Commonwealth battlecruisers, the kinds that were meant for colonizing expeditions, equipped to house a whole army if needed.

As Ia stepped off the ramp of the shuttle and down onto Nauticanne's flight deck, she looked out through the large, square entryway that lay open after their ship had anchored. The sky stretched out before her, and she saw two other battleships in the distance, one at the 200 mark and another at 1100. The three battleships were arranged in a triangle, connected together by a series of vacuum tunnels that ferried people from one vessel to the other.

"Beautiful, isn't it?" a voice said.

She turned around and struggled to hold down a groan.

"Mif," she muttered to herself.

A statuesque man in his late thirties stood before her. Tall, with broad shoulders, dark, roguish eyes, and umber-brown skin—the renowned Captain Nema. They had a history, one which included the destruction of several of his Star Force ships by her devious machinations. They were enemies once. But now—oh Deus. They were on the same side.

As the other cadets passed, they paused to salute the captain, but he waved them all away before they could even raise their arms.

His full attention on Ia, he nodded at the scene outside. "We have the academy base positioned between our best Star Force battleships, fully equipped with a new batch of Sino Corp weaponry. All of our best flyers are right here on Calvinal. We have everything we need on these three ships to win a war," he said, waving his arms as if he was the conductor of some ridiculous symphony.

He was trying to intimidate her, but it was backfiring. Nema was giving her more intel than General Adams ever had.

"Careful," she said. "Are you sure you want to be telling me all this?"

"Normally I wouldn't be sharing such sensitive information with the same brat who destroyed my battle jets." He flashed her a charming smile. "But I hear your claws have been trimmed."

She narrowed her eyes at him. "I'm not a cat." She was a *Blood Wolf.*

The corners of Nema's mouth quirked up stiffly, a grin that hid a grimace.

They scowled at each other in silence until Knives walked down the ramp of the shuttle, stretching his limbs. He stopped in front of the captain and sighed. "Do I have to salute?" he asked.

Captain Nema clapped him on the shoulder. "Nice to see you, kid."

Knives nodded. "I'm glad you're here. The general has called a meeting. We're required to attend." He flicked up a holoscreen displaying a schedule invitation.

Thank Deus, Ia thought. That meant she could leave, grab a bite to eat at the canteen, maybe even find a place to shower. She had already turned to walk away when Knives called out to her.

"Where do you think you're going?"

Instantly, she quickened her pace. She had a gut feeling about what he was going to say next.

Knives's voice boomed. "Can someone please escort Ia to the officers' conference room?"

Aaron closed in on her escape, blocking her from entering the next transport pod to the canteen.

She glared at the borg. Of course he had to follow orders, even if he was told to sit on a toilet somewhere for hours straight.

"Orders are orders," Aaron said unapologetically.

She glanced over her shoulder at Knives. "Nice try," he said.

A few steps behind him, Captain Nema watched her,

smiling. She knew what he was thinking. The Blood Wolf had been declawed after all.

* * *

The conference room was ridiculous. And by ridiculous, she meant grandiose. Each person stood on their own hovering platform, which came together with the rest to form a large floating circle. What was wrong with sitting around a table?

The platforms were equipped with their own podiums, but Ia chose to sit, resting back on her arms and kicking her legs over the edge.

Ia looked over the officers surrounding her. Some she knew because she had seen their angry faces as her starjet rocketed past them with their cargo and resources in tow. Others she recognized from the intel meetings on Aphelion, but instead of holostreaming in, they were there in the flesh. This must be a very important meeting.

The general's platform was positioned to her left.

"What am I doing here?" Ia hissed at him.

"You wanted information," he said. "I'm giving it to you."

A couple platforms away, Nema watched her with alert eyes. Thankfully, Knives was in between them, lessening the effect of the captain's stare. Knives stood there, stiff as a pole. Most definitely because his father was there, and he had to.

"Let us begin." General Adams looked over to an older woman, her gray hair trimmed down to a short crew cut. Her eyebrows were elegant, but her eyes were sharp. "First of all, I'd like to thank Headmaster Talmo for hosting this meeting."

Headmaster Brigada Talmo leaned forward on her podium. "Of course," Talmo replied. "We are saddened to hear about the incident at Aphelion. A true cornerstone to our institution. But, like time itself, all things are ever changing."

Next to her, Knives bristled.

"We are glad to extend our protection to you all," Headmaster Talmo stated.

Ia could tell there was a huge conflict between the two academies, and probably all of the academies in the Commonwealth. It was a weakness. To be fragmented instead of unified. All they needed was one dangerous idea to wedge apart the space between them, and that was it.

A middle-aged gentleman, whose missing arm had been replaced with a chrome prosthetic, chimed in. "Let's get on with it. We all know what we're here to discuss. Bastian's passing is causing quite the stir."

A murmur traveled around the room like a wave, until Talics Banyan—the Minister of Defense and the oldest of the group—pounded his fist on the surface of his podium. "If only he had destroyed that thing, GodsEye would never have gotten into the wrong hands."

Ia glanced back and forth at everyone's faces, trying to piece together the heat of their words, their arguments, the little cracks and fissures that could become deep and never-ending chasms.

"The years have confused you," the general said. "I believe *you* were the one who suggested keeping it under lock and key in case we'd find future use for it."

Ia cocked her head. If she wasn't mistaken, the general was actually defending Aphelion's old headmaster.

"Bastian's work has improved gate technology more than

any other laboratory in the Commonwealth—both private and government-funded. Bridges connect people, not divide them," the general said.

Banyan held up his finger and answered, "Connect systems, yes. Galaxies, even. But universes—that's of the highest order. In the realm of Deus herself."

Ia's eyes widened. Was that what Bastian was working on? Of course Einn wanted it, but the bigger question was why. Why would he want to open up a door to another universe?

"You've seen what happened last time," Banyan continued. "We can't let that happen again."

Ia raised an eyebrow. "Last time?"

The general tapped on his holowatch and pulled up a screen. Ia stared at the first frame. It was surveillance footage. Words were stamped across the bottom of the scene.

Project Threshold – Location: GodsEye

Confidential Status – Category 10

05.27.8901 1852

Ia stared at the date. That was twenty years ago.

Captain Nema stirred at his podium. "Are you sure we should be showing this to her?"

"She needs to understand what's at stake, so we can stop the madman who wants to re-create it."

She caught Knives's attention. *What is this?* she mouthed. He typed something and then pointed to her podium where a new holoscreen appeared. She read the word over and over in her head. Fugue.

Her eyebrows raised. That was where Knives and Bastian had encountered Einn.

The general pressed the corner of his screen, and the still image came to life. The camera eye was positioned to focus on the center of a huge white room where two half circles were placed opposite each other. Cables ran off frame to an unknown power source. At the corners of the screen, she noticed a reflection. The camera was behind a thick pane of clear glass. It was then that she realized she was witnessing the beginnings of an experiment.

Bastian's voice rose up from behind the camera. "Trial #283J. Increased the amount of charge by a factor of 9, hoping that it will be enough to pry the fissure open."

The archways spun slowly at first, but with each passing second, they gained a burst of momentum and were soon rotating at such a velocity that the arches themselves blurred, the lines appearing everywhere and all at once. A shadow of an orb. The structural beams wobbled from the speed, and when they looked like they were at a breaking point, something tremendous happened. It was tiny at first. But the intensity of it made everyone around her breathe in with a collective gasp as the tiny speck of light stretched longer and longer, like a slash of bright white through the orb's center. As it tore open, she could see the faintest illuminations of a sky much like the one over her home planet, Cōcha—the one that she was named after and the same one that was destroyed when she was young.

She saw emerald-green fields that reached far and wide to rock structures that spiraled to distant heights in the background. The vista blossomed before her in full color at first, then faded to shadow, back to color, then monotone gray, in an erratic cycle. It was as if she were viewing everything within a prism, the colors shifting and the image distorting whenever she switched angles.

And then something else appeared. A shape. A length of dangerous limbs, surrounding a muscled torso. A haze of a figure.

She remembered the story Knives told that day at lecture, the one that was supposed to scare all the new cadets. It was of a monster who ripped apart Fugue. Back then, she had imagined something like the Half-Man from the nursery rhymes or the NiteVost from myths.

But now she knew she was wrong.

She stared at the figure, her eyes sifting through the shadows until finally she saw that it wasn't a thing at all, but a *man*. With fox-like eyes, a regal nose, and a furious expression ripping across his lips.

Suddenly, the bridge to the other universe widened, and spirals of an alien black mass spilled into the laboratory like an invasion. Predatory tentacles grasped for anything they could reach—equipment, cables, even lashing out at the thick glass that separated the room from the scientists observing behind the camera. It was an unknown beast ready to devour everything from the bottom up.

"Shut it off!" "Power everything down!" she heard people screaming on the recording.

But despite the horror, Ia's gaze was still fixed on the figure who stood in the center of all that chaos. That man. She couldn't even blink for fear she would lose sight of him. And all the memories started flooding back.

This man used to sing to her. This man pressed the

blood-red feather to her heart whenever the storm clouds brewed overhead. This man had abandoned her and her brother many, many years ago.

It was her father.

She understood it all now. Why Einn was after this type of tech. And her brother, who still wore their father's white hearts on his collar, would tear apart the universe to find him.

CHAPTER 13
BRINN

THE SECOND THEY LANDED, Brinn went through all the streams searching for news of the riots, but she couldn't find anything. Even that first headline had disappeared. It was as if her imagination had made it all up. She called her brother, and when he didn't pick up, she called her parents. No one answered. She looked around at her fellow cadets, none of them from Nova Grae. She had no one to ask. No one to cry to. She felt like she was fading away.

Besides, the cadets in her class were all Citizens. None of them would sympathize with those protesting for refugee rights. They would be rooting for the other side, the same side they had chosen to lay their lives down for once they graduated.

So Brinn remained quiet, her fear in step beside her as they were ushered down to the ground for a tour of the academy museum.

The museum was domed by a large glass roof, so the light

from above flooded in, illuminating everything from old vessels from the Uranium War to early prototypes of warp drives, now obsolete according to today's standards. A huge amount of history was displayed before her. It would have excited her a year ago, thrilled her to learn as much as she could about the Commonwealth, but now she didn't have the heart to even read the words on the displays. History, she now knew, often had a way of ignoring certain facts to rosy up the truth.

Brinn looked around at the Aphelion cadets, still wearing their academy emblem on the sleeve of their flight suits. Only a handful of them remained. She counted no more than forty in their group who'd decided to stay after the Armada lay waste to Aphelion. The news of the attack was too big to keep under wraps. The media had caught wind of it the day after they had broken free from the Armada's control and landed safely on AG-9.

Despite the media's constant questioning, the Star Force was tight-lipped with their official reports in order to maintain a sense of control over the situation. Everyone blamed refugee rebels for the attack, and the Commonwealth was fine with letting that story stand. To the conservatives on the Council, it was fuel to sway the public as the vote to repeal the Sanctuary Act approached. There was tension in the air, and now, being here on the capital planet of the Olympus Commonwealth, Brinn felt it a hundredfold.

The museum was open to the public, so their tour intersected with the paths of museum visitors who were admiring the displays of engines and medals along with them. A lot of them, she could tell, were too distracted to even look at the exhibit.

Brinn felt it as they passed. Their eyes, lingering on her for seconds too long.

She reached back to raise the hood of her sweater to cover up her navy-blue hair. Liam stopped her, his fingers touching her forearm, gently nudging her hands back down.

It's okay, he mouthed. She nodded, directing her focus on him and pretending she didn't care that these people were slicing at her with their stares.

Her holowatch, set to quiet mode, flashed upon her wrist. She looked down at the new message, and despite all her worries, she smiled.

It was from Angie.

Behind you.

Brinn swiveled around, letting the rest of the class pass her by. Angie stood before her, red lacquered lips grinning from ear to ear.

"You finally made it!" Angie squealed.

Brinn gawked at her, and then her eyes began to water. A year ago when they were both in primaries together, she tried so hard to stay out of Angie's path for fear of being bullied by her. Brinn had never thought the sight of Angie would bring her to tears—at least not the tears of joy she was crying right now. Angie was her only connection to home.

Brinn rushed toward her, her feet trudging against the floor from the shock of seeing her friend.

"Oh, don't," Angie said as she wrapped her arms around Brinn in a hug. She took a step back, using her sleeves to wipe away any stray tears. "Come on, now," she said. "Crying will make your eyes look red."

"I didn't know you were assigned here."

Angie nodded. "Nauticanne accepted my transfer, of course. It was all my dad's doing. He wanted to keep a closer eye on me, especially with him in session at Council."

They followed the tour as it funneled into the main atrium. The walls of the lobby were paneled with windows that reached from the floor to the ceiling, giving them a clear view of what was going on outside. An anti-refugee protest had gathered in the large park across the street. They held signs, each filled with discriminatory slurs, while a man with a megaphone screamed for Citizens' rights. Brinn felt a wave of panic rip through as if all her bones had turned to stone.

Angie stood shoulder to shoulder with Brinn, staring out at the same sight. "It's nothing like what's going on at home."

Brinn stiffened, and the terror was back rippling up her spine. She thought back to the headlines she saw before leaving Aphelion, the same ones that gripped her with worry throughout the flight.

"You know what happened? There isn't even a murmur of it on the ArcLite."

Angie clenched her jaw. "They're trying to sweep it under the rug. That's probably why."

So it was real. The protests, the outbreak of violence in the streets of her home. Brinn felt like she couldn't move; the people around her were pressing toward her like walls of a tomb. "Angie, I haven't heard from my family."

"Oh, Brinn..." Angie grabbed her hands. But that was all she said. Not *They'll be fine. Everything will be okay.* Perhaps because she knew she'd be wrong.

All of Brinn's thoughts screamed at once, and it was too much noise. She pulled away from Angie and shouldered through the crowd. She didn't care about the looks they gave her, the muttered phrases. *Miffing mungbringer. Dirty ref.*

Brinn pushed her way through the main entrance and took deep gulps of fresh air, her lungs starved for oxygen. She tried to regulate her breathing, to quell her heart, which was threatening to knife its way out of her rib cage.

It's okay. He's safe. It's okay. He's safe.

She flipped through her contact list and dialed home. Immediately, a screen popped up with her mother's face. Her eyes were stained red.

Too many tears can do that, Angie had warned.

Brinn heard only bits and pieces of what her mother said next. "I've been... Hurt all those people.... You need to know." It was as if waves of water had crashed onto her, drowning out a few words at a time.

Brinn pressed her palms to her eyes, trying to block everything out, but somehow her mother's last words pierced through to find her. "Faren's gone."

Brinn's body went limp. Her arms swung loose at her sides, and her head fell back to look at the sky. Tears stung her eyes, and she let them. Blurred shapes of passersby walked around her, not even bothering to ask her if she needed help. She stared past them, forcing herself to look straight at the sun hovering in the sky.

The sky was clear. No clouds. Nothing except for a strange black stain in the teal blue.

But before she could make sense of what this anomaly was, an explosion thundered above, so loud that it rocked the ground underneath her feet.

CHAPTER 14
KNIVES

"LET'S GO! LET'S GO!" The orders flew all around him. "Ready for your squadron assignments."

Knives took in the view from the large service entryway that lay open at the end of the flight deck, and that slash ripping through the atmosphere. The shape of an oblong circle, its center housed a different sky with constellations not even close to being near this star system. A wormhole, he realized. But without a gate? How was that possible?

They had still been in the conference room when an earth-shattering boom interrupted the tail end of their meeting, the noise cutting off the general's final remarks. The sound crackled in the air for minutes afterward. It was only when Knives got to the flight deck that he realized the source of the noise was this thing tearing through the horizon.

The general ordered them to carry out the natural disaster protocol, but whatever this was, Knives was certain it wasn't *natural*. All officers of rank were ordered to the flight deck to prep their ships. It didn't include any of the cadets, and it certainly didn't include Ia.

That was why he was surprised to see her zigzagging underneath the wings of the parked jets awaiting flight.

What on Ancient Earth was she doing here?

If he was a good officer, he would be listening for his orders, but seriously, when did he ever do that?

He jogged through several groups of engineers and their flyers, each beelining to their own vessel for hasty prep or gathered in the center of the flight deck to await their squadron assignments. As his footsteps hastened, he pulled up a holoscreen to call Aaron. His face flickered into view, his expression as belabored as any borg's could be.

"Where are you? Ia is out here, doing Deus knows what."

"Apologies, Headmaster," Aaron replied, and he angled his screen to show the lower half of his body, one of his legs severed at the knee. "Ia disabled me before I could even apprehend her," Aaron explained.

Knives closed the screen. Sometimes he wished Ia still had that tracker in her heart.

He broke into a run. As he cleared the crowds, a voice on the speaker made announcements. "Farview. Asterix. Karien. Opo. Pronn. On the Nix Squadron." The names went on, assigning everyone into their squadrons. Knives tried as best he could to keep his focus on Ia so that he wouldn't lose her in the chaos.

Knives knew what she was searching for. A jet to take off in. But she had already passed so many of them, her attention quickly zipping all around her as if she hadn't found exactly what she was looking for.

He cut her off before she could venture any farther.

"Escaping again?" he said. *Just like old times*, he thought, but knowing her temper, he didn't dare say it.

She pushed right past him. "I know Einn is behind this. The thing that's tearing up the sky looks an awful lot like Bastian's science experiment we just finished watching footage of. So give me a jet so I can properly whack my brother in the head and stop this."

She was right. That thing outside looked eerily familiar, a tear in the fabric of space and time like in the experiment tape.

"Even if I wanted to, I don't have the clearance to give you access."

"Who gives a mif about clearance?" she argued. "All that matters is surviving past today."

A chorus of shouts came from the people passing, catching on to each nearby group like wildfire. Outside, a battleship had appeared from within the tear, half of it anchored in some other part of the All Black and the other half now peeking into their corner of the universe. It was a strange design, with a planetoid as its foundation, yet the actual structures that were integrated into it were sleek and almost too advanced for a Dark Space vessel. Still, no matter what it looked like, a battleship was only meant to do one thing.

Destroy.

It took less than a second for the enemy ship's laser cannons to charge up. They fired at full power. For a brief moment, the beams burned the color of the sky. Knives's eyes landed on the RSF battleship stationed across from them. The lasers were strong enough to penetrate its force field. The battleship had taken a hit, fragments of glass and gnarled steel breaking away, catching glints of sunlight as they spiraled downward. Another explosion sounded, this time from the engine section. Knives held his breath, watching the vessel quickly lose altitude, on a collision course with the city below. Now only two battleships of Nauticanne were left to defend.

Alarms screeched around them, and a voice on the speaker repeated "Code 24," over and over.

They were no longer working with natural disaster protocol. This was an attack.

Ia edged back in haste. "I gotta get down there."

"Down?" he interrupted. Any fool would know that the battlefield was in the air, trying to deflect the enemy's next move.

"That right there," Ia pointed out to the fiery chaos igniting the sky, "is just the diversion."

"I can't let you go," he said. "Not alone."

"Then come with me, Knives."

He looked at her in silence. If he went with her, he'd be court-martialed for going against orders. But his squadron hadn't been assigned yet, cementing his fate. He could go with her. If he wanted to.

"I heard your name," she said.

He knit his eyebrows together. "What?"

She pointed to the center of the commotion. The speakers had been cut off, and the squadron leaders were repeating their announcements, their screams growing hoarse as they went down their lists. In the center of it all was Captain Nema, who held all the flyers' attention, each one hoping to hear their name because all they had ever wanted since the day they were born was to fly with him.

"FiFo Squadron," the captain yelled, his voice booming out with enough confidence to fill a whole star system. "Joves, Irenan, Pokoy, Minnow, and Adams. You're flying with me."

"Looks like your squadron's up." Her eyes locked onto his. "So what are you going to do?"

Those were his orders. Sure, he hadn't given a mif about orders in the past. But now there was a battleship going down right before his eyes. He was a flyer, trained for situations like this. This was his city, the one he grew up in; he could help save it. He felt his jaw tighten, knowing this was what his father wanted for him. "I have to go, Ia."

She grabbed his shoulder. "Before you leave, give me a jet."

"You know I can't."

He expected a grumble of protest, but Ia had already brushed past him and stopped in front of a large cabinet. She opened it, revealing a line of windpacks hanging evenly on a metal rod. She picked one out, shrugged it over her shoulders, and fastened the clasp at her chest.

So that was what she was looking for all along, he realized.

"Well, then," she said, her voice so calculated, so certain. "I'll just have to jump."

She touched a button on a black metal band around the base of her neck, and her helmet assembled upward around her head, one smooth panel over the next, until he stared back at that red feather slashing crimson against the black visor.

Life was all about choices. He could stop her if he wanted to, but he knew he couldn't keep her. He watched her run to the end of the tarmac, and then, like the first day they met, she spread her arms wide open and leapt.

"Yeah," he whispered, "just like old times."

CHAPTER 15

BRINN

BRINN LOOKED TO THE SKY, watching as the Star Force battleship burned. It descended like a shooting star from the heavens, a mixture of gray and red smeared against a bright-blue canvas. All around her, silence overtook the crowd as the hull finally buried its nose into a tall, curving building in the city center. It left a trail of crushed steel and mortar in its wake, demolishing the entire city block before it came to a stop.

At that point, panic set in. Screams curdled around Brinn, distorting and roaring together in a wave.

The people inside the museum rushed into the street, pushing and shoving in order to get someplace safe. But there was none. Not when the city was burning. Not when the sky was torn up above.

Brinn looked around her, trying to find a familiar face, but her eyes landed on the protestors who were still standing in the park across from her. One of them looked at her, whispering to the others. Their heads turned to stare at her, and their whispers grew into shrill words that set her frozen in place.

"Mungbringer!" they cried. "You did this!"

They raised their signs overhead. Those who didn't have signs extended their fists in their air with hate.

She wiped the tears that were still fresh in her eyes, revealing what was underneath. The sadness and fear now replaced by anger. Rage. "Ignorant mifs!" she wanted to scream. There was no way this was her fault. Any average Citizen would have seen that—but no. All Citizens, she was beginning to realize, were heartless. For pointing fingers. For blaming any refugee in their sights.

For killing her brother.

The Olympus Commonwealth was the greatest governing alliance in all the galaxies. Or so she had thought. Until she started asking questions, and those questions became stones, piercing holes in her beliefs.

She was a *Citizen*, just like them, she could have said. But what was the point when she was starting to hate the word? Why be a Citizen of a place that didn't want you?

Brinn clenched her fists at her sides.

Why be a Citizen of a place you didn't want either?

The sky was coated in a black veil of smoke, and all these people wanted to do was point fingers. Their fingers became fists, and some of those fists held rocks. Soon, all she could see were blurs of black and gray as stones flew toward her. She backed away, but she couldn't dodge all of them.

A *crack* flooded her ears, and sharp pain flared at the side of her head. She caught a glimpse of a rock, slick with her blood, tumbling to the pavement as she fell to her knees. The world folded in as people crowded around her. All she could see were their open mouths screaming, their voices louder and hoarser with each chant, as if they were summoning the heat from deep inside their lungs.

But a similar fire was growing in her own core, stoked by the birth of something very new. She would no longer be complaisant.

Roaring like a beast who'd found its voice, Brinn rose, pushing and screaming at them, and she didn't even care if they pushed back.

Suddenly, she felt fingers clamp onto one of her shoulders.

She swung blindly. Those same fingers held her arm back before it struck. She stood, facing Liam, his dark eyebrows knit in a V.

Her legs went weak from shame. She'd almost hit Liam, a boy who had stood on her side of the line no matter where it moved.

"Come on." Liam wrapped his arm around her to shield her from the people still pressing close. "We have to get out of here."

He pushed his way through the protestors. Their faces blurred together. Ash was heavy in the air, coating her face, disintegrating on her eyelashes.

As they squeezed their way through the mob, the people swore at her, hissed at her, and she tried to block them all out. She wanted to forget the anger in their eyes; it was everywhere she looked.

But there was one voice that managed to find her. So

different and clear in the sea of anger.

"Brinn! Brinn!" she heard Angie cry. Brinn's eyes scanned the crowd, trying to find her friend's face. She opened her mouth to respond, but before she could call back to her, the second battleship caught on fire.

And the rumble of the aftermath drowned out everything.

CHAPTER 16
KNIVES

KNIVES SLOTTED HIS KAIKEN into Vic formation, flanking everyone at the rear. The jets before him were all Star Force-issued, so his 504 Kaiken looked out of place. Their fleet consisted of battle-ready Wakizashi 87s, equipped with the most powerful engines available on the market and built so slim they were mere slivers in the bright-blue sky. At the lead position was a Wakizashi with a black outline of a fist on each of its wings. Captain Nema's jet.

A separate squadron flew past them in the other direction, back to the base of RSF battleships, which they were losing one by one. A second battleship had been hit, leaving Nauticanne's air campus and battleship in a precariously defensive position. Half of the squadrons fell back, setting up a perimeter around what was left of Nauticanne. They would be the city's last means of defense.

To the right of the control board, a line of holoscreens hovered side by side, displaying the faces of each flyer in the squadron. But the only person he needed to listen to was Captain Nema, whose screen was magnified among the clutter of comms screens.

"If the battle gets to the ground, we'll have a lot of our Citizens' blood on our hands," Nema said. "So we stick to the skies, got that?"

Everyone voiced their agreement and followed Nema's jet as it drove its way to the tear in the sky.

By the time they approached, the enemy battleship had retreated beyond the wormhole.

"Assemble into combat formation with Nix Squadron," Nema ordered over the comms line. "We're going in."

They were what? Only a complete mung would fly into that wormhole. Wherever it was, it was in a completely different star system, and if that wormhole decided to close, they'd be cut off from backup.

Knives didn't like this plan. Not at all.

It wasn't even heroic; it was complete idiocy.

The squadrons came together, assembling into two separate but tight Finger Four formations, one jet angled behind the other. Nix Squadron stacked below their own, its formation mirroring theirs so that from the top it came together in a perfect V. As before, Knives was in the rear guard. He was thankful. To him, that meant safe. Or at least safer than the fools who were in front.

Nema's jet and Nix's lead crossed through the wormhole to the other side. In the rear, Knives was just one second behind, but that second stretched out before him like a rubber band, threatening to slap back at him at any moment. Knives felt outside of himself, as though he was watching a Kinna Downton stream, the one where she was leading her squadron to victory. How ridiculous, being in the same circumstances as the final battle in a Downton action stream. He just wanted to be in his quarters, enjoying a delicious orange imported straight from the Kiln forest on Targary because they were in season now.

Instead, he was flying straight into enemy territory.

All of the jets in formation had crossed, and he was the next and last in line. Within moments, he cleared the threshold, and the view before him, which had been just the inside of a circle moments before, had widened out to infinity. He took a deep breath as he viewed the enemy battleship, a behemoth, twice the length of any RSF warship. And behind it was something he had read about in maps reports but never experienced in person: Aokonic, the largest black hole in the whole Commonwealth, maybe even the known galaxies.

Yet despite the grand vista that sprawled before them, there was no enemy activity. It was ominously still.

What on Ancient Earth was the enemy planning?

"Behind!" Nema's voice ripped through his speakers. "They're coming from behind!"

"Rear view," Knives called out, and the Kaiken's displays reacted at the sound of his voice. A screen enlarged, hovering within his periphery, enough to focus without obstructing his view.

The enemy battleship hadn't been retreating, he realized. It was luring them.

A line of jets coated in pure stealth-black was on their tail, surfacing from their hiding place right along the cusp of the gate that held the wormhole's ring.

It was an ambush.

Knives only had a short moment to glance at the enemy jets, noticeably sleeker than the Wakizashis in their fleet. The frames of these jets were built so small that either the pilots were lying down flat or the jets were being controlled remotely.

The Royal Star Force had developed and bought the most advanced jets in all of Olympus, but this tech was unlike anything he'd ever seen. It was too advanced for a Dead Space ship and surpassed the tech of their own fleet.

His mouth hung open at what he saw next. Almost in sync, lines of light flowed through the metal surface of their ships like blood through veins, coursing to a single point at the nose of each vessel.

As if they were part of one body, the enemy jets fired all at once.

"Shields at full power," Knives yelled.

Immediately, a flash of blue rippled around the Kaiken's exterior, his force fields fully absorbing the particle-beam blast. Usually, his Kaiken was able to automatically recalibrate its thrusters to compensate for the hit, but the blast created such an impact that it veered him completely off course and out of formation from everyone else. But flight formations were useless now. It was time for the flyers to put their natural-born reflexes and field-honed skills into play.

He had programmed simulators this difficult before, but he wasn't in a simulator right now. This wasn't a pod that he could step out of whenever he wanted to. Every move he made out here would determine whether he lived or died. All the enemy needed was one lucky hit.

He flew in small arcs, trying to keep his path as unpredictable as possible. At the same time, he kept his eye on the combat. The enemy blasts weren't just meant for attack. They were using them for crowd control, corralling a few of their starjets dangerously close to the black hole that lay beyond the battleship.

"Keep your distance," he warned over the comms screens.

It was too late. Half of the Nix Squadron had already been pulled into Aokonic's grip. They were gone.

There was no time to mourn. Knives had to keep his mind on the battle.

A RSF Wakizashi soared into his quadrant, leading the enemy right to him.

Knives spotted the black fists on the Wakizashi's wings, which made it stand out from the others. It was supposed to warn those who came after it, much like Ia's iconic red feather. But it was because of those fists that everyone was on its tail. They knew Nema was the head of this outfit. Chop off the head, and the rest would flail.

Knives couldn't help but think about what Ia would do if she were there.

She wouldn't figure out overly clever ways to goad the enemy or get hero brain and rush into the thick of battle. She would stay out of the line of fire long enough to find an opening, an opportunity, a weakness. Anything so that she would come out of this alive.

And she would play dirty.

He flipped his Kaiken and headed toward the battleship. To avoid a skirmish, he turned off his engines, relying on his air thrusts, so the enemy jets wouldn't be able to track him on their heat sensors.

Like all the other vessels, the battleship had shields, even more powerful than the ones on their own jets. It would take more than a couple of particle blasts to bring those shields down.

He flew the Kaiken just above the surface of the battleship's force field, anchoring in one position like a parasite. His eyes scanned the structure. One hundred meters away he spotted a large square opening with force field chargers laced along its frame.

It was the opening to their flight deck.

Of course, it was shielded.

He pressed on his display, enlarging the image so he could get a better look at the setup. It was very similar to the ones he'd seen on Aphelion and on other Star Force bases. But then his eyes widened as they locked on the logo etched on the body of the charger unit. Sino Corp.

Mif.

Sino Corp contracted most of their military tech exclusively to the Olympus Commonwealth. How on Ancient Earth did the enemy get hold of this?

There was no time to dwell on this revelation. If they were Sino Corp force fields, at least he had an idea how to disarm them.

His gaze flew through the top of the Kaiken's glass cockpit.

"Track all enemy ships," he ordered.

Square red lights flew across the heads-up display that

ran over the glass, each one centering on each enemy ship within his field of view. Most of them were still following the Wakizashi with the black fists.

He glanced at Captain Nema's display screen, hovering in his periphery.

"Captain," he said. "I think I have an idea."

"Great, because I really would like these jets off my ass," he replied.

"Lead them to the deck entryway in the upper quadrant. If our weapons can't affect them, then hopefully theirs will."

"Risky," he said. "But I like it."

Nema's jet swooped back in his direction, a line of enemy vessels following in his wake.

If those enemy jets were going to keep attacking, this plan would make them fire where the damage would hurt them the most.

Nema flew closer and closer to the entryway, weaving away from any blasts that came his direction. Knives focused on the force field across the entryway. If those force field chargers were programmed anything like the one on Star Forces bases, they would require a data signature from each of their own jets.

"Come on. Come on," Knives whispered, tracking Nema's trajectory toward the entryway.

At the last second, Nema pulled up, leaving the enemy jets behind him heading straight to their own battleship. The force field chargers, reading the approaching vessels' data signatures, powered down, leaving the entrance wide open. With no time to decelerate, the first enemy jet crashed right through to the back end of the flight deck. Followed by another jet, and then another.

Nema's hoots filled the small space of the Kaiken's cockpit. "Kid, I can't believe that worked!" he screamed.

Nema relayed his orders to the rest of the existing squadron, and soon all of them were on their way to attack the weak spot created by the collision.

Knives was flying to join them when he spotted a different ship in his periphery, a unique cross-shaped vessel, departing from a separate exit.

It didn't look like the attacking battle jets, but there was something dangerous about its presence. The entire RSF fleet was focused in one place, clearing a very convenient path for this jet to pass without detection. But Knives had seen it. And it was heading straight for the wormhole. There was something Ia had said to him earlier. *Just a diversion.* That explosion at the entryway was a good way to mask this mystery jet's convenient departure.

"All battle jets to my coordinates," Nema ordered.

Knives had to make a choice. If he didn't follow orders, he'd be court-martialed for insubordination. His father had always taught him that only a coward would leave a fight. But there was something about that jet that raised concern. He set a targeting display to lock onto the cross ship. The image magnified. Knives scanned the whole vessel, its panels and construction broad like a shield yet sharp and dangerous. Finally, his eyes found the cockpit windows and the pilot sitting inside. Knives would never forget his face. The same one that stared back at him as he cut Bastian's throat.

Einn.

Instead of joining the rest of the RSF squadron in formation below, the Kaiken ascended, its engines still off to escape detection.

As Knives followed Einn's jet through the wormhole, he took a glance at his rear cameras, watching the rest of his squadron fighting for their lives. Perhaps it would turn out like that Kinna Downton stream after all, and victory would soon be theirs.

But then, without warning, the wormhole that joined that side of the All Black with their own shrank smaller and smaller, until there was nothing left behind him but the skies of Rigel Kentaurus.

Knives switched his rear view off and willed himself to focus on the path before him. But even then, it was a struggle.

His squadron was gone.

His throat tightened as his thoughts flew back to the battle, the bravest flyers soaring valiantly through those blackened skies. He was the only one left to remember it.

CHAPTER 17
IA

IA PUNCHED THE BUTTON at the center of her chest, feeling a jolt as the fans of the windpack worked to keep her aloft. She hovered downward, planting her feet steadily on the domed glass roof of Nauticanne's Astronautical Museum.

In the distance, maybe thirty or so city blocks away, the downed battleship lay burning, its frame so large it had crushed the buildings in its path. Even as she rushed to the edge of the roof, skyscrapers crumbled, and the skyline of the city burned to cinder.

Peering through the glass, she saw that the lobby below was already empty. The glass roof showed signs of cracks from the falling debris, and with each step she took, the fissures only deepened. Making sure to keep steady footing, she scanned the crowd spilling out onto the street below.

She lowered her eyelids just enough to set the modification in her left eye to magnification mode. She studied the mass of people before her, searching for a glimpse of Brinn's navy-blue hair. But even with her vision enhancement, she couldn't find her friend.

She banged her fist lightly against her thigh in decision. Activating the windpack around her shoulders, she swooped down into the middle of the chaos, swallowed by the mess of people running this way and that. She zigzagged through the crowds, trying to find someone, anyone that she would know. But there were no academy uniforms, not even a flash of the Star Force quartered shield among the sea of people.

She was about to scream out in frustration when she saw a familiar blond ponytail swishing in panic through the criss-cross of bodies.

"Angie," Ia yelled, sliding her helmet back off her head.

Angie Everett spun on her heel, her ponytail whipping around her. When their eyes met, she stuttered. "Ia..."

Ia pushed toward her. "Are you okay?"

And despite the uncontrollable tremble that had overtaken her lips, Angie managed a nod. Ia checked her face for any injuries. Her forehead was drenched in sweat and smeared with fallen ash from the remaining Nauticanne battleships ablaze in the sky, but she appeared to be in one piece.

"Do you know where Brinn is?" Ia asked.

Angie pointed down a narrow alley, one meant for service trucks. "I saw her head through there. With Liam."

Ia had gotten the answer she was looking for, but she didn't run. Any other time, Ia would have left Angie to search for shelter to ride things out. But with the city burning, there was no place safe. Ia looked back at her, considering her options. Angie had cadet training, and Ia could use someone to watch her back. "Do you know the layout of this city?"

"I've been living here for a month now."

"Good. Then you're coming with me. We'll find Brinn together," Ia said, and she took off into the alley. She heard Angie follow her.

Ia's feet pounded on the smooth pavement, skirting around the large cylindrical trash bins that lined the alleyway.

Then the pavement underneath her feet rumbled as a sleek battle jet passed overhead. The length of its wings, along with its upper and lower aero fins, came together at just the right angles. Like a cross. It was one that she recognized immediately. *Shepherd.*

She needed to find Brinn. Fast.

Einn was coming.

CHAPTER 18
BRINN

RACING THROUGH the city's back alleys, Brinn and Liam finally came to a stop, facing a ladder that led up the side of a tall building. With her head tilted back as far as it could, her eyes trailed up the wall to the roof's ledge, a razor-straight line slashing against the sky.

"We gotta get to some high ground," Liam said.

But Brinn was already numb. She couldn't even process the words coming out of his mouth, and the fiery scene frescoed across the sky. It was like she was stuck in a nightmare, and there was no way to pull herself out. So why try. Why even care.

The wormhole had closed a few minutes ago, but it still felt as if the universe had changed, as if it no longer belonged to them. And what was left were questions and disorder and an empty, fearsome shadow that people would need to fill with someone to blame. The Commonwealth would of course blame the refugees. They would blame her.

The air around her was thick with ash and debris from the nearby fallen skyscrapers. It was so hard to breathe that she was gasping. Not just for air, but for something. She was at a dead end. All she could do was look up. And climb. With each rung, she felt as if she was grasping for something, but she didn't know what.

"We're almost at the top," Liam called down to her from a few rungs up. "Our people will be able to find us from there."

But did she want them to?

She had spent years creating excuses for this Commonwealth. Defending these people. Fighting for them. And they had taken her brother from her. Soon, she was certain, they would take away her home. Brinn shook her head, trying to focus.

Above her, Liam cleared the ledge of the roof. He reached down to help her. She grabbed his hand, his fingers strong and callused, and hauled herself onto the rooftop. Where she expected to see the city's fractured skyline, she saw something else.

They weren't alone.

A ship the shape of a cross was lowering itself onto the rooftop, its bottom fin folding in as it landed. She scanned the surface for the Commonwealth quartered shield, but there was none.

"That's not a Star Force ship," Brinn said.

Liam raised his hands. "Don't worry. It's a friend."

A friend? She stopped in her place, her eyes frozen on the foreign vessel.

The ramp of the ship hissed, and the entryway lowered

from its center. A tall, lean figure dressed in a black flight suit walked out. A pair of recognizable white hearts had been engraved into his chest piece, and he wore a helmet with two sharp points on opposite sides of the crest.

Horns.

A spike of fear brushed against her skin. Brinn found herself inching backward. She shouldn't be here.

The figure tapped two of his fingers against a button at his temple, and his helmet retracted, revealing dark-gray eyes, golden skin, and gaunt cheekbones. His searing expression was one that she recognized and feared at the same time.

Because she had seen it before. On someone else's face.

"It's you," Brinn whispered.

An unsettling calm lay in the depths of Einn's eyes, like one that lay in the midst of a hurricane. And she knew at any moment the winds would rip her up.

Einn tilted his chin down, his gaze steady on hers. "And so we finally meet."

She turned to Liam. "We have to get out of here." She pivoted to the ladder at the ledge, but Liam held her back.

"Just listen to what he has to say," Liam insisted.

Her eyes searched his. Realization sank like lava to her core. "You're on his side? How? When?"

"Since the slaver attack—"

But she didn't give him much time to explain. She already knew who was to blame. She glared over in Einn's direction. "You brainwashed him, didn't you?"

Einn shook his head. "He was the one who found me."

Her jaw fell open. Liam was searching for Einn? Her eyes

narrowed back into focus as she twisted her wrist like Ia had taught her and broke free of Liam's grasp. She stepped away from him.

He laid his hands in front of him, trying to close the gap between them.

"The Commonwealth isn't what we believed it to be. They fed us lie after lie to get us to do their dirty work. And what do we have to show for it? My brothers. My father. Cammo, whom they've failed to honor. Nothing but dead and broken bodies."

The lines of his face grew sharp with anger, rippling past the calm that he usually wore when he was around her. That facade wasn't just for her, she realized. It was for the academy.

"Why fight for people who don't even value us," Liam continued. "He gets it, Brinn. He gets *us*."

"But he's a killer, Liam." Her voice strained, trying to get an edge in this entire conversation. Ia had told her about the Tawnies her brother had killed, the same group of people she had been trying to save when the Star Force captured her.

"I am," Einn interrupted. She turned to him, horrified that he'd admitted it. He angled his head as he continued. "But so is my sister. Yet you trust her with your life."

Her memories tore into mind. Yes, she'd been scared of Ia when she first met her. Yes, Ia had killed hundreds of thousands of Citizens during the Uranium War. But she had saved Brinn and the entire academy when they had no one else to turn to. *Then why do I still have my guard up most of the times we talk? Like we're actually fighting every time we're training?*

She had been closing herself off from Ia, keeping away her

most vulnerable doubts and fears while staying strong in front of her.

Would she have told Ia about Faren's death? If she had, would Ia even have cared?

Her heart cracked at the question.

Brinn couldn't push away the flicker of doubt that ran across her face. And she knew that Einn saw it, because he smiled.

He took two even steps toward her.

Immediately, just like Ia had drilled into her, Brinn lowered herself into the warrior's stance, her knees bent, one arm at an angle in front of her, keeping distance between the two of them.

He leaned on his right leg, observing her. "So, she's teaching you."

A second later, his flat palm rushed for her sternum, and Brinn pivoted, pushing his arm off-center. She didn't see his free hand coming. It struck her in the ribs, sending her stumbling to the side. She circled around, her fists flying toward him, exact and precise as Ia taught her, but no matter what she did, he was always several steps ahead of her. He was too fast, his other hand slicing at her neck. But before his attack could connect, he stopped.

He backed off. Calmly. The way he moved. The way he breathed and spoke. Like water when it was still.

"I'm not here to fight you," he said. He offered his hand to her. "I'm here to ask you for help."

This was a trick. Her eyes scanned his face, examining every line and angle for any hint of deception.

"Why would I ever help *you*?"

He didn't even have to think of his answer. "Because I see you, Brinn Tarver. I know how important you are. With your intelligence, you can create anything you desire. You can change the world as we know it." He walked her to the edge of the roof, so that they were looking down upon an open square in the middle of the city, filled with people running in all directions, veering away from falling columns and burning trees. He pointed at them. "All of them down there. They are insects for not understanding how important you are. You deserve *more*, Brinn. The question is... Is that what *you* want?"

The air around her stilled. What he said wasn't about the Commonwealth. Nor was it about getting revenge. It was about her finally taking control. She had been fighting against her past, her own skills and intellect, all so she could belong. But it had been for nothing. Now she could make a different choice.

To fight for herself.

Liam stepped in line, right next to Einn. Dark shadows lay heavy underneath his eyes, but the green in his irises was stoked with fiery new embers, glowing copper waiting to ignite.

"After everything that happened, I realized I was on the wrong side of this whole thing. But I think I always knew that. Somehow, I think you do, too."

Her eyes gazed at the sun. Its golden surface shone through the smoky haze. She stared right at it, letting the light sear into her vision. It was so bright and blinding that once she looked down again, her entire world was streaked with white. But through the bright haze, she saw something.

A shadow.

"I have more to offer you," Einn said. "More than the Commonwealth. More than my sister. Don't forget I was the one who taught Ia everything."

"Yeah, but you never taught me this," a voice called out. When Einn turned, Ia was before him, kicking him right in the groin.

CHAPTER 19
IA

EINN WAS ONLY DOWN for a second, his exo-armor absorbing most of the impact.

Ia looked to Brinn. "Tarver, get out of here," she ordered.

If Brinn got to the ground, Angie would find her and tell her where to go. They had planned a safe meeting point if they ever got separated.

Einn barreled toward Ia, his arms circling her body, squeezing so hard that her feet kicked off the ground.

She forced her elbows back, trying to get enough space between their bodies to twist away from him. But his armor wasn't helping her gain even a centimeter, while she was dressed in a polyaeriate flight suit, with barely enough padding to absorb any attacks that came her way. The windpack around her chest was giving her some protection, but even the metal frame was starting to crack.

Ia took a deep breath and jerked her head back, the thick of her skull colliding right into the fragile bridge of Einn's nose.

He dropped her, and she rolled back up, facing him. Glaring at her, he gripped his nose and spit out the blood that had collected in his mouth.

"I know why you're doing this, Einn," she said. "You're trying to find Dad, aren't you? You want to kill him."

Einn smiled without answering.

He was wounded, but she had to stay on guard. She kept her gaze trained on him and switched her fighting stance, squaring her shoulders and leaning on her back leg. He was too strong to take on in close quarters.

She knew their father was his weakness, so she kept talking. Trying to chip into that hard armor of his. "You can deny it," she continued. "But I know this is all linked to him."

Ia had barely finished her sentence when Einn quick-stepped toward her, so fast that he was a blur. She skirted away, but he was already two steps ahead and right in her space, a fist striking her abdomen. The wind flew out of her lungs, and she gasped, aching for the oxygen to return.

She had been fighting all her life, but with other people. Never with her brother, at least not in a real fight. They had sparred in the past, but pulled their punches so they would never get hurt. So it surprised her, receiving the full force of her brother's attacks. She knew that he was stronger than she was, but this was the first time she actually felt it.

Ia raised her chin, watching him approach her. She had to do something to gain an edge. Even if it wasn't completely fair or brave. Still gasping, she tapped the controls of her windpack. She lifted up into the air until she thought she was too high for him to reach—but with Einn, she could never be too sure.

There was something different about him. As if the air around him was on fire. She couldn't explain it; she just felt it in her blood.

"Why would I ever want to kill the man who gave me so many gifts?" Einn said.

She stared at him, trying to dissect the meaning of his words. The question in her eyes soon became a look of absolute horror as she watched him bring his palms together in ritual, something dark swirling in between his fingers. A tear. Like the one that ripped across the sky earlier. It only took a second, and he was gone.

She was too late to notice that another small tear had appeared above her.

And in that moment, Einn dropped through.

What the mif?

He dove toward her, grabbing her. With his added weight, they fell, the windpack shuddering as it tried to keep the two of them afloat. It happened so fast that she couldn't shift away. She grappled against him, but it was no use. Within seconds, he ripped the windpack off her.

And he simply let go.

Her eyes wide in alarm, she reached out to him, even though she knew he wouldn't grab her hand.

Instead, his fingers shaped another spatial tear that he disappeared into.

Then all that was left was sky, her hands now reaching for the sun. She knew the ground was coming for her.

Oh Deus, she whispered. *Oh Deus, give me the strength to survive this.*

The ground swallowed her whole, the impact shaking through her from her neck to her spine. She was still breathing, but she could tell that she was broken. Her body and mind were in shock; she couldn't feel anything, not even the pain from the breaks in her bones. Not yet, but she knew they were there.

She took in quick, rapid breaths. She couldn't move her neck, no matter how hard she tried. A shadow blurred into her line of sight. She blinked so her eyes could focus. The lines sharpened as she pieced together the details of her brother's face. His stony gray eyes. The hard line of his jaw.

Einn leaned in.

Memories flashed through her mind of the last time they'd seen each other. In the White Room, where he had knifed her in the stomach. She looked up at him just like she had back then as he watched and waited for her to die.

This time, instead of slicing a knife through her belly, he slipped his hands underneath her arms and hoisted her up. Her body was still too stunned to fight back. As her world righted itself, she saw Brinn and Liam still standing at the edge of the rooftop.

Why hadn't they run?

She wanted to scream at them to leave, but then she caught sight of Brinn's eyes, wide and weary, but not from the panicked frenzy of today. A terrible sadness weighing in their depths. Not fatigue, but as if she was *done*.

"She can't protect you anymore," Einn said. It took Ia a moment to realize he was talking to Brinn.

She felt his hands move to her neck, tightening one hand

against her chin. She let out a slow breath, knowing quite well what the next seconds would bring. A twist and final snap.

But before he could make his move, she caught a glimmer at the edge of Einn's ship.

A ghost?

No. Camouflage.

She followed the ripple of movement, still warping the light around it so that it maintained the illusion. Suddenly, the glimmer fell, the camouflage cascading downward to reveal the outline of a white skull facing her. Goner. His arm raised, the pistol pointing straight at Einn.

Was he here to help her? Deus, was she actually going to survive this?

But then, Goner's arm shifted slightly. The pistol cracked at the air, and an electric bullet surged through the gap between them. Her eyes widened as she realized its trajectory. Goner's movements were never an accident.

"Bastard," she breathed. The electric bullet tore through the light fabric of her suit and into her flesh.

Her body slid back down to the ground, and she crumpled to her side.

Einn turned to Goner. "What was that for?"

As she gasped out on the ground, she noted the sound of her brother's voice. Casual. Not at all surprised that Goner had shown up.

"Just finishing things up for you," Goner said.

They were working together.

"You mung," she hissed, her voice thin like a deflating balloon. It took all of her strength to raise her chin to look at him. "I thought we were on the same side."

Goner's eyes flicked down to hers, and the thin black line between his lip curled upward in a devil's grin. He turned to Einn. "You should go. Looks like someone found us."

Einn looked over his shoulder, but Ia couldn't move her neck to see what he'd spotted on the horizon. A muscle ticked across Einn's jaw, and she knew he was annoyed.

"I'll take care of her," Goner said, his hand returning to his pistol, a look of giddiness rippling across his face. He had wanted to be the one to end her for years.

Einn glanced down at Ia, his eyes without a trace of empathy. "Do it right," he whispered to Goner.

Her brother turned to the two cadets standing by in her periphery. Ia had taught both of them to fight, but there they were, waiting to accept their fate. Unless...did they actually want to hear what Einn had to say?

"My offer still stands, the same one I extended to Liam," he said to Brinn. His voice softened just enough to be charming. "You are welcome on this ship."

Her brother's face remained controlled, from the tension in his jaw to the darkness in his eyes. Brinn was too smart to believe him, Ia reminded herself. She'd be able to see right through it. Her gaze wandered over to Brinn, the world burning behind her.

Don't be fooled by him, she thought. It was too hard to speak, but she wanted to scream it.

Don't.

But even if she said it, would it matter? From the look in Brinn's eyes, Ia knew that she had already made up her mind.

What had happened, Ia wanted to ask her, between now and when she last saw her? What was Brinn thinking?

She realized now that was something she should have been asking all along. The gap between them had been growing larger and larger, when it could have been bridged with that one question.

As Brinn made her way to Einn's ship, Ia called out with a gasping breath. "Why?"

Brinn stopped. She looked back at Ia, her eyes cast in shadows.

"I've followed the rules all my life," Brinn said, her voice quiet. There was a hard edge that had never been there before. "It's time for me to break them."

Ia's heart cracked as she watched Brinn walk away, her navy-blue hair dark against the fire-stained sky.

When Tarver had disappeared up the ramp and into the ship, her brother crouched to look down at her. "That was easy," he said. "I didn't think she'd just leave you here."

His words stung. If she had the strength and her mouth wasn't so dry, Ia would have spit in his face.

Einn rose. Next to him, Goner stood taller, his build broader than her brother's. But the devil wasn't known for his strength; he was known for his clever cruelty. Einn clapped Goner on the shoulder. "Once you're done, meet at the rendezvous point."

And her brother made his exit.

Deus, if she died today, the last thing she was going to see was Goner's face.

When he was close enough, she tried to grab the fabric of

his cloak, but she couldn't lift her arm. Her mouth fell open into a soundless laugh.

"I don't think now's the time to be in fine spirits," Goner told her.

A hoarse whisper came out of her. "Einn beat me. Not you. Remember that."

Goner furrowed his brow for the slightest of moments. She watched him as he tried to hide the shift in his expression, which was hard to do with the skull pattern on his skin bending along with it.

"I guess I'll have to live with that," Goner said. He loaded his pistol with a fresh bullet and pointed the gun. "Now hold still."

With his finger on the trigger, he fired.

CHAPTER 20
KNIVES

KNIVES KEPT HIS DISTANCE as he flew through the demolished skyline, hiding in the plumes of smoke rising from the fallen buildings that scattered the grounds of Calvinal. It was almost impossible to see, but he managed to keep an eye on Einn's cross-shaped ship, which had landed on a rooftop in the center of the city.

Knives had turned off the navigation and comms systems in case Einn was scanning the area for other jets like his own. Without the help of his onboard, Knives had to rely on his sight and reflexes. And he laughed, because that was what Ia had wanted for him all along. He remembered the scowl that had torn across her face as they squabbled about upgrading his entire system. And suddenly, he desperately wanted another one of those moments with her. Even if she didn't care for him at all. Even if she had already lost whatever interest she had in him. He still wanted to see her again.

But to do that, he had to get through this.

The cross jet had been parked for a while, and from that distance he could see the outline of figures on the rooftop, but as he circled closer, he noticed that the roof was a little less crowded than the last time he'd been able to glimpse it through the smoke.

Knives's focus shifted to the cross jet, a glow radiating from underneath its wings. Its thrusters were activated. It was about to take off.

Knives ramped up his speed, his fingers flying to turn all of his systems back on. At this point, stealth didn't matter. His target was going to get away before he could get answers and before he could pay him back for what he'd done to Bastian. He'd made the choice to leave Nema and the rest of his squadron behind, so he *had* to take Einn down. So his actions could mean *something*. If not, then he was a coward for leaving them, just like his father had warned.

"Kai, scan that ship. Are the force fields active?"

The display shifted to sensor mode so all he saw was the dark outline of the enemy ship, a cross slashing against his display.

"Negative."

Perfect. He accessed his weapons menu, lowering the rail guns that were mounted on each wing.

The HUD flashed before him, squares centering on the main target points on the enemy ship. He needed to stop that jet before it was airborne. He flipped over the protective glass that covered the weapons trigger on the right grip. His thumb hovered over it, eyes narrowing at the target. But then he noticed who was left on the rooftop. Two people.

His eyes glanced up from the HUD and peered through

the cockpit windows. A cloaked figure, carrying someone in his arms.

She had short black hair and wore a regulation RSF flight suit, the same one he had seen on a girl who had jumped off a Nauticanne battleship a few hours ago.

His thumb readjusted, away from the weapons trigger, both hands now fully gripped onto the steering wheel.

Below, Einn's jet took off, its force field flickering on with a sheen of blue before turning clear. It took a matter of seconds for it to disappear high into the stratosphere.

Knives had missed his moment, but it didn't matter. All that mattered was *her*.

He veered toward the rooftop. The figure spotted his jet and quickly whisked Ia to the edge of the roof.

Knives circled around, aiming his rail guns for the ladder hanging off the side. He fired, aiming purposely at the ledge below to stop Ia's captor from going any further. A flurry of broken cement and dust flew up into the air, and the ladder, now detached from the ledge, lurched as it toppled over.

The man had nowhere to go. He could have climbed down on his own, but not with Ia in his arms.

Across the gap, Knives stared down his foe. For the first time, Knives could see him up close. The skull on his face was impossible to mistake.

"Goner," he breathed. One of the most dangerous criminals in all the Commonwealth. He was wanted for the destruction of Commonwealth property and resources. And that didn't mean spray-painting on the sidewalk or hacking holo-ads to play jokes. It meant completely demolishing whole

Commonwealth laboratories and information hubs. He was very good at destroying buildings and the people inside them. And Knives knew that it was one of Goner's life missions to beat Ia at all costs.

The black hollows around Goner's eyes made the lavender hue of his irises stand out, sparking like the air before the fury of lightning. His lips curled in a dare, and without warning, he jumped off the ledge.

It took Knives a second to react. No normal person could jump off a ten-story building without a windpack or a glider and survive.

Knives tapped on the camera at the bottom hull of his ship, and the display immediately tracked Goner's fall, steady and certain. He didn't even flinch when he landed; it was as if every bone and muscle in his body was built to absorb the impact. It was enough to make Knives pause, to thumb through his memory for everything he'd read about the criminal. There was nothing in any records that said Goner would be able to withstand a fall like that. It made him wonder what other skills and abilities the reports had missed.

Knives flew his jet to the opening of the alleyway, quickly blocking off his evader's only exit. He opened the cockpit and jumped out, not bothering to even lower his ladders to the ground.

Knives raised his pistol, aiming right for the skull on Goner's face. "Don't move. There's no way out."

But of course, Goner moved. As if it was second nature, Goner reached for the edge of his cape, and as he swung his arm around, he covered Ia's body. The colors on the fabric started to ripple, shifting like a chameleon to blend into the environment. The black fabric transformed from the gray, cracked texture of the pavement to the brown-and-white spackle of the brick wall in the background. His armor and cape disappeared, along with the rest of him. Last to go was his face, the skull flickering into the nothingness, as though he didn't exist.

"What on Ancient Earth?" Knives mumbled.

To the right, he heard footsteps across pavement, the skittering of gravel. Knives turned, but too late. He felt an elbow strike right at his spine. Knives tried to fight the pain, swiveling to the side with his pistol in hand, his ears craning for any signs of movement.

Nothing.

He tilted his head.

The rustle of debris near a cylindrical trash compressor on the right. Knives adjusted and fired, guessing where his attacker would be.

The bullet missed.

A clatter of footsteps came crashing toward him. An invisible hand gripped his arm, crushing the bones in his wrist. The pain seared through him, so intense he saw stars. His pistol fell from his grip.

Then his attacker let go, leaving Knives to clutch his injured wrist with his good hand. His pistol rose in midair as Goner, still invisible, picked it up and hurled it to the other side of the alley. Footsteps clicked away, the thud of Goner's soles echoing throughout the alleyway.

"Don't hurt her," Knives pleaded before the footsteps could completely fade away. "Please. Just let her go."

The footsteps stopped. Goner's skull appeared, looking back at him, the rest of his body in a translucent haze between the visible and the unseen. One black socket was larger than the other, as if he were raising an eyebrow. "You're Cōcha's friend?"

"I am," Knives said.

Goner deactivated the rest of his camouflage.

He stepped closer. From this distance, Knives could see that the skull on his face wasn't paint at all. It was very much a design etched into his skin.

Goner kneeled. With a free hand, he lifted the edge of his cape. Underneath, Ia lay still.

Knives glanced down at her. Cuts and scrapes peeked through tears in her suit, and her right arm was crooked as if broken. His heart caved in at the sight of her. It was only when he saw the rise and fall in her chest that he could let out a sigh in relief. "She's alive," Knives said, and then his voice turned to a growl. "You piece of mung. She told me about you, that you want her dead."

Knives lunged after him, but Goner raised one of his hands to keep distance between them. "Ia and I have had our fights. But unfortunately, this wasn't me." He glanced down at her. "I had to sedate her before she went into shock. She needs medical attention."

Goner lay her body gently on the ground and then stood up to leave.

"Freeze," a voice yelled out. A few feet away from them, Angie Everett stood, her face pale but her arm steady, pointing the pistol that Goner had thrown to the side.

But Goner didn't even flinch, as though bullets didn't matter to him. He nodded down at Ia, unconscious on the ground. "You have a choice," he said, addressing Knives. "You either help her, or you try to catch me. If I were you, I'd make sure she lives."

"Why are you doing this? I thought you were enemies."

"Funny," he chimed. "I could say the same about you two."

Knives looked over at Angie, who—even with a pistol in her hand—was on the verge of collapsing. "Everett, lower your gun," he ordered.

Angie raised her eyebrows.

It's okay, he mouthed, and Angie slowly lowered her arm, the orange charge of the nozzle tip now pointing to the pavement.

Goner smirked. "Good choice."

Then he raised his hand in a lazy farewell. "I'm sure I'll see you around."

The colors of his armor had started to shift to match his surroundings, and soon the outline of his body was a haze, as if between one world and the next. "Oh yeah. This rescuing thing... Let's keep this between us." Goner raised a finger to his lips, and soon there was nothing left of him at all.

CHAPTER 21
BRINN

BRINN GAZED through the front glass of Einn's ship, the observation window so wide that it displayed the landscape below alight in flames. The largest city in the Olympus Commonwealth was completely decimated, and she was fine with that. Let the whole place burn. There was nothing left for her there anyway.

She thought about her brother. Faren always knew the right thing to do. He stood up for himself way before she ever did. She heard him always, his laugh, the bravery in his voice when he told her he was marching in protest. But now he was gone, and all that was left were those memories.

Liam stood beside her. The violent light of the city fires curved upon his dark brown skin, but his eyes reflected the bright expanse of the sky above.

"Why didn't you tell me you were looking for him?" Brinn asked.

His gaze snapped over to hers. "When Ia has been training

you to fight him? I didn't think you'd be interested, but Einn convinced me otherwise. Believe me when I say I'm surprised you're even here."

"I can say the same for you. The best flyer in our year, model Citizen with a father and brothers who've served in the war."

"A paralyzed father and three dead brothers. We've all lost someone in this mess."

Ia had tried so hard to protect her, to teach her how to defend herself. How foolish she was, Brinn realized. Ia didn't know that there were things that hurt more than blades and fists. Pain. Sadness. No one could ever protect you from that.

"Those people were taken from us." Brinn placed her hand on the glass, her palm giant against the city below, like a god swatting down a fly.

"But they're not going to take you. That's why you're here," Einn said from the pilot seat. He turned on autopilot and crossed over to her, his eyes glinting like silver. "You know what I've learned from surviving for so long? The universe rarely gives you a gift. But you have one now. A new path. You've taken the first step. It's not over yet."

A new path. Those words rang loud and bright in her ears.

Brinn looked back at Einn. She felt strength in his presence. It was something intangible that couldn't be forced or created; it just existed. He was so different from Ia. Where Ia was rough and loud, Einn was quiet, his eyes always attentive, watching her movements, sensitive to any shifts in the conversation. As if he listened. As if he understood.

She pointed to the crumbling buildings and the downed battleships, with flames reaching up to the sky. This was all because of Einn. It was frightening and exhilarating at the same time. "And you, where does your path lead?" she asked him. "I've seen what you can do. All of that down there, is this really what you want?"

"Just like you, these are only my first steps. To create, you have to destroy."

Her eyes shined in the face of the orange sun. She didn't look away as the heat burned her cheeks. "Perhaps you're right."

CHAPTER 22
KNIVES

KNIVES RUSHED into the emergency medical department, the lobby overflowing with survivors from the day's attack. It was the closest medical facility in the area, located almost ten kilometers from the city center. Even so, it wasn't fully functional. Two-thirds of the building had been destroyed by the fire spreading throughout the city. The winds were strong that day, which gave the flames the ability to jump.

Knives tried to locate a free hoverbed, but they were all claimed by the wounded that had already trickled in. This event had taken many victims, and judging by the state of the people here, it would take many more.

He turned to see Angie already dragging a med facility administrator over to their corner. The man had curly auburn hair that had lost its spring, and his eyes were slow from fatigue. But when he looked down at Ia, he backed away without hesitation.

"Where are you going?" Angie asked.

The admin paused. "I know who that is."

"We just need a med borg. That's all," Knives pleaded.

Angie stepped in. "My dad is Vojas Everett, one of the most influential members of the Council. You will give this girl medical attention."

The admin looked her over and shook his head. "My uncle died during one of her hijackings. There's no way I'm letting a borg give her medical assistance."

"I can handle this one." A woman's low voice came from the other end of the hall. "I believe half of these med borgs legally belong to the Star Force anyway." Knives looked over to see Meneva Patel walking toward them. Her usually impeccable updo was now in a state of mess, but she still stood tall and confident as she flashed her credentials to the admin, whose face had grown red with anger.

"Do what you want," he said and then left.

Professor Patel stared him down until he disappeared around the corner, and then turned back to face them.

"Meneva," Knives said.

Professor Patel gave him a tiny smile as if to say she was happy that he was still alive and breathing, then shifted her attention to the girl in his arms. "What happened to her?"

Knives shook his head. "I can't say. I wasn't there when it happened."

Meneva rolled up the sleeves of her long, white lab coat. "Let's get her into one of the examination rooms."

* * *

The lights were too bright, but Knives found himself looking at them. If he glanced down, he'd see that Ia was entirely broken. The initial X-rays had shown several injured ribs, a severely cracked femur bone, and spinal compression and slight fractures to several of her vertebrae. If the damage had been worse, she'd have been permanently paralyzed.

After a quick operation to drain the fluid within her skull, they placed her in a cryo capsule to reduce the swelling. Thank Deus, Knives had come when he did. Professor Patel told him if it was five minutes later, Ia would have suffered irreversible brain damage.

They removed the modifications installed on her left eye—since the inflammation was pressing against it and could create permanent damage to her vision—as well as all of her other modifications and tech so they didn't get in the way of her body's recovery.

Once that was done, they treated Ia's spine, which had suffered the most damage. They placed her in an environmentally controlled pod made of tempered glass so it was easy to see her. Knives watched the entire procedure. He stayed planted in the same spot, never leaving her side, even though Meneva insisted it would distract her from monitoring the treatment.

Ia's body lay on a plastic platform. Above her, surgical arms were poised for their duties, but at the moment, they hung there on pause. Because everything that needed to be done was on the other side of Ia's body. A large hole had been carved out of the middle of platform, exposing the flesh along Ia's spine. If he looked closely, Knives could see the tiny surgibots, with their long, spidery legs, climbing around, operating on her. Precise cuts were made, exposing the bone, but the incisions were smothered in a gel that created an environment to keep the flesh from incurring any further trauma. The bots swam around through the goop, performing the exact repairs needed in order to make Ia whole again.

Two days passed, and Ia's treatment continued, the bots constantly readjusting the bone and reconstruction as the swelling went down, using electronic surges to stimulate nerve regeneration. They were making progress, Professor Patel had assured Knives, but every hour that passed, Ia looked the same. Frozen in place. In a world between the living and the dead. If something happened, if that capsule was opened or damaged, it would be enough to send her off, for her body to crash back to the place where he'd found her. Broken. Severed. Almost gone.

The door opened behind him, and Angie Everett walked into the room with a bag of fresh oranges in hand. "Is she awake?"

Knives rubbed his eyes and shook his head. "No."

She held out the oranges to him. They were a ripe batch, imported from Targary. He could tell by the hue of the skin, slightly reddish at the navel. He had been craving them ever since he had gotten back to Rigel Kentaurus, but now he didn't have the appetite.

"How's it going out there?" he asked Angie.

She pulled up a chair, picked out an orange, and started to peel it. "The death count is at six thousand and growing as they clear away the debris. It's still a mess, sir."

She finished peeling the orange and handed him a wedge. He ate it, to be polite. He knew what it *should* taste like. A tart but sweet flavor, cool on his tongue. It should energize him like the sun that grew it, that encouraged the crimson to blossom on its dimpled rind. But right now, it was flavorless on his tongue.

He looked toward the windows, but the electronic shutters were drawn closed. He had programmed them that way after the first day when the fires raged throughout the night. Even with them down, he couldn't get any sleep.

"Are the fires out?" he asked.

"All the major ones are under control. There are a few here and there, but there's no more danger of them spreading. It's clear enough for people to get outside on the streets."

He knew what she meant. He heard them. People were gathering. Rioting. Marching. Looting. The public was angry.

"There are rumors going around that Einn is leading the Fringe Alliance."

Knives shook his head. "Einn has other allies," he said, remembering the Sino Corp logo painted on the tech of that battleship. But he didn't bring it up, not when he wasn't sure. Einn's people could have stolen it.

"Even if it's not true, everyone's going after the refugees. They think they're all a part of it." Angie rolled her eyes. "Say goodbye to the Sanctuary Act. My dad says there's no hope anymore. Might as well call it dead in the water."

Beside him, Knives's holowatch buzzed lightly against a plastic surface. He had taken it off the first day. The messages were coming nonstop, flooding in ever since the day of the attack. He knew who they were all from.

"Do you want to get that?" Angie asked.

Knives swiped his father's message away from his lock screen. "It's fine."

Angie leaned over Ia's capsule. "She'll be waking up in a brand-new world," she said.

Knives leaned back in his chair, his eyes resting on Ia's face. "If she even wakes up at all."

* * *

Knives had drifted off to sleep. Finally. He'd felt the weight of everything pressing down on him so hard that he had no other choice. He didn't dream. It was just black.

"Wake up." An abrupt voice sliced through the dark abyss. His eyes opened, vision blurry, the light from Ia's capsule blinding him as his pupils adjusted.

Across the room, Professor Patel tossed his brown bomber jacket at him.

"General Adams is on his way," Meneva said. "He knows Ia is here."

Which meant he knew that Knives was there as well.

"I can go down and walk him to this room, or I can stall," Meneva continued. "What do you want me to do?"

Once he was back with the Star Force, they'd court-martial him for abandoning his squadron. That was certain. But most likely, his father would step in. The general would order him to report back to base, where he'd be sifted into another squadron and probably would be dispatched immediately. He wouldn't get to see Ia when she woke up. Hell, once he was on another squadron, he might be dead before then.

He stood up, quickly threading his arms through the sleeves of his jacket, minding the wrap around his wrist. His injury hadn't completely healed, but it was good enough.

He looked over at Ia, who lay still within the closed environment of her capsule. "Is she well enough to travel?"

Professor Patel nodded. "You have about fifteen minutes before he gets here."

Meneva tapped on the display at the head of the capsule. The unit hissed as the top half lifted. The sterile scent of UV rushed at him.

He grabbed a blanket from his chair and draped it over Ia's body. He placed one arm under her knees and another around her shoulders as he scooped her up.

"The gel sealants on her wounds will hold for a few more days." Professor Patel placed one of the surgi-bots in his chest pocket. "She'll need to be stitched up once you settle somewhere." Then she reached into one of the pockets of her lab coat and pulled out an amber bottle. "And you're going to need this. Just a few drops on her tongue so the bio-bots can get into her bloodstream. She'll be in a lot of pain, but don't go overboard, or her body will become too dependent on it. Do you understand?"

She looked him straight in the eye, and he nodded.

"Good." Meneva slipped the bottle into his chest pocket, where it settled on top of the depowered surgi-bot. "Do you even know where you're going?"

"I know a place," he said. It would be a gamble, but it was something.

He moved toward the door, but before he left, he turned back. "Thank you, Meneva."

She nodded with a tight smile, and then he passed through the doorway.

"Wait," she called out, running into the hallway after him. "Your holowatch."

"I don't need it." He knew that the Star Force could track his location if he brought it with him.

"Good luck, Knives," she said. It was the first time she had ever said his first name. All it took was the world to end for them to actually become friends.

With Ia in his arms, he ran.

CHAPTER 23
BRINN

EINN'S SHIP, *Shepherd*, flew for days before Brinn noticed them slowing to a stop. She glanced out the window at their destination, a chunk of rock floating dangerously close to a gigantic black hole.

She stared into the swirl of matter in the black hole's center. "That doesn't look like a wise place to anchor."

"That's Aokonic," Liam said. "The flyers learned about it in class. It's the largest black hole in the known territories, and it's still growing."

Brinn recognized the name. Aokonic was located right at the edge of the Commonwealth territories. There was strategy behind Einn's decision to place his headquarters at that exact corner of space, she realized. So she took back what she had previously said. It was the perfect place to anchor. No one, not even the Royal Star Force, would dare to venture close to it.

She was so far from home. Her thoughts went to her

parents. She had to hope that they were safe, even if she hadn't heard from them since the attack on Calvinal.

To forget her worries, Brinn turned her attention to the structures built all around the planetoid's cragged crust. The chunk of rock wasn't just a dead planetoid. It was an actual colony, and Einn's headquarters. She'd expected a mishmash of old space stations welded together. A rust bucket of scrapped parts jigsawed into a somewhat functional amalgamation. But what she saw was a self-sustainable space station with enough advanced tech to rival those in the Olympus Commonwealth. There was no way that all of this was stolen. Einn must have aligned himself with some powerful backers.

She glanced over at Einn, wondering about the shadows in his history. He caught her gaze and then gestured to the sight before them.

"It's beautiful, isn't it?" Einn said.

"This is your headquarters?" she asked.

"No." His features softened, his sharp brow for the first time appearing less severe. "I call it home."

And she remembered the way Ia used to talk about her brother when she and Brinn first met. No matter how far Ia had drifted, Einn was the anchor who would always pull her back. To where? Here? This same place Brinn was looking at right now? How strange that she was the one seeing it in Ia's stead.

But it was Ia who had made that choice. To fight her brother like that and die. To never see this home again. Faren was the same. He'd decided to go to that protest despite the risks. And now they were gone.

Everyone made decisions that hurt her. Now Brinn had made her own selfish choice. This was the only way she could ignore the holes that were eating through her heart.

A new path. That was what Einn had said. The Star Force was no longer her destiny, but as she looked up, Brinn saw something that could possibly take its place. A massive structure that stilled the breath in her lungs. At first glance, it looked like an intergalactic gate, but larger than any of the ones she had seen, which wasn't many since space travel was expensive and heavily regulated by the Olympus Commonwealth. This grand circular structure was large enough to fit a whole planet in its center. Work vessels had been deployed, crawling all over to repair the damage it had withstood. She had gathered that this was on the other side of that wormhole that tore open the skies of Calvinal.

"We call it Penance," Einn said as he marveled at it.

There was something about it that gave Brinn a strange sense of déjà vu. As if she had seen this exact thing before. She dug through the pit of memories, trying to piece it together.

"This was Bastian's work," she said, her breath fogging the glass on the window that separated her from the structure before her. She had seen it so many times, drawn in the pages of his journal while she worked through equations at the other side of his desk. She never asked what it was because she thought a structure like that could never actually be built. But here it was, staring back at her, a goliath brought to life.

This was what had created the wormhole to Calvinal without a receiving gate, which in itself was a marvel of engineering. But it wasn't all this structure could do. She knew from her work with Bastian that more was possible.

"You want to tear open the universe, don't you?" she asked Einn.

He gave her a wicked grin. "Don't *you*?"

This universe was violent and erratic. It made no sense to her, and the people along with it. The only thing that she understood was the logic set by science, numbers, and that monstrous structure that hovered before her.

"Well, then," Brinn said. "Let's get to work."

CHAPTER 24

IA

THERE WAS NOTHING for Ia to grasp onto. No thoughts, ideas, or even the notion of time. All she had was the pain. Her eyes opened, and there it was—an unwanted companion, the first thing to greet her. It rippled throughout her body, delighting in the splits in her pieces.

Her vision blinded her at first, that wave of reality that rushed into her, but after a few blinks, it dimmed to what was actually there. She looked up at an old metal ceiling with rusting beams crisscrossing from one wall to the other.

Her hands clutched the cloth bedsheet at her sides, rough yet almost bare-thin. Even curling her fingers felt foreign to her. As if this body was not hers.

With every ounce of strength, she tilted her chin down, gritting her teeth all throughout to bear the sharp pangs ripping through her body. She saw the apparatus gripping her right arm. A thin, angular spider made of metal crawled on her skin, sticking large, sharp pins into several points of her wrist.

She cried out. Not from the sight of it, not even from the pain. And oh, there was pain. But she was faced with a revelation more alarming than that. No matter how much she willed it, she couldn't make her body move.

Ia heard the sound of metal scraping against the floor as the door lumbered open at the other end of the room.

Eve stood in the doorframe, holding a bucket. Her eyes locked on Ia's. The bucket slipped from her hands, water cascading across the floor.

What was this? A memory? Was she even awake, or had her dreams taken her back to the last time she had set foot on Myth? *What the mif are you doing here?* she wanted to scream, but her voice came out a garbled mess, as if every syllable had sloshed into one. When she blinked, the world jumped.

"Don't panic," a calm voice floated toward her. Knives was now in the room. He was wearing his brown leather jacket, but his flight suit was old and dirty, as though he'd worn it for weeks straight.

How did he get here?

Ia looked behind him to the empty doorframe, where Eve was no longer standing.

How much time had passed since she'd seen her? Her eyes widened, and then she looked down at her arm. The vise that was holding down her wrist had disappeared, and the metal spider was nowhere to be seen.

"I had to give you a sedative," Knives explained. "You woke up too soon."

She tried to move her wrist, but all she could manage was a slight twitch in her fingers.

Knives reached out, his hand stopping hers.

"Don't overwork yourself."

She looked at his hand over hers, and she knew she should feel something. His fingers against hers. That warmth that flushed against the surface of the skin.

"I can't," she said as she tried to find the words. "I can't feel you."

His eyes tensed, and for a split second she glimpsed shock reflected in the blue, darkening for an almost undetectable moment before he blinked. "Professor Patel said it was all going to come back."

His voice was soft, pleasant, but she could tell he was trying too hard to keep it that way. She closed her eyes, wanting to shut everything out, to return to that empty space of slumber, a place where dreams didn't even dare to lurk. But she was awake, and everything was crashing back toward her.

If Knives was still holding her hand, she couldn't feel it. Was it the sedative that was barreling through her veins, numbing her whole entire body? Or was it a fate worse than that? In the dark, she was alone with her thoughts, and there was nothing she could do to stop them.

Her last memories played in slow motion. Goner staring down at her with his pistol pointed. Einn letting her fall from the sky. And Brinn, that look in her eyes. Was it sadness? It seemed more like what Ia was feeling now. Numb.

She opened her eyes and found Knives's face. Her throat felt like sand. "Where is everyone?"

"Everyone..." he repeated. "Hopefully as far away from

us as possible. The last I knew, Professor Patel was back on Calvinal, and the rest of the RSF are gathering their forces." He looked away as if the memory was something he didn't want to stare in the face. "That attack was big, Ia. Nema and half of our squadrons were lost once they crossed that wormhole."

Each word required her to fill her lungs with enough oxygen to speak. "Then how are you still here?"

He looked down. "Because I turned back."

There was something he wasn't telling her. She could see it, that weight in his shoulders dragging him down. It may not have been something she needed to hear. Not the facts and statistics of the events, death counts and explosions, because he was being very forthcoming about the news he shared. It was something a bit more buried. An emotion or a fear. Or perhaps a guilt he didn't even want to confront just yet.

"But if I didn't," he continued, "I wouldn't have found you. You wouldn't be here right now."

"And where is here?"

A knock came at the door. "Can I come in?"

Knives turned his head. "Yeah. She's awake."

The door slid open, churning to a stop at the midpoint. Long, slender fingers grabbed onto the edge, pushing the door the rest of the way. Eve stepped out from the shadows of the hallway. The dying light from the ceiling flickered onto her face, glistening with sweat and dirt.

So it hadn't been a dream at all.

"We're on Myth," Ia said.

Knives nodded.

Eve walked in. "You should have seen him. He was almost on his knees begging for a place to stay."

Eve stopped at the corner table, unscrewed her canister, and poured some soup into the lid. She crossed to the bed and knelt beside her.

Ia couldn't quite move, but she eyed Eve up and down, unsure whether or not to trust her. She had asked Eve before what side she was on, and she never answered. She was a wild card. Unpredictable. Ia was surprised Eve had even gotten her message to Goner. And look what happened there. He shot her.

Well, Ia thought, that was entirely her own fault for trusting him.

Eve held up the cup of soup. "You need to get your strength back if you want to go after your brother."

"He already has what he wants," she said. Einn sought Brinn just as Ia knew he would, but instead of using force to steal her away, to snatch her from Ia's side, all he'd needed were the sweet words in his mouth.

Her brother was better than she was.

Ia let out a slow breath. A sigh. A release. Einn was stronger and faster than she'd ever seen him. Yes, she had the confidence. She had the ego, but Einn didn't even need all that.

Einn wasn't just better than Ia; he was *more* than her. He could tear open physical space. Something that no being should ever be able to do. If he could do that, what would happen at their next fight?

She looked at the cup of steaming soup, brownish-green from the algae baths where it was cultivated and full of the right kind of nutrients to get her back on track to facing him again.

Instead of eating, she closed her eyes.

Because there wasn't going to be a next fight.

CHAPTER 25
KNIVES

IT'D BEEN ABOUT a month since Eve took them in at Myth, and almost two weeks since Ia woke up. Since Knives had left his holowatch back at the hospital, he watched the program streams that floated in the center of the barroom to gauge how much time had passed.

Which meant he often had to watch the news. The two Queens' press conference ran on repeat. "We will find them, and we will retaliate." That was the sound bite that was used the most.

When it played on the streams, the bar patrons always laughed, and he joined them.

Retaliate with what? The Star Force was cut down by half, and one of their most respected captains was gone and left for dead all in one swoop. General Adams was the last leader on the field, but Knives knew his father. He was an angry bull toeing the dirt, ready to follow this all the way through.

Knives sat at the corner seat of the counter, his elbow propped on the sticky tabletop and head cocked to the side, watching the general take over the press conference and go on about the rest of the details.

"We have a designated team combing through our territories."

That was all fancy military talk. It meant they were flying in circles and finding nothing. Knives rolled his eyes.

"I saw that," Eve snickered. She leaned up against the ledge of various archnol concoctions with a smirk on her face.

"Why do you even play this stuff here?"

She blew out a steady stream of mint vapor and pointed her vaporizer out at the crowd. "Because we're all celebrating."

The inebriated patrons who were sprinkled through the room shared the same look of delight on their faces. Knives assumed it was great watching the Commonwealth fail and fail and fail again. Especially after Olympus had *colonized* their planets. More Commonwealth code for taking people's homes and resources.

Knives dug his hands into his pockets, his fingers curling around an object he found inside. It was Bastian's pen, its metal surface cool in his palm.

Knives should be happy. Hiding out like this, he was free from his responsibilities to the Star Force and to the Academy. No more worrying about being a headmaster the cadets could look up to. But why did his heart feel so heavy?

A sharp scream tore toward them, coming from down the hallway. Eve looked over to her customers, some of whom had turned their heads and noticed.

Eve's eyes whipped over to his. "Quiet her down."

"I'm not going to stuff a rag in her mouth if that's what you're thinking," he snapped.

Eve crossed the gap between them and tapped at the name tag on his jacket, which was the exact place his inside pocket was located. The amber glass cylinder knocked lightly against his chest. He knew what Eve was getting at.

Meneva had told him to be careful with Ia's dosage. Since Ia woke up, it was something he'd had to give her to dull the bouts of pain she was experiencing. He thought it was mercy at first, seeing the effect it had upon her. But after a few days, he had started to notice a change. That ravaged look twisted upon her face the moment he produced the bottle from his jacket, and the sweet solace that fell upon her eyes when just one drop landed on her tongue.

"We shouldn't be using this all the time," he said.

"Don't think it's a good idea if these people actually know that the Blood Wolf is here. Dead Spacers are gossipy folk. One way or another, it will get back to Einn. If you're too scared to dose her, I will." She reached over the counter to dig out the contents of his pocket.

Knives stood up before she could reach him. "I'll take care of it."

He turned and made his way down the hallway. Eve was right. If people found out Ia was there, they'd have a field day. Ia had more enemies than her brother. Many knew she had switched sides; others had very deep grudges against the Blood Wolf of the Skies. She wouldn't be able to defend herself, not in her condition. What's worse, Knives was sure she wouldn't even try.

He tapped the door sensor over and over again, but the door took its time to slide open. The screams from inside fell harshly on his ears. He gripped the edge of the door and slammed it to the side.

His eyes landed on Ia. A slick layer of sweat coated her entire face. She had ripped the bedsheets right off the mattress, clutching what she could, her fists so tight that her knuckles were a stark white. She screamed out in agony.

He knew that the microscopic bio-bots in the sedative were losing their charge. As a result, her body was purging them, resulting in a high fever and more pain than humanly possible. It would have been easy to give her another dose, a new surge of bio-bots to numb her pain sensors while the old bots were getting flushed out of her system. But that was how the addiction usually started.

Ia looked at him, shaking. "It hurts." She tried to pull herself upright, her body trembling.

Knives kneeled down and scooped her up. He placed her in a nearby chair. He glanced over at her bed. The sheets were soaking wet from sweat. He started pulling them from the corners to replace them with a new set.

"Knives." Her voice was tiny, cracked. "Please."

"Listen to me," Knives said as he turned to meet her eyes. "Not this way, all right?"

He thought she'd understand, but her eyes hardened at him. She screamed, her voice curdling the blood in his veins.

"Ia," Knives said. "This sedative is highly addictive. I don't want to even chance it."

She looked down to the ground, her eyes drifting. "If you wanted me to suffer," she whispered, "you should have let me die."

His heart deflated. If there was some way he could share

in all the pain she was feeling, he would, even though he had way too much weighing down his soul as it was. He would do it. Because it was her.

"Ia." But that was all he could say. All other words were lost to him. *Fight*, he wanted to tell her. He knew she could. Where was the Ia that he knew? Where was the girl who never gave up?

When he didn't move to help her, she screamed, "Get out!"

Knives could have refused, could have brought over a chair and sat down right next to her. Instead, he took a deep breath and left.

* * *

He stepped back into the main bar, what used to be a captain's deck before it was renovated into the local watering hole it was now. Ia's screams echoed behind him, reverberating throughout the hallways.

He glanced over at Eve, whose brow was furrowed at the sight of him.

"You didn't give her the meds?"

Before Eve could even finish her question, he pulled the amber container out of his pocket, opened it. He leaned over the counter and tipped its contents down the drain.

Eve raised her voice. "What the mif are you doing?"

Instead of answering, Knives reached over and grabbed her holopad, turning the music up to high volume. It was loud enough to mask the sound of Ia's screams.

There was no way he was going to let Ia sink farther down into that hole. He cared about her too much to do that.

"You don't want people to hear her?" He slid the holopad over to Eve. "There. Problem solved."

CHAPTER 26
BRINN

BRINN STOOD in the elevator, waiting as it completed its ascent. Since she'd arrived almost a month ago, she had been working nonstop. The testing laboratories were on the other side of the ring, and she needed to get to them to check on everyone's progress.

As the elevator crossed the gap between Nirvana and Penance, she gazed up through the glass ceiling, admiring the gate's large arches. It was bigger than its predecessor, at least according to what the blueprints from Bastian's journals suggested.

The new structure was a replica—*no*, an improvement—of the original, which had been torn to scrap by the Commonwealth before Einn could actually make any use of it. They had called the prototype GodsEye. Einn used another name for this one. Penance, to punish everyone for their wrongs.

As they reached the arch of the upper ring, an entryway in the metal paneling opened, and the elevator was swallowed up. The lift came to a stop, and the doors slid open to a large workshop with multiple stations, some for construction and others for research and development.

When she stepped onto the floor, everyone's eyes were on her. She would never be used to the attention, but Einn had given her lead on this project.

In the sea of white lab coats, her navy-blue hair, now grown into a pixie cut, was easy to spot. She was the only Tawny in the Nirvana colony, which made her valuable to the team. She made connections and solved problems that no one else could figure out. More than that, she knew Bastian's work. That, paired with her Tawny intelligence, was an unstoppable combination that would finally create that bridge from one universe to the next.

It also meant there were a lot of expectations for her. To perform. To actually succeed.

As she walked down the path to the testing labs, a man in a white coat approached her to sign off on some calculations. She looked them over, making corrections as she made her way to the testing labs. When she was done, another engineer stepped up. And another. And another.

With each one, she blinked the fatigue out of her eyes. It was a lot of information. But she was the only one who knew how it'd all work.

"You're back." She looked up to see Einn beside her. He stood out in the crowded room, his flight suit tailored to fit close to his body. A mesh of gray iridescent webbing patterned the sleeves, accentuating the corded muscles underneath. It made him appear strong, intimidating to anyone he met. Still, after seeing him take down Ia so easily, she no longer needed the suit to be reminded of his strength.

"I didn't want to miss the test," she told him.

Brinn had insisted on running the experiment on a smaller scale before trying it out with the larger structure. So they'd replicated another unit, a smaller version of Penance, within a controlled space in the laboratory.

This wasn't known physics they were tampering with. If they created a bridge between their universe and the next, they had to get it right. Most nights, Brinn worked without rest. As a result, dark circles had appeared underneath her eyes.

Einn handed her some H_2O jelly, and she grabbed it thankfully. She was dehydrated, so focused on her work that she had forgotten to drink or eat throughout the day.

As she slurped up the contents of the foil pouch, Einn nodded over the testing site. "It's looking good."

The engineers on her team had already finished re-creating the replica of Penance. It was an immaculate copy, she had to admit. Her engineers were a disparate group of Fringers, Dead Spacers, and even some who'd defected from the Commonwealth. Quite a few of the workers were former slaves whom Einn had bought from the Armada. Once they set foot on Nirvana, they were freed and presented with a choice: to go back to their normal lives, or to contribute to a greater purpose, one that would ultimately change the entire universe. Most of them, Einn said, had stayed.

Everyone worked well together, while the builder borgs carried out their plans, executing the precise instructions on Brinn's updated designs. This model would be better and more power-efficient than the GodsEye in Bastian's blue-prints. And it would *work*.

Brinn walked to the main console and took a seat, her fingers finding their natural place on a floating set of holokeys. She nodded to the test site. "Let's begin."

Her fingers flew like they were on an instrument, but the music was the drone of machines. Soon everything was powered on, the hum growing like a crescendo. The archways began to spin, around and around, building enough momentum to create a gravitational force large enough to withhold a spatial tear within its arches. Everything was working perfectly, and all they needed was to see a glimpse of something new in its center. Stars that were never discovered, beasts that would never roam their universe, particles and atoms that existed only in another space and time.

Yet nothing happened.

Not even a pinhole to peek through.

Brinn had scoured over every detail, every equation, every outcome. It should have worked.

She had failed.

* * *

Brinn and Einn walked slowly down the length of the hall-way. She stared at the view of Nirvana, the planetoid colony floating outside, but her mind was elsewhere, swamped with a maze of thoughts trying to troubleshoot her own failure.

"Don't be hard on yourself," Einn said. "It's going to work. Eventually."

"How can you be so sure?" she asked.

"I wouldn't have been born if this wasn't possible."

She stopped and stared at him, her eyebrows crinkled as if weighted down by an immense gravity.

"From the look on your face, it seems like your people haven't told you," Einn said. "The Commonwealth was successful in opening the bridge several years ago. And when that happened, someone stepped out of it. My father."

"Does Ia know?"

Einn nodded.

Brinn glanced away. Yet another thing that Ia had failed to mention. She had built a shield of secrets around her, and she never let Brinn get past it.

"Is this why you want to open that gate? To find your father?" Brinn asked.

He shook his head. "My father left me with nothing but a hole. A hole that was filled with ambition," Einn added harshly. Then his voice grew calm and even. "You asked why I want Penance to work. But do I need a *why*? I want to do it because I *can*. To do something as great as Deus herself. Isn't that enough?"

"We're not gods," she said.

He backed away, his lips turned upward in a mischievous smile. "What if I am…?"

If anyone else said what he did, she would have laughed. But with Einn, she wasn't so sure. She was a Tawny, her brain seeped in numbers and science. She didn't know anything about Deus, or if she really did exist. But she had seen what Einn could do at Rigel Kentaurus, something that was physically impossible by the laws of their universe.

In the corner of the sky, she saw the blink of lights, growing intense with each ticking second, too fast to be a passing comet.

Someone had arrived.

Brinn glanced over at Einn, who had stopped to watch its approach. He had noticed it, too. It was hard not to. The ship was large, a giant silhouette against the blazing sun. She squinted to make out the lettering on the side. Her jaw grew slack.

Sino Corp.

* * *

Brinn followed Einn to the docking bays to meet the new guests. The ship came with ten envoys. Fighter jets with enough firepower to take down anyone who'd mess with the main ship. Anyone could see it for what it was. A small fleet.

Brinn stared at the Sino Corp logo brandished across the ship's frame. No matter which way she thought about it, this was a bad idea.

As they approached the vehicles, Brinn started to slow her pace. Einn turned, noticing one less patter of footsteps ricocheting through the open space. "What's wrong?"

She nodded back to the main atrium. "I don't think I should be present."

"Nonsense," he said as he shook his head. "You're the main engineer. You're coming with me."

"But, sir—"

He held up a hand to interrupt her. "I've always hated that word. Just call me Einn."

She was taken aback by his lack of formality and casual manner, especially when he had just nearly destroyed one of the largest cities in the Olympus Commonwealth. If it was Ia, she would have insisted on being called Sovereign, or Blood Wolf, or something of the like.

"Einn," she said. "I'm sure you already know this, but the Sinoblancas family is very public about their opposition to the Sanctuary Act. The act is dead now because of them."

The vote had happened a few weeks ago, almost immediately after the attack on the Rigel Kentaurus system. Thank Deus she had already been on Nirvana. She heard about the refugees rioting in the streets afterward, accompanied by the beatings they took from the Citizens and the roundups made by the Commonwealth guards. They were all being herded and shipped off. No one knew where. Just away.

She couldn't sleep some nights, wondering what her parents were going through. Even if the mobs were turning against them, she wanted to hear *something*. Because at least then she'd know that they were still alive.

"Their political ties have no weight here," Einn said. "This isn't the Commonwealth."

"That's not what I mean." Brinn pointed over to the massive ship settling in to anchor at the edge of the docking bay. "The Sinoblancas family doesn't like refugees. Or Tawnies. They won't like that I'm here. Trust me, Einn. One of them was in the academy with me. He hated me."

Einn's eyes landed on hers. They were a startling storm gray, so sharp it crackled at the air around them. "They won't touch us, because we're going to get them what they want. Money. Greed. That's why they're here."

"What are you trying to say?"

"They come because they want the resources beyond the gate."

Brinn furrowed her brow.

"It's a partnership. Where do you think we get all this tech?" He swept a long arm at the space around them, motioning from the drone-controlled starjets to the large unit of builder borgs stationed in the corner. He raised an eyebrow. "You didn't think I stole all of this, did you?"

She did, but she didn't say anything.

She swallowed, trying to quiet her fears. Here she was again, playing the same role of scared little Brinn, facing down an even larger monster, one that had its own set of teeth the shape of money and weapons.

Einn leaned in as if he could sense her worry. "If they do anything to you…" He unlatched one of the pistols at his side and tossed it toward her. She stumbled forward, managing to catch it. Einn nodded at the pistol in her hands, that calm smile still plastered across his face. "…you shoot them."

She nodded, her fingers curving tightly around the grooves of the handle. Einn didn't make her any grand promises. He never told her he'd protect her, or lay down his life for her. And somehow his response tore right through her. There was an old saying from Ancient Mars. *If you give a starving man a fish, he'll eat for a day. But give him the tools and teach him the way, then he can actually fight for his own existence.*

Ahead, the entry ramp to the main Sino Corp ship cracked open. It lowered slowly until it boomed onto the floor. A line of men in crisp tailored jackets stepped out onto the deck. Surprisingly, only two of them had the Sinoblancas dimpled chin. One she'd recognized as Kilio Sinoblancas, who had led the repeal vote in the Council. Once the vote had passed, he had stepped down from his position, resuming his leadership as CEO of Sino Corp, and now this man who had displaced millions of refugees from their homes stood in front of them. Her stomach churned with sudden anger.

Einn waited for the new visitor to be the first to speak. A power tactic, she noticed. He'd used it whenever anyone new had come to Nirvana. Except for her. He always spoke first when it came to her.

Perhaps that was a strategic move as well.

"Galatin," CEO Sinoblancas said. "Good to see this place is shaping up. We've brought new goods for you to play with."

Einn nodded at the fleet that was parked beside the main ship. "And those?"

Kilio Sinoblancas smiled, the dimple on his chin raising ever so slightly. "The Star Force has been crowding us lately. I think that general suspects something. You never know when they'd want to come onboard for a *routine search*. Those ships are for when things get a little less routine."

Brinn angled her head. Were the Star Force and Sino Corp at odds? That was the first she'd heard of it, especially since Sino Corp was the Force's main weapons supplier.

The CEO's gaze shifted, settling on the shock of navy-blue hair on the top of Brinn's head. From the flicker of disgust in his eyes, she knew instantly what he was thinking. *Mungbringer.*

"And who is this?" he asked.

But before the man could inquire any further, a voice snaked in, interrupting the conversation. "So this is what Nirvana looks like..."

Brinn glanced over as a very recognizable skull on a very recognizable head materialized before them, the photo sensors on his suit mimicking the melanin-shifting cells on his skin. She could ask him where he'd gotten that camo armor, but she'd already suspected that a Sino Corp tag could be found underneath the hem of his collar.

"I see you finally got it together for this inevitable rendezvous," Einn said.

"These whelps were kind enough to let me hitch a ride."

Kilio Sinoblancas's expression hardened as if he had no idea Goner had been on the ship for the duration of their trip. Goner's white lips lifted up in pleasure. When he saw Brinn, his grin grew wider, dripping with mischief.

"Well, well," Goner hissed. "If it isn't Cōcha's friend..."

Again, all eyes turned to her.

"This is Brinn Tarver, our head engineer," Einn cut in. "She's the one who's going to turn Penance from an average interstellar gate to a bridge between universes. Then it'll all be yours, gentlemen, a wealth of resources for the picking."

Brinn expected them to scoff at her presence, to order their guards to drag her from the room. Instead, they all nodded in approval.

"Of course," the CEO said, and then his voice softened to a more accommodating tone. "Please let us know if you need any of our assistance."

A ripple of shock ran down her spine, and all she could manage was a slight tilt of her chin as a response.

Einn place a hand calmly on her shoulder. "Why don't you show Goner around while I bring our guests to their quarters?"

Brinn was glad to make her escape. She looked over at Goner. "Let's go."

Goner followed her until they were out of sight. She was starting to motion over to the equipment when he turned and waved her off. "I don't need a tour."

"Then why are you following me?"

He sighed. "I didn't want to stick around." He nodded back to the Sino Corp group still standing on the flight deck. His eyes landed on Einn and then snapped back to hers.

"You better watch yourself, little girl. I see that look on your face."

What look? She scrunched up her eyebrows and pulled her lips up in a snarl to hide whatever he thought he saw.

Goner pointed over to where Einn had disappeared. "Einn is a bigger monster than Ia ever was."

Brinn's face went red. "I disagree. He's more rational than Ia. Grounded, in a way."

Goner snorted. "Einn only believes in chaos. He doesn't have reasons for doing anything. At least I've never figured them out."

"And you do? You had a reason for killing Ia?"

Brinn stood by her decision to leave with Einn, but that day still haunted her, watching from the window of *Shepherd* as Goner pointed his pistol at this girl who was fiercer and braver than anyone, this girl who once was her friend. She wouldn't mourn her, she told herself, trying to harden her heart.

"She's my nemesis," Goner answered. "Killing her was something I've always been destined to do. All it takes is one bullet." He jabbed a finger at his temple and exhaled with glee. "That was one good day."

As he stepped away, Goner pointed at the weapon in her hand. "Careful there. You don't want to shoot the floor."

Brinn looked down at her arm. Her knuckles had gone white from clutching her pistol so hard. Her finger was already on the trigger as if she wanted to strike.

Apparently, her heart wasn't as closed off as she'd thought.

CHAPTER 27
KNIVES

KNIVES PACED in front of the rusting metal door that led to Ia's room. He wanted to go inside, but he couldn't bring himself to tap his finger against the sensor.

"She'll be okay," he muttered to himself. "She'll be fine."

He dragged his fingers through his hair, now greasy from the lack of showers on Myth. The old space station was on water rations until the next ice haul from the nearest asteroid belt came through. But even then, Eve had explained that their budget for ice purchases wasn't on her priority list.

Showering was the least of his concerns. He stopped pacing and stared at the door. His life was full of doors, and most of them he wanted closed. There were always things he didn't want to face on the other side.

She'll be fine. That was what Meneva had told him. She would heal. Her body would be whole again. But it'd been a few weeks since she woke up, and Ia still hadn't tried to walk, or even sit up on her own. *Can she move?* he wondered. He couldn't just barge in and ask.

Finally, he tapped his knuckles on the sensor, and once he could get his fingers around the edge of the door, he grabbed and pulled, helping it on its way. Inside, the room was dark because Ia had at some point insisted that the fluorescent light hurt her eyes. She was asleep, her forehead slick from night sweats and her body straight like it was when she was back in the hospital. Because she wasn't yet capable of rolling over, or curling up, or moving her body to get comfortable.

If he had brought her in to the hospital five minutes later, Meneva had said...but if he had found her minutes earlier, then she'd probably wouldn't be stuck in this bed. He'd have been there. He could have tried to save her.

Not tried. Yes, Knives told himself, he would have saved her.

He could have saved so many people. If he was faster, stronger, better. Maybe if he was more like his father.

Marnie would be alive.

And so would Bastian.

And Ia would stand in front of him once again and smile.

Normally, he'd have called out to her. Put on the brightest grin that he had buried deep in some hidden crevice inside him and persuade her out of bed. But today he backed out of her room, trying not to make any noise.

* * *

It was after hours, and most of the patrons had already left for the night. Knives was on the couch, facing the observation window, his gaze lost in the All Black. He wondered where the Star Force was in that sprawl before him.

A trace of shadow lengthened across the floor, and he

looked over to see Eve leaning against the pillar, looking at the same view. She glanced down at him. "If you're going to sit on your ass, I need you to at least be useful."

"Productive sitting isn't a thing," he replied.

He propped his elbows on his knees, resting his head on his palms while he studied her. Even with the fluorescent lights crackling above, he knew a scheme was hatching behind those eyes.

Eve nodded to the distant stars as she blew out a fresh trail of vapor. "You fly," she pointed out. "I need to send someone out for a pickup."

"Where?"

"At a race space," she said. "The Harix Corridor. You know it?"

Of course he did. It was one of the hardest, most dangerous racetracks in the known galaxies, and his sister had flown that course in ten seconds. He'd always wanted to see that space for himself.

"There's been one victor for the past year," Eve explained. "Remind him that there's a world outside that race."

That's when Knives realized he wasn't picking up some-*thing*, but some*one*.

"Is this guy really that important?" he asked.

"Ia is our best shot at taking Einn down," she said. "It's not because she's strong or quick. It's because there are still people out there who would rally alongside her. And the guy I'm sending you out to find is one of them."

But Knives couldn't just walk into that race space and say hello. He had seen the streams for the Allmetal Cup. The victors were placed on sky-high pedestals before and after the race. It would be the same at Harix. "If he's the victor, it'll be hard to even get close to him."

Eve leaned in. "Not if you win."

He stared at her as he realized what she was saying. She wanted him to race.

But before he could protest, Eve winked at him. "And it wouldn't hurt to have that prize money as well."

CHAPTER 28

IA

IA HADN'T EVEN BOTHERED to try to take that first step on the cold, hard floor. To connect. Because that would mean she'd be awake.

What's more, she couldn't feel when Knives's hand was on hers, or the rough cotton wrapped around her arms. She could barely feel anything, except for the pain. It was the only thing that was left, smothering her so that she couldn't see the world around her.

Not that she wanted to anyway. She kept her eyes closed whenever she could, even when she was no longer asleep.

The pain would be gone once the bots were all flushed out, Knives had assured her. Words she knew were repeated right from the doctor's mouth. The pain would be *gone*. Or would it? Her body would still remember. It wasn't systematic like that. The body always remembered. It remembered every decision you made. Every failure. It was all a part of her. Even if her memories were gone, wiped somehow by that accident, her body would prod and poke her until it all came flooding back.

There was no escape. Floating in this place between death and life, where the days blended together like waters of an ocean. A slosh of seconds that ebbed into each other, became each other, dissolved into the same thing.

It barely registered when Knives came to visit her.

"Ia," he said. Whenever she saw him, he was always calling her name.

And then one day, the voice became female. Low. Smoky.

"Ia." It snaked quietly into her dream. It found her, caught in the middle of worlds, a place where nothing ended and nothing began. And then something wet landed on her face with a slop.

Ia's eyes shot open, her sight blurry, blinking until she could focus. Finally, she realized the blur wasn't from her vision at all, but from the thing that was on her head. A muslin cloth, drenched in cold water.

"Wake the mif up already," Eve said.

Ia lay quiet, trying to outlast Eve's very short patience, hoping the surly bartender would soon give up and leave. But she didn't.

"Do you want me to throw more water on you?" Eve's voice was loud and agitated.

There was no use pretending anymore. Ia blew one corner of the cloth off her face, exposing her mouth and tiny bit of right eye. "What do you want, Eve?"

"My room back."

Ia's right eye swiveled around, spotting the red fabric draped across the doorframe, the terrible travel posters of planetary destinations on the wall, and the fake gold accenting on everything, now sadly losing its luster. All touches of Eve.

Which meant she'd been sleeping in Eve's room, on Eve's bed, sweating all over Eve's bedsheets for Deus knows how long.

"You're kicking me out? I'm injured." She had no shame pointing it out to her. "I might even die."

"And that's why I want you out of here. Because if you do croak, I'll have to get dead-person smell out of my mattress, and you know how hard that is to get rid of."

"But I can't even move." It was something she had already grown to accept. It was her new truth. She hadn't been able to get up since the fight with Einn.

Eve glared at her. She placed a heel on the edge of the mattress and kicked. The vibration rattled her bones.

"You're the Blood Wolf of the miffing Skies, Ia." She leaned in. "You can try."

Eve kicked the bed frame again and again. Each kick harder than the last.

Ia clenched her teeth with every kick. She felt it each time. The impact searing right through her.

And then her mind stopped.

Because she *felt it*.

Each.

Time.

From the chatter of her bones to the reaction of her nerves. It was all very numb, but it was *there*. And for first time in a very long time, she realized that there was something else besides the pain.

"So are you going to just die in here, Ia?"

Ia looked Eve right in the eye. "No."

CHAPTER 29
KNIVES

THE HARIX RACE SPACE was exactly how Marnie had described it. Crowded and noisy, and that was just on the observation platform right by the finish line. For the most part, that was where everyone docked.

The track was even more chaotic. One of the dangers of navigating the course was getting past broken wings and engine hulls—remnants of races past. Not to mention the occasional dead pilot. They were ghosts, haunting this place of spoiled dreams.

Knives looked at the old bottle cap that Eve had given him before he left Myth. It was worn on its edges, painted with red lacquer, and meant only for the guy he was here to see. The victor. His face was hovering all over the place, on holobanners and marquees. A mess of thick dark-brown hair whisked into a very sharp knot on the top of his head. He wore a cloth face mask, covering his nose and mouth, which wasn't uncommon due to the racing fumes.

Underneath his image was his ID. Minotaur.

At the Harix track and every other race space—both legal and illegal—across the galaxies, the pilots never used their own names. They used the name of their ship. Not the model, because that would get confusing. Most people picked trendy names. Like *Viper* or *HammerHawk*. Even *Bebop* was popular among the racing crowd.

So *Minotaur* was an unusual choice. It was an old word; not many people knew it. But when Knives was young, he was forced to take a class called The Classics of Ancient Earth. A fancy class for the fancy school his mother had insisted on enrolling him in. Fancy, in this case, meant boring. But at least he knew where the name had originated from.

If this guy had won this race that many times, then *Minotaur* was a suitable name for his ship, which had been traversing the labyrinthine paths of the Harix Corridor for so long.

Knives looked up to the victor's tower, where he caught a glimpse of him. The pilot's dark-green flight suit was halfway zipped, the upper half shrugged off, with the sleeves swinging down around his ankles to expose the black compression shirt underneath. The victor leaned against the safety rails, staring at the course.

A standing platform lowered down to the challenger's lounge. An announcer with long arms and legs, the effects of gravity growth, swayed on top of the platform. "Racers, get ready."

As everyone made their way to their jets, Knives raised his arm to get the announcer's attention. "Is it too late to sign up?"

The announcer scratched a long fingernail across his eyebrow. "What's your ship ID, kid?"

He'd never thought to name his own ship. Star Force flyers rarely did, since they never needed to own, especially with a wealth of high-quality vessels to borrow in the fleet.

"Theseus," he said finally.

The announcer curled his upper lip at the sound of the name and then shook his head. "What are you waiting for? You better get to your *Theseus* before the race starts."

If Knives wanted to win, he needed a mifload of luck— and names were lucky. It was Theseus who brought down the Minotaur in the myths. In the unlikely event that he actually did win, *Minotaur*'s pilot was going to look up at his name and be pissed.

* * *

Settling into the pilot's seat, Knives positioned himself at the far end of the starting line. He sized up the other models, the majority of which were modrockets, regular transport vehicles overhauled with scrap and refurbished racing engines. They weren't high-speed vessels like his Kaiken, so he'd have an advantage.

He craned his neck trying to catch a glimpse of Minotaur in the center of the starting lineup. Knives did a double take. The ship was covered in burnout, but there was no mistaking that silhouette. A Yari 4. Not many of them were made, hence the 4 in the model name. They were luxury racers. He had no idea how anyone in Dead Space could get hold of that, unless that person stole it.

A holoscreen clicked on in his periphery, and the announcer's voice rang through. "Racers, on your mark."

Knives placed one hand on the steering wheel and slipped

the fingers of his other hand through the grip lever on the side. Asteroids of all sizes stared back at him. So still, as if they were suspended in time.

"Set."

Knives blew out a deep breath to relieve the tension in his jaw. It did nothing to help.

"Go."

He punched the lever forward, his front thrusters igniting.

Of course, *Minotaur* was in the lead, its dual hypersonic engines supercharging its ionic thrusters. A bright light in the otherwise dark sky.

Beside him, the other jets jockeyed for second, third, and fourth position. Anything that could get them as close to the front as possible. To do that, they had to fight for the center. After all his time programming flight simulations, Knives knew that a cluster of jets heading right through an asteroid field never amounted to anything good, so he hung back.

It wasn't long before a wing was clipped, and then another, each collision knocking the asteroids around them. Soon, jets were going down left and right, detached wings and broken engine parts spiraling out of control. A chain reaction that was impossible to contain. And just like that, the moment of stillness had passed.

If Knives waited any longer, he'd lose his chance to get through the chaos that was brewing. And from here on out, it was only going to get bigger. His eyes darted back and forth, tracking the trajectories of everything colliding around him. Finally, *there*. An opening. A direct shot right through, only clear for a couple of seconds.

Knives whispered a quick prayer to Deus and charged forward. He dipped the Kaiken low, avoiding the bulk of the debris, trying to outrun the chain reaction before it reached the rest of the path. He held his breath as he weaved through the remains of the asteroid field like a needle threading in and out of a seam.

Finally, he reached a clearing, and he exhaled, his whole body jittery with adrenaline.

But he wasn't completely in the clear yet.

The Kaiken approached a section of the path that was immersed in total darkness. He looked up and saw why. A behemoth loomed in the distance, blocking the light from the system's star. From Marnie's stories, he knew what it was. An enormous asteroid, known for the complexity of its tunnel system.

But there was one major route that everyone knew about.

His eyes focused on a slim opening on the face of the rock. Knives's heart rattled against his rib cage. *This* was the actual start of the course. The Harix Corridor.

If he thought navigating through an asteroid field was a pain in the ass, then traversing directly through a giant asteroid was even worse. He'd have to be as precise as possible. The passages inside were tight; only room for one racer at a time.

There were at least five or six other jets in front of him, including *Minotaur*. And he didn't even want to think of the gap that existed between the second- and first-place racers. For him, it seemed victory would be impossible.

If he wanted, he could stop right there, turn back, and he'd be guaranteed to wake up to see another day.

But there was something he'd remembered. A memory, not from Marnie, but from someone else, whispered to him over flickering candlelight: the reason why the best of them continued to fly.

It's something you chase, Ia had said to him.

This whole thing wasn't about winning or losing. It wasn't about receiving VIP treatment in the victor's tower, getting that cash prize, seeing his face floating all around that observation pavilion.

It wasn't about any of that at all. It was about feeling *invincible*.

Even if it was for one brief moment.

Knives took a deep breath, and with all thrusters fired, he went in.

The Kaiken raged against the dark. The headlights were only strong enough to see a few meters ahead, so he focused on the taillights of the jets in front of him as a guide.

Suddenly, a blinding light flashed on the course ahead.

His jaw grew slack. A light that bright could mean only one thing. A crash. And it was a big one. The explosion was quick, the fire extinguishing within seconds as it burned up all the unfortunate ship's oxygen reserves.

The starjet directly behind the wreck got clipped by a ripped panel, sending it backward in a tailspin, hitting another jet.

Quickly, Knives maneuvered the Kaiken backward to a larger pass, angling his jet against the wall to avoid the jumble of metal and debris.

The pileup was a major setback, burning through precious seconds he needed to challenge Minotaur at the lead, whose finish time averaged at the thirty-second mark.

He needed another plan.

He thought back, his sister's account unfolding rapidly before him. Marnie flew the Harix Corridor in ten seconds. In recent years, no one had even come close, not even Ia.

"There's a reason why," his sister's voice echoed in his memories. Just as he remembered it. Clever, haughty.

His eyes widened as it all came back to him. Hands on the wheel, he tilted his jet back, zooming past each curve and corner, searching for that little something his sister had told him about.

A secret passage.

And if he remembered Marnie's story correctly, the entrance to the passage would be coming up on him right about—

He swerved left, navigating around a rock column until he spotted a tiny opening slashing diagonally along the rock wall, blocked from view by a large spire.

He squeezed the Kaiken through the crevice. Its force field sparked green from contact at the wing.

From this passage, it would be a straight shot out to the finish line.

His eyes flitted down dangerously to the stopwatch. It had already been twenty seconds since he entered the Harix Corridor. He wasn't even close to beating Marnie, but he never imagined flying faster than his sister. That was not what today was for. No, today all he needed to do was be quicker than Minotaur. Even if it was by a nanosecond.

His eyes narrowed as he stared at the end of the tunnel. Where there should be an opening, there was a wall.

A barrier blocking him from a chance at victory.

He fired his rail guns at the thick layer of rock, little bits and pieces of debris clouding the space around him. The light from outside seeped through, cutting through the darkness. Soon, hundreds of crooked holes stared back at him like rows of peeping eyes. But still, the opening wasn't big enough for his jet to fit through.

He glanced down at the stopwatch, another second ticking by.

Slamming his palms into the steering wheel, he cursed. "So close. So miffing close."

Marnie never had to worry about this problem. She always had luck on her side. For her, it all fell into place. As if it was her destiny.

But Knives always had to claw for whatever scraps destiny was willing to give him.

There was another girl who had to do the same. She clawed and scraped until she was close enough to bite off a chunk of destiny and spit it out at its feet.

So that was the real question he had to ask himself. Just as he had during Einn's attack. What would *Ia* do?

Knives glared at the sheet of rock.

He knew what she would do. She'd break it down.

The barrier was already full of holes, and his jet was the perfect hammer. He ignited his thrusters. The Kaiken surged forward. His body jolted backward in his seat from the sudden shift of speed. The nose of the jet buried right into the barrier's weakest point, a cluster of bullet holes that landed off-center. All the while, his thumb was on the trigger, his rail gun blasting away at whatever surface it could get. At this point, the Kaiken's force field webbed a bright green around him before overloading and fading away.

With an extra surge, his jet scraped through, its once pristine hull now damaged and completely vulnerable. But at least it was free.

Knives looked down at the timer. He had three more seconds. Glancing in his periphery, he saw that Minotaur hadn't cleared the corridor yet.

Eyes forward, the finish line in sight, he pushed the thrusters to their limit.

But then he caught a flash of movement in his rear view. Minotaur was behind him.

Comparing the specs of their jets, Knives knew the Yari would quickly overtake his Kaiken, and he glanced over to see Minotaur pull up to his side. The victor of the Harix Corridor angled his head at him and brought two fingers up to his brow in salute.

It was enough to make Knives falter for a second too long.

And just like that, Minotaur had taken the lead.

In the past, Knives would have conceded defeat, but not now. He felt his heart thrumming inside, chasing this need to go faster, to be better, to completely ignite.

His eyes narrowed as an idea took hold.

Knives tapped hard on his displays, discharging all the fuel and power he had into the afterburner. At the same time, he redirected the Kaiken's batteries to give the burn some extra oomph.

He pressed the button, sparking an explosion that tore through the back of his jet. The Kaiken kicked forward with a burst of furious speed.

The HUDs and enviro systems went down. Knives punched the button at the collar of his suit. His helmet came up over his head, visor down. His grav suit was fully activated, already pumping in a steady stream of oxygen for him to breathe.

He couldn't look left or right to track where Minotaur was. Because all that mattered was that finish line, marked by two giant red beams floating in the distance.

He had to bet all his luck on this one moment and hope to Deus that Minotaur was behind him. His racing ID was *Theseus* for a reason. Theseus slayed the Minotaur by being clever and resourceful. He faced the impossible, and he won.

The lights of the finish line blinded Knives as he passed over it. The Kaiken was depleted of all its fuel and charge, and without power to its thrusters, he couldn't even slow down to see who had won.

Blood still rushing through his veins from the thrill of the race, he swooped toward the landing pad. His heart pounded inside his chest, and he wanted to yip out in glee. Being invincible. Was this how it felt?

His jet flew through the atmos field that circled the landing deck and adjacent observation deck where most of the bystanders awaited. The gravity generated from the atmos field slowed him down, but his jet was still flying at a furious speed.

This was going to be a dangerous landing.

He careened to the deck, his wheels touching down on the flat surface. His knuckles rattled as he clutched the manual brakes with all his strength. The friction was so intense that one wheel popped, and then the other.

The Kaiken slid to a halt, the bottom of its hull scraping against the landing pad. Once he was at a stop, Knives reached up, prying the cockpit open. Immediately, his ears drowned in the roar of chants, thundering around him like an unrelenting storm. Knives stared back at the crowd, their fists punching the air in unison.

"Minotaur," they cheered. "Minotaur!"

His chin lowered, his confidence deflated.

Victory screens circled around them, all with the same face he'd seen when he first arrived. Those green eyes followed him, even as the holoscreens arced throughout the space. Taunting him.

"That was a close one, kid." The announcer's hand stretched out for a handshake.

But Knives's gaze was fixed upward, watching Minotaur's pedestal rise up toward the victor's tower.

Knives tightened his fist around the bottle cap, feeling the edges dig into his skin. He reached out and gripped the announcer's hand. As Knives pulled away from the handshake, the announcer's expression shifted, his eyebrows arched in question at the bottlecap now resting in the center of his palm.

"If you see him, give him that," Knives said.

And he turned back to his jet, signaling for the mechanics on deck to deliver a new batch of fuel pods, a charged battery, and a fresh set of tires. Then he climbed back into the driver seat of his Kaiken.

"Theseus," he muttered. So much for a lucky name.

CHAPTER 30
BRINN

BRINN LEANED AGAINST the railings of the upper plankway of Nirvana. The domed roof made it the perfect observation spot. But instead of looking up into the All Black, Brinn's head was tilted downward at her holowatch. Her button tapped on a command. Refresh.

Her inbox was empty.

Every morning, Brinn secretly sent a message to her parents. Faren was gone, but she had to hold on to the hope that they were still out there. That was what she *had* to tell herself. Because with each new day, her soul sank farther into the ground. There was no way to climb up. The feelings that had carved their way through her—sadness? grief?—she couldn't say it was one thing or the other. It was much more complicated than that. As though she was being hollowed out inside, layer by layer, slowly being replaced by someone she didn't recognize.

"Are you all right?"

She glanced over her shoulder and saw Liam on the plankway. A smile on his face, that mask that he always wore. In the quiet moments, he often found her here, standing in this exact hallway, staring up through the observation plexiglass at Penance hovering before a tapestry of distant stars.

That was where her future lay. In that bulk of heartless steel.

Her eyes met his. "We're not kids anymore, are we?"

The smile on his face vanished, and she saw all the turmoil churning within. He shook his head. "No, we're not."

"That day we decided to leave with Einn," Liam said. "You mentioned that you lost someone, too."

She gripped her hands against the side rail, the sweat on her palms against the metal unleashing the heavy scent of iron around them. "My brother died in the riots of Nova Grae. And my parents, I don't know where they are. They could be…"

She couldn't say the word. It was too final.

"Death is easy to accept. It's the memories…" he said. "They remind you how happy you used to be. It makes everything so much harder. "

The pain in her heart pulsated through her. It brought up questions she had never asked before. *Why do we even keep going?*

If it was for the people you loved, if that was where happiness dwelled, then it was gone now. It wasn't just her family she'd lost. She had also lost the chance to ever experience that joy again.

Perhaps that was why she was willing to work on Penance. It filled the hole inside her, if only temporarily. It gave her purpose where there was none anymore. A chance to piece all the broken fragments back together. Just for this tiny moment in her tiny life. That was a good enough reason for her. Anything to keep from falling apart.

"Do you think your parents would be proud of your decision to come here?" Brinn asked.

"My dad lived and breathed for the Star Force, but now he's paralyzed. I want to say that I'm fighting for him, for everything he's lost. For all the brothers *I've* lost. But it's not just about that. I'm fighting because I'm angry. I'm *so* angry. And I'm alone with that. I want people to see all of it, to know that it's real."

She understood him. Perhaps that was what everyone else on this rock felt, too. Maybe that was why they were all there.

Liam leaned against the railing, his eyes lowered. "And now with the Commonwealth sifting existing Citizens into send-off ships, this is the only place that makes sense to me anymore."

"What?" She craned her neck to look at him. "What did you say about Citizens being sifted?"

"They're sending everyone from refugee planets away, even Citizens," Liam said.

Like her mom. Her blood stopped cold inside her veins.

They were stripping away people's rights. If her mom was still alive, then she'd be on her way to a refugee camp.

She didn't bother to finish their conversation. She was already up and running.

* * *

Brinn knew that Einn had harmed Tawnies in the past, using their brains as power sources for GodsEye. When she'd found this out, she was horrified. But the more she thought about it, it was a resourceful thing to do. Einn needed to get the job done, one way or another, and he used the tools he had to do it. These were thoughts that she shouldn't be thinking. They went against her heart, even if they didn't go against logic.

That was how she realized that she and Einn had something in common. They were both logical people. Like her, he calculated every move he made.

Perhaps that was why she wasn't scared of him. If Einn was ruled by logic, he wouldn't kill her. He needed her too much. When someone was that precious, that integral in achieving one's greatest accomplishment, one would do anything to keep that person happy.

That was the logical thing to do.

And *that* was the very reason why she stood in the doorway of his war room.

Einn was alone, his eyes fixed on the holoprojections on the spherical ceiling. He swiped on the holoscreen, zooming from one star system to the next. Colorful lights streaked around him as constellations shifted with each new location.

He grumbled in dissatisfaction. It seemed like he was trying to make a decision, but nothing was good enough for him.

"Are you trying to find a new place to target?" she guessed.

He glanced up, lips already tight in a sneer, but when he saw it was her, he smiled. She didn't know if it was genuine or not.

"I'm trying to pinpoint the location of Olympus's remaining fleet." His eyes returned to the transforming skycaps above him. "I know they're hiding somewhere. All it takes is one battle to wipe them all out."

Brinn scratched a finger behind her ear. There was no easy

way to ask for this, so she had to just blurt it out. "I'd like to go to Nova Grae."

"Nova Grae..." Einn whispered. Then he swiped on the screen to pull up the map of the planet.

"That's where I'm from," she explained. "It hasn't been long since Olympus started deploying send-off ships. I just want to find my parents, to make sure they're all right."

His fingers drummed against his chin as he stared up at the holo image of Nova Grae slowly spinning in orbit before him. "A medium-trafficked port of import-export. Population of 4.5 billion people." After a moment of silent thought, he turned to her in decision. "I'll find your parents. I'll go to Nova Grae."

"Really?" Her voice swelled with a sudden burst of hope.

"We'll assemble a few units."

"A strike force?" she asked. "Why would you need that?"

"You've got me thinking. The Star Force fleet is nearly wiped out. They must be reserving all of their resources for a decisive confrontation. If one of their colonies was attacked, would they even answer the call?"

Her eyes widened in horror. She already knew the answer. Nova Grae was the perfect place to terrorize. It was mostly a residential planet, with only one military base to defend itself. "Why wipe them out when you can humiliate them first..."

His eyes fell to hers, a glint of chaos stirring deep inside.

Perhaps she was wrong. Maybe Einn wasn't ruled by logic, but by something else entirely.

Her heart shriveled within her chest at the thought of her old neighborhood—the streets she used to walk, the buildings she saw on her way to school—completely destroyed, an echo of what happened at Rigel Kentaurus.

"And my parents. You'll still try to find them?"

Einn looked at her, his eyes a little less wild than the moment before. "I will do everything I can."

A small victory. Nova Grae was going to burn. But at least there was still a chance of finding the only family she had left.

* * *

Two weeks later, Brinn rushed to the flight deck, weaving in and out of the line of returning starjets. A fleet had recently arrived from their mission to Nova Grae. Her eyes darted back and forth at the soldiers disembarking from their vessels.

She passed a group of refugees. Some even had blue hair like her own. Her eyes traced their features trying to find some likeness to her mother—the soft eyes and mouth, hardened into a grim line from all the days she'd had to hide. All the days Brinn forced her to because of the shame she felt about who she was. The tears swelled in her eyes, blurring her vision.

In the thick of the crowd, she saw a woman with her hair pulled neatly atop her head, just the way her mother used to wear it. Her eyes locked on the shock of blue, on that burst of hope, bright like a flare in the sky guiding her back to where she should be.

Brinn's fingers shook as she reached out to her. She tapped her on the shoulder, and the woman turned.

The woman stared at her, her eyes warming to see someone of her kind. But they weren't eyes Brinn recognized, the eyes that she wanted to see. Stern and gray, gazing at her with a complicated love that a mother has for the child she wants to protect.

The woman's lips parted. Before she could say anything, Brinn turned away. No matter how quickly she blinked, the tears fell.

Like a ghost, she wandered the grounds. There were moments where she'd briefly come back to life at the sight of someone slightly familiar, but when she found out it wasn't her mother, she'd fade out once again.

"Brinn," a low voice said.

She turned to see Einn. He stood tall, his figure like a dark sword ready to strike. Even now, even when they were safe.

He flinched slightly at the sight of the tears slick against her cheeks. "I found your home." For a moment, her heart rose, only to sink again when Einn paused to find his words. "Your parents are gone, Brinn. I'm sorry."

Her spine curved forward as if it lost all willingness to move, and she turned away. In her head she started to rationalize that simple phrase. *I'm sorry.* That was what a normal person would say. What did that even mean? What were they sorry for? There was nothing they did to cause that loss. Not unless they were holding the gun, or slashing the knife, or throwing that fatal punch.

She staggered away from the noise of the arriving crowd, and she looked up to see Liam standing in the corner. He was still in full combat gear, head between his hands. She rested a hand on his shoulder, and he looked up, his face weary.

"What happened over there?" she asked.

He closed his eyes as if trying to will the memories away.

As if they were still with him, even now. Not just the sight of it, but all the sensations. The smell of smoke. The thick blood on his hands.

"Do you think our parents will ever forgive us for what we do?" he asked.

She no longer had any parents, but she still knew the truth. "No," she said.

* * *

That night, lying in her cot, Brinn pulled up her sent folder and tapped on the last message she sent to her parents.

Her own image played back on the screen. "Hi, Mom. Hi, Dad." The girl on the screen paused. "I don't have anything else to say. I just wanted to say 'Mom' and 'Dad' again. I want to remember how that feels."

There was more to that message, like how she'd promise to never fight with her mom about how all bokhi blends tasted the same or how she'd go with her dad to the museum he always wanted to visit. But instead of watching the rest, she clicked out of the recording.

It was her SOS message, a reminder that there were still traces of the person she used to be and the daughter that her parents wanted her to become. Her thumb pressed down on the file until a command dialog appeared. She tapped Delete.

CHAPTER 31
IA

SHE LIVED IN THE MIDDLE of dreams. In the atom of space between one and the next. And in those dreams, memories floated toward her, dancing like an orchestral reverie. They painted the scenery of the bright-white interiors of the Sinsia township, the rise and fall of an alarm, a pistol gripped loosely in her hand.

Sights and sounds played together like notes racing to the end of their measure, and by the finale of the first movement, she saw her brother.

Ia wasn't always the Blood Wolf.

When she was twelve, no one except Einn knew her name.

"Ia," he called.

At fifteen years old, he was still small, but the captain of the ship knelt captive and quivering before him.

Einn waved his hand, motioning for her to join him.

Jogging up, she stopped beside him. He smiled so she would forget the man sweating next to her. Einn grabbed her pistol and slipped a combat knife between her fingers. The wooden handle felt rough to touch.

"Hold it tight," he said, examining her grip. And she dug her fingers down until her knuckles were white.

He placed a hand on top of her head. "Don't be scared. You can do it."

It was only when she nodded that he backed away.

Her grip was unstable, and her knife shook in her hand. The vessel's captain kneeled before her. A trickle of blood dripped from a gash across his eyebrow and down into his sharp, guarded eyes that darted back toward her brother. Einn had backed off to the far end of the hall.

The captain's gaze came back to her. She saw the decision cycling through his head, and soon he was no longer quivering.

The captain rose, and with his broad palms, he shoved her backward. Her body, her muscles light and her bones still soft, slammed into the metal wall. She slid down to her side.

Ia was frozen from the pain, but her eyes moved until they found her brother who stood still, watching. She needed to learn, he had told her, in order to survive. But she was too afraid.

Her eyes drifted back to the captain, who was on his way to her, his hand already reaching for the pistol at his side. *He won't shoot*, she told herself. What kind of man would kill a little girl? He would let her go. Because in another life, on another planet, with his crew, with his family, she was sure he was kind.

The captain raised his pistol, his finger tensing against the trigger.

It only took that instant to see how wrong she was. People can do very bad things, she realized. People of all sizes.

She rolled onto her knees. Gripping the handle of her knife with both hands, she lunged.

The captain's body slumped forward, and as the tip of her knife tore deeper into him, his heat and his sweat enveloped her. The weight of him made her stumble backward, his body rolling off her in a thump.

She looked up to see her brother's extended arm.

"You survived," he said.

Seeing him before her, she drew out a staggered breath and wept.

Einn wiped the tears from her eyes.

"It'll get easier," he said. "I promise."

He held her hand, and her fingernails dug into the skin of his knuckles. But that fear, it was still *there*.

* * *

Ia woke up, sweat coating her skin. She pulled herself into a sitting position. Her hand combed through her messy hair, now drenched from the effects of her night terror.

Her body trembled, not from the cold, but from the strange feeling inside her. Like a plug had been pulled, her life force completely drained.

As her breathing slowed, she glanced up. A chill ran up her spine. There was someone in the room. A dark outline, the sharp angular lines of an exo suit along its body. It stood with its back to her.

The phantom figure turned slowly, and she saw the demon tips on Einn's helmet. "It'll get easier," it whispered.

The muscles in her body turned to stone.

"Einn?" she asked. Her voice felt small, as if the word

itself was a parasite, stealing the oxygen from the confines of her lungs.

Suddenly, its features shifted so that another vision stood before her. The Blood Wolf's feather drawn in fresh blood across the visor. As the figure stepped closer, Ia saw its hands around its belly, blood dripping out of a gaping wound, a peek of pink intestines slipping through.

"It'll get easier," it assured her.

It walked toward her, and she felt the life jolt out of her.

She grabbed what was closest to her, a dinged thermos on the side table, and hurled it before the thing could get any closer.

The phantom vanished.

The thermos clanged against the metal wall, falling to the floor in a clatter.

She stared at it as it rolled to a stop.

The lights flickered on. Eve stood in the doorway, her eyebrows raised in alarm. "Is everything all right?"

Ia looked down, too ashamed to face her. "I knocked it over in my sleep."

Eve looked down at the canister and picked it up. She poured more water into it and then returned it to the bedside table. It clinked on the tabletop, the sound so loud in Ia's ears that it made her flinch.

Eve furrowed her brows, and Ia turned to face the wall.

"You should get some rest," Eve said, her voice calm. "We start physical therapy this week."

After Eve left the room, Ia closed her eyes, but even as she did, that image of the phantom was there, staring back at her.

* * *

Ia fell, her knees cracking hard against the metal grating.

"Pick yourself up," Eve said. Normally, Eve's thick, dark eyebrows followed an elegant arch, but at this particular moment, they tipped downward with a mix of frustration and annoyance.

Eve had wheeled her off on an old mechanic's dolly to a closed section of the space station—the chapel. It was sanctioned off for good reason. The paneling was falling apart. Chunks of ceiling hung down and squeaked on old rusted hinges, threatening at any instant to fall on their heads as they passed underneath. But the bronze statue of Deus was still there, with beautiful thick hair almost as long as her robes, her one palm held against her heart, and the other holding a sword to the ground.

Only older space stations had chapels for worship, and Myth was no exception. Ia thought of all the prayers that were said in this space, the sins that were confided, and the favors that were asked. Perhaps a few pairs had even sought their bonding here. There used to be so much dignity in this room, and now it was empty, the pews unscrewed from the floor panels and pushed to the sides.

Here, the air was stale. The stillness stuck to Ia's skin, burrowing into every curve and sharp line on her face. But it didn't matter how the air felt. It was the oxygen that mattered, and thankfully she could breathe just fine.

She was hunched over on the ground, her legs and limbs so weak she thought she'd crumble at any moment. Luckily, Eve had scrounged up a muscle-assist exo suit for Ia to wear. It was from her old days on the mining rigs, Eve explained. The suit reinforced the joints, and in Ia's case, it helped stabilize her. Without it, she knew she'd topple to the floor in the least graceful fashion. She was happy her crew wasn't here to see this. She had been someone to fear for so long, and now look at her. Helpless. She didn't even want to think about how she'd be able to fly, given the way she moved now.

"Stop it," Eve said. "I know you're wallowing."

Ia glared at her, eyes narrowed.

"You're thinking," Eve cleared her throat, adjusting her pitch higher. "'I was the Blood Wolf of the Skies, and now I'm on the floor crawling around like a pathetic little insect.'"

How funny. It was only a month ago that Ia was training Brinn. Now the roles were switched, and she was the one getting picked apart for her lack of resolve.

"Is that really how I sound?"

Eve nodded and then sat down right next to her, her ankles crossed, one over the other. "Look, there's no shame in this."

"I don't need you to tell me that," Ia said through gritted teeth.

"Yeah, but you need to hear it." Eve glanced at the dirt underneath her nails. "Maybe if that kid was here—that Bug of yours—he could say it a bit more sweetly. But he's not. Right now, you got me."

Knives had been gone for over two weeks, leaving Eve in charge of Ia's care—physical therapy, bringing her food and water, helping her with personal hygiene tasks like washing her face and going to the bathroom. That was embarrassing enough. But the worst part was the conversation.

"Just leave me alone already," Ia asked. "I can't walk right now."

"That's a lie, and you know it," Eve said. "That suit can help anyone. Yes, the steps will be weird and clunky, but one step in front of the other still qualifies."

Eve was right. These suits had been used to aid people with limited mobility and in all types of grav situations, but Ia had already learned that it wasn't the walking that was the problem. It was her endurance. Every step took so much energy; it drained her where there wasn't even anything left. She gazed at the exposed pipes in the ceiling. There was a time when her body would have been able to swing from one end of the room to the next with ease.

"Yep, that's the face of a wallower," Eve's voice said, breaking through Ia's thoughts.

Eve crossed over to the far end of the room where her pouch lay. She kneeled down and pulled out something from inside. Ia's helmet. Eve dusted the dirt from the top and placed it on the ground in front of her.

Ia's eyes widened at the sight of it. She'd thought it was gone, that they had sawed it right off her, like her eye mod and her vocal enhancer. Everything that had become so much a part of her, a part of the Blood Wolf of the Skies.

It could be a replica, she thought, but even from this distance, she could tell. It was hers. It wasn't the feather that gave it away; it was the mold of the helmet itself. The way the panels assembled and melded together as if it was one piece. Not many makers could achieve that. Her helmet was one of a kind, made by an old armor smith from the Meridian system, using techniques that had been passed down from generation to generation. The smith was the only one left in his family, so the knowledge died along with him when the Commonwealth invaded and wiped out his entire planet.

Eve nodded down to the helmet on the floor, going so far as to rest her foot on its crest. It made Ia cringe, but then, for a terrifying second, she saw it: the phantom figure watching her from the shadows, its horns so sharp that they would make her bleed. The terror seeped back into her. She had no armor. Nothing to shield her. If she put her helmet on, if she became the Blood Wolf, she would have to face it. She would have to face her own death. Again.

"Here's the thing," Eve said. "Do you want this or not?"

Ia stared at the helmet lying across the room, the Blood Wolf's feather bold against the black. Every scuff and scratch told a story of her life. It gave her courage. It gave her hope. And she always wore it proudly. She never cowered behind that visor. Never.

She pulled herself up and clambered to her helmet. Plucking it off the floor, she crossed back to the other side of the room and placed it right next to the statue of Deus, where day by day it would gather dust and eventually be forgotten.

CHAPTER 32

BRINN

IT WAS LATE in the evening, and Einn had ordered Brinn to her quarters to get some rest since it was something she often forgot to do. As she lay on her cot, she undid the latch of her holowatch, now linked to a Dead Space private network to mask her location from anyone who was searching for her. But with her family and Ia dead, she didn't know who would be. Besides, she didn't need to be connected to do what she wanted to do.

She dragged her finger against the touch screen. The watch illuminated in the surrounding darkness. She opened her photos folder, quickly selecting the one she wanted. A holodisplay flickered in the space before her, like an apparition appearing on its regular haunting hour.

The photo was over a year old by now. It was the one they took the day of the Provenance Day parade, the same day Ia was captured. In the image, Brinn's eyes were bright with wonder, and Faren was looking at her, his lips upturned, caught in the middle of a laugh.

It was painful to see her brother's face, but it hurt even more to see her own. So she set her eyes on Faren, the one person she missed the most in this universe. Brinn always had so much to tell him. So much.

"Hey, Fare," she said. But those were all the words she could manage now.

She left the rest of her words in the tight confines of her throat, swallowed them, so they crowded up all the space in her chest. No matter what she'd tell him about why she was doing what she was doing, she knew what he'd say.

She got out of bed, leaving her brother to haunt her space without her.

* * *

Nirvana's residence halls were different than the dormitories at Aphelion. For one, they were a lot darker. Einn certainly had the infrastructure to install lighting grids everywhere, but the darkness was his choice. Instead of overhead lights flooding every crack and corner, LEDs were embedded along the walking path to guide the way. As Brinn walked down the hallway, all of the doors looked the same, but she knew which one to stop at.

Brinn stared at a red metal door. She knocked three times. No answer.

She tried once more, but the door remained closed.

Liam must be gone.

Strange. It was already late, and most people's activities were done for the day, though a few people preferred to do their lurking at night.

Ever since Liam had arrived back from the mission on Nova

Grae, it had been hard to find the time to see him. Brinn was too preoccupied with work. She didn't have room for other things. Or people.

It was easy to shut everything out when she had already settled on a certain truth. That the world was broken. That the hope that remained was quickly slipping through all the giant cracks, taking her along with it.

To stop from completely disappearing, she had to remind herself that there was *more*. That there was still something out there for her. It felt like the only thing that could fill that void was Penance. But even she knew that it was merely a distraction, a way for her to numb herself and forget.

She didn't know if Penance would suddenly change everything, but she did know that it was the only thing she could control right now. The only thing that she could fix. One thing was certain: she would open a bridge to another universe. There was no telling what would be on the other side. It could better the world. Or it could destroy it. Brinn couldn't be bothered with those details. All that mattered was that she succeeded.

As she turned away from Liam's door, her forehead knocked into something flat and hard. She glanced up but all she saw was the length of an empty hallway.

She waved her hand in front of her, and her palm brushed up against something. An invisible obstacle to her path, tough and textured underneath her fingertips. Like metallic fabric. The hard sleeve of a suit that someone was wearing.

Immediately, Brinn stepped backward and glared at the empty space. "I don't know why you always have to walk around like this."

"Like what?" the air whispered back at her.

She rolled her eyes, having absolutely no desire to continue with the conversation. She knew it would be frustrating and filled with useless questions.

"Do you know where my friend Liam is?" she asked.

Eyes the shade of ghostly lavender appeared before her, followed by the sharp, white lines along the jaw and chin, completing the outline of the skull on his face. She had seen it a few times already, but it still was unsettling when it appeared out of nowhere like that.

"Why are you asking me this?"

Brinn crossed her arms. "Because you always know where everyone is. Isn't that your specialty? Sneaking around and spying on people?"

"No," Goner said. "My specialty is destroying things."

"Well, this place is still standing."

He blinked his eyes slowly as if he was trying to ignore every single word she had said. Then he turned away from her and started walking back to where he had come from. Before he rounded the corner, he looked back at her, his white cheekbone cutting hard against the dark.

"I thought you said you wanted to know where he is."

* * *

Goner led her down paths and hallways she had never seen before. From what she could tell, he was bringing her deeper and deeper underground.

They stopped before a pair of tall doors. Thick metal sheets with intricate carvings etched into the surface. The carvings took the shape of circles, layered on top of one another. Some concentric, some intersecting. Like ripples across water.

No, like the tears in space itself.

Her eyes traced the outline of the doorframe, looking for the glowing square sensor that would open the doors before her.

"They're not that kind of door," Goner said. He pointed out the circular brass doorknobs on each of them.

Brinn reached out, grabbing a doorknob. It twisted easily, but getting the door to inch open was another story. Brinn wedged her shoulder against the thick metal, every muscle straining as she pushed with all her strength.

Goner leaned back lazily against the wall, watching her as she struggled. "If you can't muscle your way through, maybe you don't even deserve to see what's behind it."

Brinn glared at him, then heard the rumblings of noise beyond. She pressed her ear up against the cold metal, the jagged carvings scratching against her cheek. Shouts, followed by the crunch of heavy impact.

Her eyes narrowed on Goner. "What the mif is going on in there?"

He smiled, as if savoring the fear on her face, and then he placed a broad palm on the door and pushed.

The door gave way easily for him, as though he was a child brushing away sand in the sandbox.

Was she really that weak? she wondered. Or was he really that strong?

He waved a hand for her to make her way inside. "Personally, I don't think you're ready to see this, but that's why it's so much fun."

The door opened to a dark, spacious arena. Crystal spires

hung low from the craggy ceiling. The walls were made of rock, bare of metal beams or paneling. The place was a natural cavern deep within the subsurface of the floating planetoid.

A grated walkway lined the perimeter of the cavern. It was crudely made, with no safety railing to keep people from falling off the edge into the pit below.

The noises she heard through the metal doors grew louder as she made her way along the perimeter. From outside, it sounded like a light scuffle, one with bruising and gashes involved, but inside, the danger was thicker than she'd thought and more apparent. She was walking into a battlefield.

Brinn stayed close to the rock wall. Behind her, Goner had disappeared. His vanishing acts were starting to aggravate her, but there could be a reason why he didn't want to be seen in a place like this.

Shouts came from down in the pit. She froze midstep, a rush of fear crawling up her spine. She could go to the edge and investigate, but she stayed stuck in place.

And then she saw it. A glimmer of light rippling above. The light stretched and tore beyond all natural order until a gash appeared, revealing another view through its center. Just then, a figure tumbled through, followed by another.

Brinn's eyes grew wide.

She recognized the dark silhouette, his sleek black flight suit topped with the horned helmet. It was Einn, but that wasn't what made her freeze in terror. It was the boy he had dragged through that wormhole with him.

Liam. Punching and clawing, not to get away from Einn, but to escape gravity's clutches. Because if he didn't, he'd hit ground. And he'd be dead.

She had seen this moment before, when Einn had dropped Ia from a similar height.

Ia was a clever and resourceful fighter, but there was no way to fight gravity. The sound of the impact had been terrifying. Brinn had expected it to be filled with the crunch of bones, the splatter of blood all across the pavement. In actuality, it sounded clean. A quick crack against the cement. But that was what had made her pause, that something so quick and clean would take down the strongest person she knew.

All Brinn could do at that moment was watch her fall. It served as a reminder. People weren't equipped to go against nature. They needed tools, wind packs, starjets, eye mods. They were feeble creatures. Nature could wipe them out in seconds, if it wanted to.

So that was why it was terrifying to watch Einn defy the forces like this. In a way, he had placed himself above the order of the universe. And he truly *was*.

Liam tried to anchor onto him, but Einn had already twisted away. Einn weaved a pattern with his fingers, opening up another spatial tear. He dove through, leaving Liam to fall.

Brinn ran to the edge, watching her memories repeat themselves. But instead of Ia, it was Liam.

And that was when she felt it, this *more* she was searching for. There were threads that still held her to this world, to this life. He was one of them.

Was there still good in the universe? Yes, if she could feel this way, then yes.

"Liam!" she yelled, and his gaze met hers. Perhaps it was

the shock of terror, but his eyes remained surprisingly calm.

Snapping back into focus, his body spiraled so he faced the ground. He reached to a device strapped around his waist and tapped on the center button. Another wormhole appeared directly in front of him, and he flipped his body right through.

And the other end—where was it? Her eyes flew up and then down, locking on to a small cylindrical tear hovering near the ground. It was perpendicular to the other wormhole, and only a few meters away.

Liam's feet appeared, along with the rest of his body. He landed in a crouch, his back curved, chest heaving up and down from the adrenaline.

Einn, who had landed moments earlier, walked over to him and offered him a hand.

When he stood, Liam's eyes went to hers. There were others gathered next to him, young soldiers dressed in combat gear, and they all had the same device. Einn had more plans than Penance, she realized. And more weapons for war.

* * *

Brinn followed Liam into a room lined with lockers for the soldiers in training. Some of them were in the middle of changing out of their gear, but she didn't care about the flash of skin.

She stared at Liam's broad back, her anger firing. He could have killed himself today. If he landed wrong, he could have severed his nervous system. Liam would end up paralyzed, just like his father.

"Give me that device," she demanded. "Do you know how dangerous that is?"

But he kept walking. She grabbed him by the crook of his elbow, but he shrugged away from her.

"I'm prepared for all this. To fight. To die. I'm a soldier," he said, and his glare cut through her. His words stung with the acid of truth. "I'm not your brother, Brinn."

She tried to bite down whatever sadness had welled up inside her. She hadn't realize it before, but perhaps he was right. Was this how she was dealing with her brother's death?

"Give me that device, Liam," she said softly.

Grumbling, he passed it to her, and she turned it around in her hand, examining the delicate wiring, the shoddy frame, powered by a microcanister of uranium. Whenever it was activated, a wave of radiation would be unleashed upon its immediate surroundings. And on the user himself. It was dangerous. A weapon. If she wanted to, she could break it apart with a quick twist of her wrists. Then it'd be just a tangle of circuits and wires.

"If you're going to fight, you need rad meds," she said. She handed the device back to him and then pointed at the display on the center of the belt. The indicator was almost near the empty mark.

"And keep an eye on the power gauge. If you get caught in between spaces when this thing goes off, then you're cut in two. You could be beheaded if you aren't careful enough. Okay?"

"Thanks," he said. "For the advice."

She gazed up at his face.

No smiles. Not anymore.

CHAPTER 33
KNIVES

AFTER A WEEK of repairs, the Kaiken was ready for flight. Knives estimated that it would take another week to get back, not because the Harix Corridor was far, but because he wasn't excited to report back his defeat. He decided to stop by a nearby system to grab some ramen from a noodle joint he had always wanted to try. The place was called Nowhere Ramen, which wasn't exactly the most appealing title for a ramen restaurant, but it did fit in with the planet on which it was located. Classified as a gray planet, with very little water or vegetation, the place was pure desert. The planet had no registered name, but the residents called it Armpit. No one knew about it except the people who lived there and extreme foodies. The noodle house matched its surroundings, a shack built of dried clay and decaying wood.

Inside, it was dark and cramped, but packed with customers. The hand-rolled noodles were supposedly formed in unique grav conditions, which made them chewier. No one knew exactly how the ramen chef made them, but Knives did know that for a brief moment, eating those noodles made him forget about his humiliating defeat. Probably because he had paired the ramen with a couple bottles of barrel-brewed archnol. But then, after a satisfying burp, the shame returned.

As he sipped at the dregs of his drink, pondering whether or not to gorge on another set of noodles, he looked around the ramen joint. He hadn't noticed until now that white hearts were pinned or patched onto almost everyone's flight suits, jackets, and wrist bracers. Most of the patrons were Einn's supporters. There were a few, like him, who wore no emblems. Thank Deus, he had long changed out of his Star Force gear. He wore whatever he found in the discard pile at Myth, which was a stained white undershirt, and a dinged-up flight suit with scuffs on the knees and elbows, but enough thread to maintain a barrier when he needed to make use of its enviro controls. Oh, and his brown leather jacket with the Pete name tag stitched onto it. It didn't hurt to have an alias when he was wandering about.

But that was the only thing that marked him. No red-and-white quartered shield, no flight patches or fancy gold pins, not even an insignia of his favorite Poddi league team.

Here, he was Pete. Neutral Pete. Being neutral wasn't supposed to draw any attention, but here it did. It made him stand out among the crowd. The absence of white hearts on his person was a telltale sign that he was not one of them.

"I know what you're thinking. Don't worry. It's not a cult. They won't force you to join," the owner of the ramen joint said to him as she wiped down some nearby counter space. She was a tall woman, with long gray hair pulled back into a tight braid. At full height, she would hit her head on the beams of the building's low ceiling, so she stood in a slouch, her hunched body draped in long, loose indigo layers of clothing.

"I'm telling you, Kami," one of the patrons said. He was an older man with a round belly. "You should reconsider."

Kami turned back to Knives. "I take it back. Maybe they are a cult."

"This"—that same patron tapped on the pair of white hearts stitched to his sleeve—"can offer you protection."

Kami spooned a fresh batch of noodles into a bowl and served it to a new customer who had taken a seat at the counter. "Protection from what?" Kami asked. "This joint is in the middle of a dust zone. There's no blue planet around for stars and stars."

The patron shrugged, but then a different voice jumped in to answer. A woman this time. "You know the Bugs. They won't stop until they control everything."

Knives cringed. There were so many times in his youth when he'd dreamed of leading colonization campaigns, the same large-scale missions that took all these people's resources, their planets, their homes. Now, after hearing the other side of the story, he understood why they called Star Force troops Bugs. Because they infested every star system they came across. Like bleach-locusts, flying from field to field, eating everything until the land grew infertile.

"I've had most of these patrons for years," Kami explained. "It was only recently that they started wearing those white hearts, ever since that attack on Rigel K."

"You heard what they're doing, right?" one customer said.

"Oh, do tell," Kami said with obvious disinterest.

But everyone else perked up, eager for any bit of space gossip.

"White Hearts ships have been attacking convoys. Olympus vehicles as well as big corp liners."

That was odd, Knives thought. They were going after corporate vessels, too?

"And it's the way they're doing it that's freaking the other side out. They call them ghosts. They appear, do their damage, and then vanish."

"But how?"

The customer slurped up some noodles. "No one knows."

Knives would be lying if he didn't admit he was interested in how they were doing it. There was something familiar about this story. It reminded him of his short time on Fugue, seeing Einn vanish from one place and reappear in the next.

Kami leaned in, interrupting Knives's train of thought. "You know, I've lived long enough to know that people like the White Hearts don't last. There's always war. There's always death. But when there's night, the sun will always rise." Kami's eyes caught the light. "Can't wipe out hope, my friend."

Knives snorted and pushed his empty bowl forward. "You could say the same about rats."

Kami took Knives's bowl and placed it in the sink. "True," she said, "but you're too young to be this cynical."

Knives reached into his pocket to grab a pay cube that Eve had given him for food and fuel charges. He scanned over his credits on the pay sensor and then got up from his stool. "Thanks for the meal."

Before he could turn, Kami called out. "I know you don't buy in to that hope nonsense, but you know what I always say? And my customers can attest. Hope comes in the form of steaming hot ramen, and you just had some, son. Make sure you come back for more."

She handed him a handwritten receipt. Knives straight up blinked at the sight of paper, curled at the edge where it was ripped. It was something he thought he'd never see again, not since Bastian passed away. He stuffed it in his jacket pocket.

"Thanks," Knives said, stepping away from the counter. He passed through the white cloth covers that hung down from the entryway, the light from inside following his dusty footsteps into the wasteland.

* * *

After that pit stop, Knives decided it was time to return to Myth. He had to swallow his pride and check in on Ia. Sure, he'd have to admit to Eve that he had lost the race, but there was no reason to bring it up with Ia Cōcha, the girl who had flown that corridor in fifteen seconds.

A small grimace flittered onto his lips at the thought of her teasing him. On second thought, perhaps it'd be a good thing. Insults meant conversation. Something they haven't had together in a while, not since her accident. And the type where she was screaming at him didn't count.

Finally arriving on Myth, he lowered his Kaiken and parked. As Knives stepped down the last rung of the ladder, he glanced at Eve walking toward him in the docking bay.

"I see you were successful," she said with a smile.

Knives stared at her for a second. He hadn't commed back his news. So he had no idea how she had heard that tidbit of fake news. "What do you mean? I lost."

She pressed her lips together. "I know. I saw the results on the race space feeds. Perseus, right? Nice touch."

"Actually, it was Theseus," he said.

Eve shrugged. "Whatever."

Great, he thought. So everyone in the universe knew that he lost that day. Well, not him—Theseus.

"Then why are you celebrating?" he asked, unable to mask the bitterness laced into his voice.

She jutted a thumb over at another jet, already parked at the far side of the bay. The model was unmistakable. A Yari. The same Yari he'd raced side by side with to the end of the track. The same Yari he'd lost to.

Minotaur was on Myth, and so was its driver.

"He's been unloading for thirty minutes already," Eve said.

"Unloading what?" Knives asked.

"He traveled with cargo," she said.

Knives crossed the docking bay and walked around the Yari's port side until he found his opponent unlatching another jet from the tail end of his vessel. The jet wasn't a model he recognized, definitely not a superjet like the Yari or a known racer like his own. It wasn't a remod either, which was a mishmash of recognizable parts. Nope, this one was a custom build. And a dirty one at that.

He dragged a finger on the metal siding, the black burnoff so thick all over that it didn't even move from his touch.

It was a piece of junk.

His old opponent stopped what he was doing. His mask covered the bottom half of his face, the loops on each side stretched behind his ears, but his eyes made an impact, focused as if they were about to shoot lasers right at him.

"Hey, chien," he said. "Hands off."

"Did you just call me chien?"

"Yeah, it's French for dog."

But Knives already knew that. What was strange was that French was an old language, and something only the wealthiest members of the Commonwealth knew. They spoke in Français during their dinner parties, traded secrets and gossip using this ancient language. There was something familiar about this guy, and Knives couldn't shake the feeling that they had met before.

Impossible. Could he be a Citizen?

"It might not look like much, but this thing is a beast," the champion said.

"So why didn't you ride it during the race?"

"Because it doesn't belong to me." The champion swiveled toward Knives, the dark-brown curls knotted on top of his head bouncing as he moved. From this distance, Knives got a better look at him, his eyes searching for anything recognizable, which was hard since he could only see the top half of his face. His eyebrows were thick, and his eyes were a jade green. A splash of freckles dotted the bridge of his nose. Nothing too out of the ordinary.

Eve planted a hand on the wings of the custom-built jet, but somehow the victor didn't blow up in her face about it.

He reached into a side pocket and pulled out the red bottle

cap. He tossed it back to her. "Why'd you drag me all the way out here, Eve?"

She ran a finger against the flattened edge of the bottle cap and started walking back to the bar of the space station. "Because I thought you'd want to see her, Vetty."

So this guy had a name, Knives observed. Vetty. Somehow he'd heard it before. It was a name from his childhood, a popular pick back then. Many of the older boys in his social class bore that very same name.

Vetty ran after her. "See who?" he asked, his voice low.

Eve took a drag from her vapor stick and raised her eyebrows as if Vetty should already know. That alone made Knives question everything about him.

Vetty stormed past them, navigating the space as though this wasn't the first time he'd been there. Seeing that no one was inside, he stared at the entryway to the space station's small residential wing.

"Is she in there?" Vetty asked.

Eve nodded. "In my room."

Vetty lowered his face mask, revealing a sharp jaw and a distinct dimple in the middle of his chin. It only made Knives stare.

Without even asking permission, Vetty opened the door to Eve's room and closed it right behind him.

Knives's jaw tightened, his molars grinding down hard. "You can't just let him go in there."

He barged past, but Eve stopped him. "They need to talk."

"Talk? She barely even talks to me. What makes you think she'll even say a word to that guy? And was I seeing things?"

Knives motioned to his own very dimple-less chin. There was only one family who bore that distinctive mark. "Is he—"

"Yes," Eve said, angling her head at the room the victor disappeared into, "that guy in there is the true heir to the Sinoblancas Corporation."

That was why the name was familiar. The young men in the elite were all named after *him*. Vetty Sinoblancas. He was a golden child of the Commonwealth, until the news dropped one day that he was gone. It wasn't a kidnapping. It was a choice.

"The runaway heir," Knives said. "So why does he need to talk to Ia?"

"Because," Eve said, "he's her ex."

CHAPTER 34

IA

IA'S EYES WERE WIDE as she stared at the boy lurking in the doorway. Vetty looked almost the same as ever. But stronger. His shoulders broad with the added thickness of muscle.

"Great," she muttered. This was the last place she thought she'd see him again.

He took a step into the room, his face catching the lone light cast from the ceiling.

"It's been years, and that's all you have to say? Great?" Vetty asked.

She sat up in her bed, using her arms to help pull her legs close to her chest. "I knew Eve would tell you guys. Is Trace here, too, and the rest of the crew?" She wouldn't be able to bear the looks on their faces when they saw her in this state. A traitor to their kind. And no longer a warrior because of it.

"No," he said. "It's just me." She held her breath at the sound of his voice, so familiar that it stirred up buried memories. Some good, some bad.

But surely that wasn't why he was there, to take a nostalgic trip down memory lane. Hell, maybe there was another bounty on her head, but this time from Dead Space instead of Olympus.

Wanted: Ia Cōcha, for betraying her people. Kill on sight.

"Well, if you're here to shoot me, do it now. I'm the weakest I've ever been in my life." She glanced down at her thin, stubby knees poking up from underneath the shred of blanket. When she looked back up, she saw that he hadn't moved. "Don't have a pistol? I'm sure Eve keeps one around here somewhere."

He leaned a muscular shoulder up against the far wall. "This isn't like you at all. I mean, the first thing you'd find out is where all the weapons are," he joked.

She studied the mirth in his expression, his relaxed pose. "So you're not here to kill me…"

"Why would I do that?" He moved to the center of the room, brought over one of the stray chairs, and sat down. "A comrade who I never thought I'd see again is sitting right in front of me."

"Comrades, huh?"

The left corner of his mouth quirked upward into a classic Vetty half smile, and again those ancient yet familiar strings tugged at her heart.

He leaned forward in his chair, voice lowering. "What happened to you?"

"Einn." The answer was short and simple, but steeped with so much of everything. Anger, most of all. But there was also pain, loss, regret. Humiliation.

"Your brother?" Vetty's eyebrows raised. "But he'd never lift a hand against you."

"There's a lot we need to catch up on." Ia snorted.

Vetty stood up, so tall that his head almost hit the low middle beam across the ceiling. He offered her a hand. "Let's get some food then, and you can tell me everything."

Just like old times, she slipped her hand into his.

* * *

She hadn't put on her suit, so it took a lot longer than usual to walk the length of the hallway. She had to stop for a moment to catch her breath and hold on to the energy she had left.

Beside her, Vetty rested a hand on her shoulder. She looked back at him, his eyes still so kind even after their years apart. He held up a sturdy arm. Gladly, she slipped a hand into the crook of his elbow. He had always been such a gentleman, unlike the other Sinoblancas that she knew.

"Your cousin was at Aphelion," she said. "Nero."

"That little scant," Vetty muttered. "You didn't kill him, did you?"

"Almost did."

"Well, thank Deus you didn't. If that kid was dead and out of the picture, I'm sure my father would invest more of his money into trying to find the rightful heir, and I really don't want to deal with that right now."

"You've never considered going back?" she asked.

"Go back to what? A future of never-ending business meetings?" He rolled his eyes at the thought of it. Vetty's father was once again president and CEO of Sino Corp, a company that had been controlled by their family since the days of Ancient Earth. It was to be passed down to the eldest son of the next generation, and that was Vetty. But Ia hadn't met him as Vetty

Sinoblancas. She'd met him as a drift runaway off the rings of Nurelia. He was charming and smart, an amazing navigator with a wealth of knowledge, knowledge that she later realized he got from years of elite-class tutelage.

To this day, she had never known what exactly drove him to leave that life of privilege. She never asked.

"But what if going back could help stop the war?" she asked.

"Hardly a war," Vetty said. "It's just your brother being chaotic as always."

She stopped, placing her other hand on his forearm so that he would know she was serious. "It's a war, Vetty. People just don't know it yet."

The hallway opened up to the bar, chairs still strewn about from the night before. It wasn't opening hours yet, so the place was empty save for two pairs of curious eyes staring back at them. Well, one pair of icy-blue eyes was a little bit more annoyed than curious.

Knives stood at their appearance, his eyes narrowed—not at her, but at Vetty standing beside her. There was obvious tension between them, and not all of it seemed like it was because of her.

As Vetty helped Ia into her seat, Knives turned to her, his eyes softening. He offered her a plate of food. "You look better."

Her eyes turned to the floor. Perhaps she looked better, but she didn't feel it.

"Of course she does," Eve said. "I've been whipping her back into shape."

Knives craned his head at Eve with obvious judgment.

"What? She needs to do something if she's going to stop Einn."

"Eve..." Knives warned.

"Stop," Ia said, banging her fist on the tabletop. The action was weak, but it still had an effect. "All this talk about me going after my brother. None of it makes sense. Look at the state that I'm in. I'm not even at 100 with an assist suit on."

She didn't want to tell them about the nightmares, about the ghost that haunted her in her sleep. And sometimes even when she was awake. His horns were slick with her blood. If the visor was lifted, would it even be her brother under there? Or a monster smiling back at her, excited to finally devour her?

"Fine," Vetty said, grabbing a protein cube from her plate. "I'll go after him." It was a Vetty thing to do, to rush headfirst into anything that smelled of danger.

"No, Vetty," she warned. "He's different now. He's stronger." *He's the devil himself,* she thought, but she didn't say it.

"Well, it's not like I haven't been training while we were apart."

"It's not that," she said. It was so hard to explain what Einn could do, because she didn't quite know what it was herself. "He has abilities."

Vetty leaned in, along with the others.

"I don't know if it's tech or what, but he can jump."

"Anyone can do that," Eve said. "I mean maybe not you, in the state you're in."

Ia narrowed her eyes. "Not that type of jump."

Knives's shoulders tensed. "She's right. I've seen Einn do it before in Fugue. It was like he opened his own personal interstellar gate, but on a smaller scale."

Ia's heartbeat quickened inside her chest as the images flew back at her. She saw them so clearly, the small tears that Einn ripped through space so that he could leave her to fall. She had no idea how he had acquired such unnatural power, but then his words echoed through the folds of her memories. *Why would I ever want to kill the man that gave me so many gifts?* She didn't know exactly how, but it was linked to their father.

Eve unscrewed her vapor stick and refilled the fluid. "I think we need more intel. Maybe we can get someone from his camp to tell us something. Do we know anyone who's over there?"

"Brinn," Knives suggested.

Ia scraped her fingernail against the warped metal surface. Her voice grated against her throat. "She's on his side now."

The air hung heavy with silence. It had been a while since she had spoken about Brinn Tarver, but there wasn't a day when Ia hadn't thought of her. She wondered how her brother was treating her, and most of all, she wondered why Brinn had switched sides.

Was it her fault? Of course it was. Of course it was.

Eve tapped her vapor stick to settle the fluids, then glanced at the clock on a nearby holoscreen. "It's almost time to open up shop."

Across the table, Knives stood, presumably to help Ia up, but Vetty had beat him to it, already at her side, one arm around her shoulder.

"I'll bring Ia back to her quarters," Vetty said. "There's still something I need to show her."

She cast her eyes from one to the other, watching them ramp their glares up to maximum aggression. Knives turned and made his way to the storage room behind the bar.

As Vetty helped her pass the awning into the residential wing, she tried to catch a look at Knives, but he had disappeared.

"I gotta tell you," Vetty said. "You're keeping interesting company these days."

"What did you do to him?" Ia asked.

"Nothing." Vetty shrugged. "I just beat him in a race."

"Of course you beat him. You were in your Yari."

"Hey," Vetty said. "I also learned from the best."

She smiled at him. It was nice that they could talk to each other like they used to, that even after all this time, they could still feel at ease. He was a link to her past, to those glorious days when she was at her peak. When people called her the Sovereign. But she didn't want to think about those days. The past was called the past for a reason. It would never come again.

"I've been seeing signs of your brother around," Vetty said. "I know he's building something big. Whatever it is, I thought perhaps you'd be in on it with him."

"This one is all him. I think he wants to finally make a name for himself, and he'll do it if he rips a hole in the universe. It'll be a signature for everyone to see."

Vetty was on a lot of missions that Einn had orchestrated, using the feather of the Blood Wolf to strike fear into everyone's hearts, but when Ia had started to reclaim that feather as her own, taking on jobs that helped refugee groups, even formulating attack strategies for the resistance, Einn wasn't exactly pleased. Usually, Einn pulled his strings in the shadows, but now he seemed to be racing to the finale, like a puppet master ready to step out and receive his applause.

"There's another thing. You know how the crowd at Harix talks," Vetty said. "They say the White Hearts are on the search."

"For what?"

"Not what," Vetty said. "It's whom. Einn's been sending his people to find the Half-Man."

Ia cocked an eyebrow. "The Half-Man? But that's just a nursery rhyme."

Everyone knew the song. Even her mother had sung it to her when Ia was young, when she was alive. The tune itself was catchy and upbeat, but the lyrics recited on their own were quite the opposite. *Watch out. Watch out for the Half-Man. He lives neither here nor there. The Half-Man comes from nowhere. He'll take you and break you. Watch out, watch out. Before you disappear.* It was the type of song that scared kids rather than put them to sleep.

But everyone knew that it was just as it was—a nursery rhyme. Yet all this time, Einn thought it was true?

She could have laughed at her brother's foolishness, but Einn always had a knack for being right.

"Hey," Vetty said. "Before we turn in, there's something you need to see."

Vetty helped her slowly to the flight deck. To the right, she saw two starjets parked side by side.

Vetty's Yari and...

"*Orca*," Ia breathed. It was her jet. The same jet that had outmaneuvered Captain Nema and led the ambush at the battle of K-5 Neptune. The same beast that had torn through the Harix Corridor. After she had separated from her crew to keep a low profile while the Commonwealth was after her, she stashed *Orca* in a large fissure of an asteroid near the Gipia moon. There was a part of her that thought she'd never see her beloved jet again, but here she was now.

This jet was a part of her, a lost limb that magically had returned.

She should have felt complete, but instead, she felt a thread of fear and anxiety stretch through her. *Orca* was a beast made of metal, and even if she crashed, there was still a good chance the ship would be fixed, with the right mechanic and all the right parts. But what about her? Her body was slow. Her muscles were weak. Those were things that couldn't be replaced. And a ship was nothing without its pilot.

"You don't look happy to see her," Vetty said.

Ia took a deep breath. She didn't want to admit it, but with *Orca* there before her, perhaps it was time. "I don't think I'll be able to fly."

The tears were hot as they streamed down her face. But she let them flow. What was the point in stopping them?

"You're the best pilot I know," Vetty said. "I'll keep telling you that until you believe it yourself. It'll be annoying. I promise you that."

She couldn't help but laugh, even through the tears.

Vetty took her hand. "You have to let us be there for you."

Ia looked down at her feet. She had never been on this side of it all. On this side, she wasn't the Blood Wolf. She wasn't the Sovereign. She was just Ia. Ia, who needed help.

She looked at Vetty and nodded.

CHAPTER 35
BRINN

BRINN STARED at the screen, looking at the scans she'd taken of Einn's vitals in an effort to apply whatever it was he could do to their own technology. No matter how she looked at it, the results, while shocking, were clear as day. Parts of his body were made of a different kind of matter.

There had always been questionable constants in the universe. Dark matter and antimatter were a few of them. Usually, these new types of matter were categorized to fill in the holes that appeared within people's knowledge of how the universe worked. There were always things that couldn't be explained.

The matter in Einn's body was unlike anything Brinn had seen. At least not in this universe. It had more mass and was much denser than the matter she knew. On a scale, Einn weighed three times more than a normal man his size and age, but gravity didn't affect the excess grams that were on his body. He could move and jump just fine, almost better than anyone else. More importantly, this matter was how he could create those wormholes.

"Are there more like you?" Brinn asked.

"There was my father, yes. But I believe there were more in the past. That beings from other universes have traveled into our own. Those with an array of abilities. Some like me. Some maybe even more powerful," he said. "You call them gods. This Deus you all talk about is one example."

"You think she's real," Brinn said slowly.

Einn nodded, and his words came out sure and certain. "All legends come from something that was once true."

Brinn sat back in her chair, trying to piece together her thoughts. The origins of Deus had never been explained in such a way. Anyone could have heard Einn's theory and dismissed it as a result of having one too many OPiodes that day, but she knew what he could do. And she had seen what he was inside.

"Then Ia was like you," she said.

A tight line cinched along his jaw. "Perhaps. But she's dead now." There was glee in his response, as well as a slight hint of relief. Maybe because he would never find out if it were true.

Einn strolled through the aisles, angling his head at the machines on each workstation, each unit at different levels of completion. He stopped at one specific prototype. "Is the new tech ready?"

He picked up the unit, turning the tiny metal orbs in his hand. It was her new invention. It created mini black holes using the same uranium charge units that were attached to the wormhole devices she had seen Liam and the soldiers practicing with.

"Yes, but they only work for seconds at a time."

Einn tossed it up in the air, as if it was a toy. But Brinn knew it was more dangerous than that. "That's all we need. Finish this batch, and load them up."

"What for?"

Einn turned to her with a smile, a light in the dark. "We're going out with them."

That only meant one thing: they were preparing for a mission. And if he was considering putting her new invention in play, it would be a dangerous one.

Brinn could reason it out for hours in her head. That this research would benefit their understanding of black holes and thus their understanding of the universe. But in reality, she knew what these things were. They were bombs. And she was the one who had created them.

CHAPTER 36
IA

THEY SPENT A FEW DAYS going over all the basic moves. Ia felt like a child again, relearning everything that had taken her years to perfect. Walking, running, climbing, fighting. But she had to admit, the assist suit helped.

Every night, when Eve helped her take it off, Ia collapsed into the hard foam mattress of her bed. Well, Eve's bed.

The movement was all there. Ia just felt weak and uncoordinated. Which meant she'd be easy to take down in a fight.

Vetty took over her sparring sessions. Out of everyone, he was most familiar with Einn's fighting style.

As she went through all of her movements, she understood how Brinn must have felt during their training exercises. Ia was angry at her body for not doing what she wanted. Still, she repeated each pose, reteaching her body the precision it needed to deflect any attacks. Uppercuts, a right hook, a fist to the center of the chest. It wasn't just that; it was also speed. If she wasn't fast enough to block a punch to her sternum, her rib cage could shatter. And that would be it. End of the fight. And thus, the end of the universe.

That day, Vetty had convinced her to train without the assist suit, which meant there wouldn't be much power to her attacks, and her balance would be thrown off easily.

She focused her attention on the details of Vetty's stance. One angled arm in front, palm upward to either attack or block. His other fist was already tightly recoiled near his chest, ready to dart out at the next opportunity.

She took a deep breath, trying to center her breathing, bringing her weight and balance lower into her stance.

"Are you ready?" he asked.

Her brother wouldn't ask her if she was ready. He wouldn't even give her a hint of an attack. But she nodded at Vetty anyway, grateful for the warning.

His upper hand, already curled in a fist, flew toward her face, and thankfully, she was able to sidestep in time without straight up falling on her backside. Vetty shifted, moving in quick arcs toward her, his feet trying to trip hers, but she wobbled away.

"Take him down, Ia," Eve hooted from the sidelines, cheering her on.

It was a surprising turn of events. She was actually able to keep up. Maybe she could do this. Maybe she could *win*.

Suddenly, instead of Vetty's face, she saw a black helmet and two sharp horns. Her muscles froze, stuck in a mess of eternal sludge. A palm struck hard in the center of her chest. She staggered backward, her eyes catching the first milliseconds of Vetty's next attack.

But she couldn't twist her body in time. His fist landed hard on her shoulder, knocking her completely off-balance. Her feet wobbled underneath her. She fell hard on her hip, the pain knocking through the inside of her body, so sharp it felt it would rip through her skin.

She looked up, and the phantom image of Einn was gone. Instead, Vetty stared down at her, eyes wide with concern. He rushed over to her, offering his hand.

Instead of slipping her hand into his, she burst out, a torrent of uncontrollable emotion pouring out of her. She was crying, she was laughing, she was about to vomit. Everything rumbled out of her throat in a force, her sharp cackling bouncing off the thin and rusting metal walls.

"Are you okay?" Vetty asked, then looked back to Eve, who was also staring over in shock. "Is she okay?"

Ia waved her hand as if it was nothing. "Yeah." She roared with even more laughter. "We're all going to die, but I'm fine. And the universe as we know it will be completely gone—but the universe is overrated anyway."

"I think she's losing it," Eve said.

"The universe *isn't* overrated," Vetty said, trying to reason with her. "What about kitpups? And seeing the aurorealis of the Jinoran skies?"

Ia rolled her eyes at him.

"What about chocofluff?" a voice called out, and she turned to the figure standing in the doorway.

Knives stepped into the training room, his golden hair a mess and his chin dark with stubble. He was more unkempt than ever, but he stood tall and unshaken, his eyes always defiant. It was something that she wanted desperately to see in herself yet again.

Somehow, a smile reappeared on Ia's face. "For that, maybe I'd reconsider."

Knives turned to Vetty, disdain searing in his eyes whenever they were in the same room. "I'll take over."

Vetty ignored him, stepping back into his stance. "I can keep going. I'm not even breaking a sweat." He looked over at Ia, and his expression softened. "Sorry."

She shrugged her shoulders, knowing it was true.

Eve pushed away from the walls and crossed the room. She grabbed Vetty by the elbow. "Come on. You can help me dredge up the new batch of archnol brew. I'll even give you first sip. It goes down the smoothest."

Vetty relented and let Eve drag him off.

They were gone, and it was just the two of them left with the smell of sweat and rubber in the air.

"I guess we should keep going." Ia rolled over to get herself up when Knives crouched beside her.

"Just sit with me for a second," he said.

"But I have to get ready. I don't have time to just sit. Look at me, I'm not even strong enough to kill a bug." She stared at him, realizing that she was staring at another type of Bug.

He settled down into a sitting position, legs akimbo. His knees were so close that they grazed against hers. "You were the one who showed me that I should watch out for fighters like you. You're small, and you aren't strong."

She bit the inside of her cheek, trying to keep herself from yelling at him, and instead settled into her usual glare.

"But none of that matters," he continued, "when you're fast and agile."

Knives was right. These moves were meant to overtake even the largest opponents. That was something she had been trying to dig into Tarver's mind all those times they trained.

Ia was so hard on Brinn back then, but look at her now, giving up so easily because her body had forgotten. The fear had always been there, she knew. Somehow she had managed it, stuffed it down and trusted that her mind and body wouldn't give up the fight. But now, after facing death and coming back, the fear was paralyzing.

"There's more to it, isn't there?" Knives asked as his eyes studied her. By the way he said it, she knew that he had already figured it out.

"I see him," she said finally. "Every time I close my eyes, Einn's there. And he's ready. *So ready*, Knives. How can I even fight him?"

"You're the Blood Wolf of the Skies," Knives said. "This is all mental. I hope you realize that."

"The last two times I fought him, I nearly died. You can't count on me for this fight," she said. She'd been around the group's conversations long enough to know what they thought. They'd made the decision for her. That *she* would be the one to fight her brother. But it wasn't possible. She wasn't going to win. She could feel it in her bones, in her dreams. It was as if Deus herself were warning her to stay away.

"It's fine to doubt yourself," Knives said. "But when the time comes, you have to move."

Suddenly, his arm darted toward her. An attack to her right

cheek. She dodged, then pushed herself to the side and swung her leg, stopping it right before her shin hit Knives in the face.

Knives grinned. "See, you still got it."

Her heart was beating so hard she heard it in her ears. She could have torn him apart for what he just did. Pure rage flared up inside her. Rage, she noticed. Not fear. And that was something.

"Let's go again," she said finally.

* * *

She relaxed, her body collapsing to the floor in exhaustion after hours of sparring. She lay on her back, staring at the lights in the ceiling. She raised her hand, shielding the glare from her eyes.

She saw his profile come into view. Knives sat beside her, his eyes dark in the shadow. But even in the dim, she could see the expression on his face, one that had only gotten more dented and creased as the days went by. There was a wealth of things bothering him. She couldn't decipher all of them, but at least she knew one.

"Vetty told me about the race," she said.

A weak groan escaped the confines of his throat.

"He beat me. I flew the Harix Corridor in 31.92 seconds," Knives said, looking at the floor. "Not even close to your time, or my sister's."

She sat up to face him, her eyes glowing with excitement from everything he'd told her. It seemed like centuries since she'd been in the pilot seat. It scared her, even. Especially now, since she wasn't sure she could fly.

"But that feeling? Was it there?" she asked.

His eyes flicked up to hers in question, the light blue like frozen shards against the white.

He nodded. "Invincible."

Ia grabbed his hand, letting her fingers intertwine with his. She remembered how she couldn't feel him when she first woke up, but now it was there. That warmth. "Then I consider that a success."

Ia didn't know if she could fly, but she remembered what it felt like. She remembered the thrill, the speed. That was where the victories lay. And she felt sadness seep deep into her veins. Would they only be memories? Would her heart pulse like it used to?

The universe was overrated, in a way. There were things that didn't matter. She didn't care two mifs if she never saw the Jinoran skies again, or gushed over next year's kitpup calendar filled with cuddly polka-dotted beasts. But there were other things that were worth holding on to. Yes, she remembered now. What was worth saving? It was deep inside. It was *hope*.

Her lips turned up in a smirk, an expression so rare to her now, but yes, Deus, it was there.

CHAPTER 37

KNIVES

KNIVES SAT ON THE WINGS of his Kaiken, looking up at the distant stars. The space station was set on a twenty-four-hour rotation, and at this hour of early morning, the sun was about to come into view.

He hadn't been able to sleep. There was too much on his mind.

"You're a Bug, aren't you?" a voice called out.

Knives looked over his shoulder, down to the landing platform. Vetty Sinoblancas stood with his chin tilted up at Knives, that dimple very prominently in view.

"Why do you want to know?" he asked. He rolled to his heels and settled into a crouch so he could stare down at the runaway heir.

Vetty kept his face mask around his neck for easy access, Knives noticed. He didn't want people to know who he was. At least they had that in common. One of the reasons he was worried about Vetty being there was that it'd bring the wrong type of attention back to Myth, and not the kind from the

Dead Spacers or the Fringers who frequented the place. He didn't want word to get back to Commonwealth. With the Sinoblancas family backing them, it'd be possible that a unit would be dispatched out there to investigate. The last thing Knives wanted was to be found by his father, not even when the Commonwealth needed him the most.

Knives had been running most of his life, for different reasons. This time, he wanted to say it was for Ia. But there was another explanation. He was a coward. For deserting his squadron while they all perished. They were all better men than he was, yet he was the one who survived.

Looking at Sinoblancas's face made him feel even worse. Because in addition to being a coward, he was also a failure.

Vetty squinted, his pupils darting back and forth as he studied Knives's face. "There's something strangely familiar about you." Then his eyes widened. "You're Marnie's brother, aren't you?"

Knives stood up at the mention of her name. "How do you know my sister?"

"She was older than me, but we shared the same tutor. Guess I was a smart one for my age," Vetty said with a smug grin. "I was about to commend you on your flying skills, but now that I know you're an Adams…"

"What are you trying to say? That I'm not that good?"

"Well, in comparison to everyone else in your family…"

"Oh my Deus." Eve stood at the entryway of the landing dock, wrapped in a grungy sleeping robe. She held an icy cup of caffeine in her hands. "Just fight and get it over with."

Knives jumped off the wing, shouldering past Vetty as he

headed back to the main atrium.

"She's still asleep if you're going to visit her," Vetty called after him.

Knives gritted his teeth, trying to fight the urge to swing at him.

"Careful, Romeo." Eve stopped him, placing her cup of caffeine in his hands to distract him. But it didn't work. He still wanted to punch that dimple right off Vetty's chin.

"I still don't understand why you brought him here," Knives said to Eve.

"In case you haven't noticed, we're losing one big stink of a battle out there. We need allies, and good ones. Besides, I think you two could be friends," Eve said, to which Knives promptly laughed.

"Friends? You're kidding me, right?" Knives said as he walked away.

Eve called after him. "Maybe you haven't realized it yet, but you and Vetty are more alike than you think."

Sons of the Commonwealth who hated their fathers and were also possibly in love with the same woman.

Yeah, Knives thought, they were too alike. And *that* was the problem.

CHAPTER 38

IA

IA FOLLOWED THE SOUND of music, haunting and eerie as it echoed through the metal corridors. It was a traditional Solstice tune. Powerful yet joyous—a song that prevailed beyond borders. Most people, no matter what planet they hailed from, celebrated Solstice. If anything, it was reason to relax, to drink, to forget your worries.

So for her, Solstice came at the right time. She had been reconditioning her muscles and retraining her coordination nonstop for the past few months. But her soul was still weary, still drawn so tight from everything that was running through her mind at every minute, every second of the day. Solstice was a reason to pause, and she needed that right now.

The barroom was awash with strings of orange lights, to praise the sun's generosity. Without the stars, they wouldn't exist. But that was all the holiday decoration Eve had bothered to put up. Ia was surprised she had put up anything at all.

The large room was empty. Its ugly, cracked-leather couches sagged sadly from the lack of drunkards asleep on their cushions. Without the thick of people, it was easy to see the wear and tear on the place. Minus the small handful of patrons drinking solemnly in the corner, Eve and Knives were the only two people in the bar. Vetty had gone on a supply run to the Raserie district.

Eve had positioned herself in front of the bar counter instead of behind it. Probably because there weren't enough customers to justify working.

Beside her, Knives poured himself another drink.

"Easy with that," Eve cautioned. "The fumes in the new batch haven't completely dissipated yet."

"Yeah, I know," he said as he waved her away. "I could go blind."

Ia stiffened at the sight of them together but quickly dismissed it all, blaming the uncomfortable tightness in her chest on her messed-up nerve endings.

She tapped a slender finger on the counter. "I'll take one."

Eve arched an eyebrow. "Are you sure that's a good idea?"

"Archnol is never a good idea," Ia said.

Knives reached over the bar and grabbed an empty glass, setting it down for Eve to pour. Eve tipped the large bottle of new brew. The liquid tumbled in. The drink was a beautiful amber with specks of black that settled at the bottom of the glass. Ia swallowed the shot of archnol in one gulp, allowing the thick liquid to burn the inside of her throat.

Eve glanced over at the other patrons, her paranoia over Ia being discovered as blatant as ever.

"It's Solstice Eve, and they're all drunk off their spirits," Ia reassured her. "They won't remember my face even if they see me."

Eve didn't laugh. "If Einn finds out you're alive, he's going to come knocking down our doors. Do you know how long it's taken me to get this place in shape? If only we had one of his weapons to turn the tide. And an army, that'd be nice," Eve ruminated.

More importantly, they needed someone to lead. And she knew they wanted her. Ia thought about taking up the Blood Wolf's feather yet again, and her jaw tightened. Her brother's face seared into her vision, his demonic smile as he watched her fall to her death. Her stomach turned. She took a deep breath to calm herself down.

"Looks like you're moving around better without the suit," Knives noticed. She had changed outfits earlier that day, deciding to train without the added weight of the alloy frame at her joints. She wore baggy nylon training pants and a tattered white tank top. Her arms were bare, showing off the feather tattoos on both her forearms that she had gotten years ago on a trip to Eden. She would never forget the look on her brother's face when he saw them—completely pissed off.

"Not for much longer, if I have another sip of this," Ia said, a hint of a smile appearing on her lips.

Knives grinned. Perhaps because it had been awhile since Ia dropped a joke into conversation.

"Well then," Knives said as he stood up. He looked at her and extended a hand. His cheeks were flushed a rosy red. "Care to dance? Before you take that second drink, that is."

A rush of heat flooded her cheeks. She told herself it was from the drink and then slipped her hand gently into his, her fingertips resting against the hardened skin of his palm.

He led her to a little bit of open space between two tables, big enough to qualify as a dance floor. The music had changed from a festive carol to a more solemn tune. Knives wrapped an arm around her hip, and she rested a hand on his shoulder, and they swayed side to side, letting the music guide them. They'd spent a lot of time in close quarters together, but for some reason, seeing him in front of her so clearly like this was strange. As if she hadn't seen him for quite some time. Those cold blue eyes, striking in the orange cast of the sun lights.

"I'm sorry Vetty isn't here to dance with you," Knives said.

She pulled away and looked at him, studying the expression on his face. What was that question in his eyes? Why couldn't he just ask her directly?

"Vetty and I are just comrades, Knives," she said.

"Oh," he said sheepishly. "I just thought... I know he's your ex."

"He's my ex for a reason." She laughed. "It's true that I'm happy that he's here. I wouldn't be standing if it weren't for him and Eve." Her gaze rested on his, and the mirth in her expression left, replaced by something a bit more precious. Her voice softened. "And I wouldn't be dancing if it weren't for you."

Those icy-blue eyes warmed for a glimmer of a second, and her knees grew weak. She took a step forward in case she fell, and he held her closer, just a bit closer, so that her cheek was almost touching his. She thought back to when they were at

Aphelion. To that kiss. There was something between them, that was certain. But did she have the courage to face that, especially now when she had to face everything in her life? Usually when the universe was at the brink of destruction, feelings changed. They disappeared. Or they grew stronger.

How did he feel about her now? she wondered. And how did she feel about him?

She felt like Tarver, overanalyzing everything when she shouldn't be. She felt the corner of her lip lift up in a smile as she remembered her old friend, but then stopped herself. That was the thing about memories. They only existed in that one moment in time.

Ia took a deep breath. This was Solstice, Ia reminded herself. *Relax, you munghead.* She rested her head against his chest, letting him guide her. She heard his heart beating steadily, and his warmth surrounded her.

The music ended abruptly, barely in the middle of the song. She glanced over to Eve, who was standing at the bar, raising the volume of the holodisplays.

Ia was about to yell at her for ruining such a perfect moment when she heard Knives whisper. "It's the Queens."

Ia's gaze turned to the holoscreens floating in the center of the room. The majority were designated race streams for the gamblers in the crowd, with a few reality programs about redecorating vacation vessels sprinkled throughout. But one by one, they all switched to the same image. The two Queens of the Olympus Commonwealth stood in front of the cameras, neither in their usual regal attire of long, flowing gowns of silk and lace, but in golden flight suits. Judging from the bare furniture on their set and the lack of flashing text scrolling across the screen, this wasn't the usual press conference. This was something different.

The Queens wore an emblem on their breastplates. It wasn't the Olympus quartered shield but a new crest, one she had never seen before. Its backdrop was the golden sun of the royal family, with a simple copper swallow flying through the foreground.

Queen Lind's dark-brown hair was swept to the sides of her face, soft waves trailing down her olive skin. Her expression was weary, but her hazel eyes were determined as ever.

Queen Juo was taller than Queen Lind. Her shoulders were broad and her black hair, thick and coiled, framed her wide eyes and sophisticated cheekbones. Her dark brown skin was a clean canvas, with no makeup, no lip stain or eye shadow.

There was no pedestal to hide behind, just the two Matriarchs standing shoulder to shoulder, hands clasped together in support.

Queen Lind took a deep breath and spoke. "I would like to greet you all. Not as Queens, but as equals." Ia shuffled closer to the holoscreens. *Equals?* Ia pulled a lock of hair behind her ear so she could hear more clearly. For as long as she knew, the Queens have never addressed the people outright with a statement of equality. They were symbols of Commonwealth history with roots that reached back to the old worlds. Ancient Earth and Ancient Mars.

She looked at Knives. His eyes were filled with a mixture of surprise and hesitation.

Juo continued. "By now, you have heard of the unrest within

the Commonwealth. Of the atrocities our government has let pass. The abolishment of the Sanctuary Act. The refusal to acknowledge hundreds of thousands of people who are not our enemies. They are families. They work side by side with us. These people are our peers, as we are yours."

Juo looked to Lind and nodded for her to continue. A small smile passed between them, an intimate gesture only those close to them had seen until now. Their expressions were entwined with strength, transferring courage from one woman to the next.

"That is why we are announcing our separation from the Commonwealth, an institution we no longer see fit to lead." Lind stared into the camera, her eyes shining with glimmers of a brand-new future. "We are no longer your queens, but we are here to fight with you. Freedom is something that everyone deserves. Citizen or not."

"Holy mif," Eve said. "Is this seriously happening? What does this all mean?"

"It means," Knives said slowly as if he couldn't even fathom the news, "that there's a civil war."

Ia stared at the Queens. Queens no longer. A weight lifted from Ia's shoulders. With the split in the Commonwealth, there was a chance that the refugees would find their freedom. But there was a pit forming at the bottom of her belly. Because none of this would help stop Einn.

"We are not alone. There are others who are brave enough to join us. Like us, they believe that there is a better way. And we promise you, there is," Juo said, her eyes flashing with conviction. She was no longer Queen, but that didn't matter.

Good leaders didn't need titles to stoke that dying spark. "There is still goodness in this universe. We cannot forget that. We cannot let it die."

Lind brought a delicate hand to her heart. "We'd like to extend an offering of peace to Einn Galatin. Together, we can bring balance to the cosmos."

The broadcast ended abruptly, cutting straight to a garbled image, pixels of multicolored noise. A drone of static flooded through the barroom.

"Well, that was unexpected," Eve said.

"Do you think Einn will agree to meet?" Knives asked.

Ia stared at them, her head flooding with thoughts. Einn wasn't interested in the Commonwealth or the refugees. She thought back to the look in his eyes when he forced her to make her first kill.

"My brother doesn't care for peace," she said. "He just wants to watch things burn."

A storm was brewing in the horizon, and Einn was in the center of it.

Ia wasn't strong enough yet, and she wasn't ready. But time wasn't going to stop for her. She could keep running. But her demons were vicious, and they would catch up to her soon.

CHAPTER 39

BRINN

"WHAT IF the fight is actually over, Brinn?" Liam asked.

She looked over at him, a small smile creeping across her face. A fake, one that she had used thousands of times before when she had to pretend she wasn't Tawny. She had no idea what to tell Liam because she didn't know how to feel about it all.

The two of them sat side by side, just as they had when they left Aphelion, strapped in to their flight seats, chins tilted high to see what lay ahead. They had just departed from Nirvana along with almost their entire fleet. In moments, they would all pass through an open gate within Penance's arches, connecting their location to a private star system in Commonwealth territory. They had been invited by Lind and Juo, along with their new group, the United Cause, to meet and discuss the terms for peace. Once they came to an agreement, there would be no more need for bloodshed or to complete Penance.

She knew she should be happy, but Brinn felt an emptiness inside as her work approached a premature end.

Despite the promise of an armistice, Einn had ordered everyone to carry their new jump belts, along with the black-hole prototypes Brinn had developed. Just in case, Einn had said.

Brinn looked over to the other soldiers in their ship—refugees, Drifters, and defectors of the Commonwealth who had joined their cause. They all sat still and tense. None of them had expected that this day would come. That the Queens would address them as equals and invite them to create a new government together. But was that enough to make up for everything that had happened? All the homes and planets that had been taken? All the families that had been broken apart?

Einn walked up and down the lines. "In moments, we'll be touching down on solid ground. It will be new for some of you. To see grass. To see the sky. To see the women who once were queens." His eyes connected with every one of theirs. He knew their value. Their worth. "You are all here because this moment belongs to you."

"Are you going to accept the terms?" Liam was the first to ask, but Brinn knew everyone else was wondering it.

Einn's voice never wavered. "I will make my own choice, and I give you the freedom to make yours."

He stopped at Brinn, glancing at the clunky edge at the side of her hip. The pistol he had given her, concealed by a black shawl she fastened across her right shoulder.

Their units had grown stronger since their last clash against the Commonwealth. With each mission to take down Star

Force envoys protecting refugee send-off ships, they had more followers, more soldiers to add to their cause. They were more powerful than ever before. *She* was stronger, too.

Brinn was on the lead ship along with Einn and a small unit of elite troops. Liam was their point of command. He had led dozens of missions so far, all of them successful. She hadn't asked about the casualties, the bloodshed that he'd seen. But she knew that it had hardened him. He was different from when they had first met, always doing things by the book. But now there was no guide. It was just them figuring it all out. Not just their tactics and strategy, but their own moral compass. Their own reasons to fight, or not to fight. To kill or not to kill. Everyone had a different vision of what lay at the end of the road, of what all their actions would amount to. It was blinding, so much that you couldn't see all the details. But it was there. They just had to keep clambering toward it with everything they had.

Some people, she was sure, saw peace. Some people saw the death of the Olympus Commonwealth as just payment for all the suffering they'd caused.

And what did she see at the end of that road?

Absolutely nothing. She didn't feel the need for vengeance or the desire to make things *right*. Because there was nothing left. Everything had already been taken from her. Faren was dead, and so were her parents. Even if they had survived, nothing would change. How could there be a chance of happiness for them, or for her, after everything they'd gone through?

They landed on a field filled with long grass and wildflowers the color of the setting sun. Lind and her advisers were already waiting for them, the royal villa in the background. A new banner with the copper swallow of the United Cause flew at its entrance.

As they disembarked, Brinn trained her eyes on Lind. She was more beautiful than on the holobanners that were marched up and down the streets of Nova Grae during the Provenance Day parades. Her hair was a long, glossy brown, the same brown Brinn had dyed her hair for years and years.

She hated Lind at that very instant. Her life of privilege, of not having to worry about being socially shunned for how she was born into this world.

A hand rested on her shoulder, and she swiveled with a start. Her eyes landed on Einn's. They were a deep gray like the sky before dawn. Staring into them, she should have been afraid. But they were calm and steady. A pool of unknown mystery—something that should be feared but was instead a thing of beauty. Because it meant anything was possible. It meant that destiny had not yet been written.

Einn took his hand away and extended it to the former Queen Lind. Lind accepted his hand, grasping it firmly between her soft, slender fingers. Her fingernails were clean and perfectly shaped.

"Juo couldn't grace us with her presence?" Einn asked.

"She is attending to refugee matters," Lind said. Behind her was a line of men and women whom Brinn used to think were important. She saw heroes of the Uranium War, captains and commanders and even scholars who were known for their ideas of peace and philosophy. General Adams was there, the same man who had captured Ia and dragged her to Aphelion.

Brinn almost laughed. Ia was captured by that man but dead because of the young man who stood by Brinn's side right now. It was funny how people's paths converged, how they pushed people in directions they would never expect.

"As you know, we've come to negotiate the terms of the treaty. We both seek the same goal, freedom for all." Lind's voice was as clear and dignified as birdsong, but somehow it grated harshly against Brinn's ears. Her brother's blood spilled across the dirt of Nova Grae because he had wanted that same freedom. Where was Lind then?

"And what is your definition of freedom, Lind?" Einn asked.

Lind smiled at him, a perfect smile, one that had probably been taught to generations and generations of royal queens. "That would take quite a while to explain. I have studied the subject for years. Shall we walk by the river while we discuss?"

Anger rose up Brinn's throat. She knew what was to come. Lind would talk of the ancient philosophers, of their examinations of the very ideas of liberty.

But they were just words, Brinn thought. More words that did nothing. Regurgitated like vomit for all to gather around and clap.

She saw through the copper swallow's rising melody, trying to rouse all of them from the dead. A gift of hope to keep them alive. But no, it was your lungs, your blood, your cells—*that* kept you alive.

Hope was a lie. A lie that could burn through everything. All her plans. All of her work. The destiny that *she* chose.

Lind wanted to fight for her freedom? No, she wanted to take it away. So Brinn would have to claw onto it, clutch it in her desperate fingers, because there was nothing else.

"Wait," Brinn said. Lind turned, looking at Brinn for the first time. But Brinn's gaze wasn't on the former queen; it was on Einn. "You told us that we are here to make a choice."

Brinn pulled out her pistol, and the shot rang throughout the field.

The bullet flew, meeting its mark. It buried itself deep into Lind's stomach and she fell. Within moments, the woman who was once queen was just flesh.

General Adams reached for his pistol, but before he could draw, Einn had unsheathed the knife at his hip. The blade pierced right though the general's neck. Blood trickled slowly at first, then sprayed out around them. The general crashed to his knees, clasping the knife, unable to pull it out to grasp onto the few seconds he had left.

Einn leaned down, listening to the general's dying breaths. "How wonderful it is to see you at this very moment."

Like clockwork, the first troops quickly swooped in on Lind's personal guard. She couldn't see him, but Brinn knew Liam was there, valiantly leading the attack. A series of spatial tears formed around her, and new soldiers jumped into battle. Gunfire erupted on both sides.

From the front lines, Brinn saw her inventions at work. She had created, and her creations had power. Words meant nothing compared to what those soldiers held in their hands, what she held in her hand. A circular metal disk that she had been developing for the past few weeks. She pressed down on the activation timer and hurled it as far as she could at the approaching enemy. She counted five seconds, and the black-hole bomb detonated. A swirl of darkness appeared, the absence of light, a mouth that swallowed everything.

There were no more words. There was absolutely nothing.

* * *

It was a quick victory. Brinn crouched by the river and soaked her hands in the water, washing off the dirt and blood that had dried into a thick, speckled brown on her skin. A shadow fell over her, and she looked up. Einn stood beside her. His expression was that of stone.

"Are you horrified by me?" she asked.

But Einn didn't answer. "Do you know why I asked Lind to define freedom?"

Brinn shook her head.

He looked up at the sky. "It's because a lot of people don't even understand it." Then his gaze lowered to hers. "You made a choice," he said. "That's what freedom really is. Everyone has their own reasons for being here. This isn't my dream. This is yours. We just happened to collide. That's why you went along with building those bombs. That's why you're working on Penance. This is the work you choose to do."

Brinn stood there frozen. Einn made her feel seen for the first time in her life. And she felt as if she was finally in control.

"Thank you," she said.

He shrugged. "I was going to kill her anyway." Then his eyes seared into hers. "Like I said, we just happened to collide."

Goner was right. Einn was chaos personified. But there was something free in the way he lived. His choices were his own. And now so were her own. She had chosen to stand on this side of the battlefield with him.

As she walked through the piles of casualties, she heard her name.

"Brinn." The voice was faint, barely a part of this world.

She looked down, and her eyes grew wide.

Liam lay slumped on his side. His hand was on his chest, using all of his remaining strength to cover his shredded flesh. He didn't have much longer.

Her strength drained, and she dropped to her knees beside him. She tried not to look at the blood. It was everywhere. Yet his eyes were still the same as on the first day she met him. Even though she was different now, even though her skin had hardened, and her emotions had gone distant and cold, his were the kind of eyes that still made her heart thunder inside.

There were strings that tied her to the Brinn who used to be. A compassionate girl who wanted to love, needed love, and was willing to give it. And over this past year, with the loss of her family, a lot of those strings had been cut, like a boat from its anchor.

And soon she would feel that cut once again. So deep. So sad.

With great suffering and great strength, Liam's hand closed the gap between them, his fingers grasping hers. His skin was warm with his blood.

"Don't feel bad," he gasped. "I told you I was prepared."

Her eyes stung, and she blinked to keep the tears at bay. She didn't want that string to sever, but here it was, already unraveling.

"Is there anything you need?" she asked. There wasn't much time left, but she could give him comfort in the remaining moments.

His hand squeezed hers. A light touch. The warmth in his hand faded. "Tell me I fought hard."

Brinn thought back to Einn's words. *This is the work you choose to do.*

"You did well," she said. The tears streamed down her face. A sob was trapped at the base of her throat, but she grappled with every ounce of her being to hold it in. "Liam, you did well."

Satisfied, his lips turned upward in a final expression. His eyes left hers to gaze at a different beauty. Brinn was thankful that during his last moments, he was staring up at the sky.

CHAPTER 40

IA

THE DEMON STARED back at her. No matter how many times she blinked, he was still there. Ia rewatched the broadcast of the peace treaty over and over, staring at the holoscreens, at that black helmet with two sharp horns on top of its head. Every time she saw Einn on-screen, her brain stuttered as if it was on pause. A very dangerous hiccup that she couldn't quite get rid of.

"Turn it off," Knives said.

"No." Ia's voice clawed its way out of her throat. "I need to see it."

Knives got up abruptly and left. It was only then that she realized he was asking her to turn it off so he didn't have to watch it again. He had just seen Einn murder his father. Of course he didn't want to face that over and over.

Instead of getting up to check on him, she reached for the control screen and replayed the footage all the way from the beginning. This time, it wasn't her brother that she was fixated on.

Brinn Tarver shot Queen Lind. It was an impossible sentence, one that she'd never have thought of conjuring up, but here it was. A statement of truth. It had happened.

She paused the recording the exact second before Tarver pulled out her weapon. She recognized it as Einn's pistol by the white pearl engraving on the grip. He had given it to Brinn, just like he had given Ia the knife the day of her first kill. Einn was the type who liked to give people the matches for the fire.

Ia magnified the image to study Brinn's expression. The lines of her face were deep and weary. There was darkness where there used to be light.

It was as if Ia was looking at herself. Back when she felt like all was lost. She was very familiar with that anguish. When the Star Force destroyed her planet, killing her mother in the process, that was the first time she had become acquainted with that terrible feeling. Every time it came for her, it was stronger and stronger, until hope was merely a childish memory.

And that was how she knew there was another explanation why Brinn did it. And it had nothing to do with Einn. Her brother was just very good at showing Brinn the way. If Ia was there to talk to her, maybe it'd be different. Maybe the face on the screen wouldn't be so angry and so ready to throw herself right into the pit of despair.

Ia's heart cracked inside, vessel by vessel, piece by piece. She stormed out of the chapel, raging with each step, and burst into the employee lounge. Eve and Vetty looked up from their game of Goma.

This whole time she had been so scared of Einn, of facing death so soon after she had pulled herself away from it, that she had forgotten there were other people tangled up in this fight. So she would cut those cords. She would point them back toward the light.

She was going to get Brinn Tarver out of there. That was her mission, and she had been a fool for forgetting it.

Ia pulled up a chair to their table. "It's time we talk strategy."

CHAPTER 41

KNIVES

WHEN JUO AND LIND announced the secession of the royal lands from the Commonwealth, the first thing Knives wondered was which side the general was on. General Adams was a man who valued tradition and discipline. He'd fought for the power of the Commonwealth all his life. It was hard to imagine him leaving all that.

"There are others who are brave enough to join us," Lind had said. More than anything, Knives had hoped his father would choose differently this time.

So when he saw him on the recordings, Knives was relieved. As one of the greatest generals of the Olympus Commonwealth, there was a grand narrative that his father had lived, and it was no longer his after that one decision—to join Lind and Juo. Erich Adams had thrown away the title, the prestige, that place in Commonwealth history. Knives had admired his father at that moment.

But then he saw the blade plunge into his father's neck, and the moment was gone, replaced with the horror of watching him die. And this sadness of possibly never being able to feel that again. That admiration he'd had just moments ago.

A knock sounded at his door. "It's me," Ia said from outside his room.

The door slid open, and she peeked inside. "Are you all right?"

Knives sat on his bed, staring at his hands. He didn't answer.

She took a few small steps inside his makeshift bedroom, a storage closet for ration supplies back in the day. There was enough room for a cot and his few belongings, which weren't much. His jacket and his old Star Force flight suit, whatever he had on him when he left the hospital.

He didn't have to run that day, he thought to himself.

What was he running from? What was he *always* running from? He rubbed his knuckles across his tired eyes.

"Listen," Ia said slowly. "I came to tell you that I'm leaving."

"I'm still trying to wrap my head around everything." He ran his fingers through his mess of hair, and his eyes rose to hers. "Did you just say you're leaving?"

"My brother needs to be stopped. If I can't fight him, then I need to find the person who can. There are rumors of someone called the Half-Man."

"Don't be ridiculous," Knives said.

"I know. I mean, the Half-Man is just a nursery rhyme. But that's what you thought about Fugue, and it ended up being real. If this guy exists, then he should be on our side. Not Einn's. It's worth looking into."

"No, not that," Knives interrupted. Since the accident, Ia

hadn't been alone. She had help. She had support. Because she needed it, or at least Knives thought she did. "Are you sure you're ready to go out there?"

She sat beside him on the edge of his cot and rubbed the weariness from her face. "It doesn't matter if I'm ready or not." She looked at Knives. "My brother wants to turn that gate on. That's why he stole Bastian's journals, and that's why he was after Brinn. That gate is his endgame. You saw what happened on Fugue when Olympus opened it in the past."

Memories flooded toward him of his journey to Fugue. Torn metal. Destroyed planets. An entire star system—dead. All remnants of the GodsEye experiment that went wrong over a decade ago. The new gate that Einn was building was dangerous.

"Why now?" Knives asked. "You've been running from this fight for so long. Why do you all of a sudden want to go after him?

"Because," she said as she picked the frayed thread at the seams of her pants, "I can't stay here and do nothing anymore. Besides, I'm not the only one who's been running." Her eyes peered back at him, ripping through the invisible shield he had been constructing and fortifying every second of every day. "You never talk about the Star Force, and you never talk about the day that wormhole ripped open the skies of Calvinal."

For the past few years, his father had wanted him to take a high officer's position in the Star Force. He wanted Knives to follow in his footsteps, to become a general, to be a leader of Olympus—but Knives refused it all.

Because in a way, he was scared. He didn't want to die in

battle. He didn't want to asphyxiate to death like his sister. He didn't want to look death right in the miffing face. Wasn't everyone scared to die? Wasn't his father frightened those last moments of his life?

Instead of answering her, Knives looked away, his fear so thick that it couldn't be turned into words. Words could lessen its power. Words could make him understand, but maybe he didn't quite want to. Not yet.

Ia stood up and made her way to the door. He looked up at her figure silhouetted in the low light. And he felt it again. That same admiration he'd felt for his father before his dying moments. He felt it from looking at her. All because she was making a choice.

Before she left, she looked over her shoulder.

"General Adams...I hated that miffing bastard," Ia said. "Except for today. This was the first day that I truly thought we were fighting on the same side."

A complicated pain rippled through Knives's body, a wave of sadness, weakness, and denial. His muscles tensed to keep it all away.

Ia's voice slashed through his sinking thoughts. "But you, you've been by my side for more than that. It's a shame your father won't be able to see the things you'll do." Her eyes found his for just a second before he turned away.

He should have been grateful for those words. It meant that she saw him, that she had pierced her way through that shield of his.

When he looked up, she was gone. For a long time after she left, Knives stood in the empty hallway. He turned the same string of thoughts over and over in his head. His father had pushed so many of his own dreams onto his son, because what were your children if not a way to live forever, to continue making a mark in this sorry world?

But Knives always had to ask himself, was that the mark he wanted to make?

One day, he'd have to make that brave choice.

CHAPTER 42
BRINN

WHEN SHE RETURNED to Penance, Brinn lived in her lab. Now she could get back to her real work. Even at her workstation, Brinn kept the pistol on her, fully charged and ready to shoot. She knew she wasn't in any danger here in the laboratory. It served as a reminder of what she'd done.

No matter what planet they hailed from, people were frail. All it took was one bullet to make them crumple like Lind did that day. Like Faren did the day he lost his life during the protest. It would have been through the head for him. Yes, they were Tawny, but they needed to think—for their brains to process—to actually heal.

Brinn was the last person in the labs that night. She looked over her calculations, her fingers trembling as they typed, when she saw a shimmer. The world around it curved and concaved.

She groaned. "When are you going to stop doing that?"

"It's kinda my thing," Goner said, and he appeared sitting

at the desk beside her. He nodded at her hands. "I saw that, by the way."

She curled her fingers into fists.

"Still shaking from the kill, aren't you?" He twirled around in his chair. "And I thought maybe you'd be worthy of being my new rival. The girl who shot the Queen." He leaned forward to study the look on her face. "You have crossed a line that you may never be able to come back from." He grinned. "Aren't you proud?"

It wasn't a question she wanted to answer. She didn't need to feel good or bad about what she did. All that mattered was that she was still here. That she could do what she wanted to do.

"She spoke about peace like it was that easy..." Brinn said.

Goner laughed. "But you never wanted peace. Why try to pretend?"

She glared at him. He wanted her to give him a real answer. The true answer.

"I would be without purpose if peace happened," she said, turning back to add more scratchings in Bastian's journal.

"You wouldn't be working on this," Goner said, sweeping his arm around him. He chuckled. "We are selfish beings, aren't we? Doing things for our own purpose of existence."

She tilted her head at him, latching on to the way he had used the word *we* as if they were alike. What was his purpose of existence? Being a massive mung?

He scanned the contents of her table, and a twisted smile snaked across his face. "Is that the same pistol you used?"

Brinn grabbed the weapon and slid it closer to her. She still had no idea what went on inside that thick skull of his.

"You couldn't kill me with that even if you tried," he said. "My skin is thicker than any armor."

"And you couldn't kill me," she warned him. "I'm Tawny. I can heal."

He shrugged. "But you could decide not to if you wanted. I could slice your throat right now, and you could still decide whether or not to put your energy into healing yourself, into living. After all you've gone through, all you've suffered, why would you even choose to keep going?"

She hated him because she knew what he was getting at.

The blacks around his eyes narrowed as he studied her. "I see it. A sliver of something deep inside you. It's bright and shiny and filled with hope."

"Stop it," she screamed. She grabbed her pistol, cocked it, and fired.

The bullet bounced off him, clinking to the floor like a broken toy. Smoke smoldered on Goner's chest, and he burst out laughing. "I told you, you couldn't kill me. But you killed a woman without armor. You killed a woman who hoped for peace. Do you know what all this means?"

"This is a war we're fighting, and we're winning," she said. That was what it meant.

"No, it means the real ghosts are coming for you."

Brinn sneered at him. "There's no such thing as ghosts."

"Maybe you're right." He smiled as he walked away.

* * *

Brinn tried working after Goner left, but her mind kept running away from her, her fingers still shaking as she tightened the screws on a brand-new utility belt.

She slammed her palms onto the table's hard surface, and in a fit of anger, she swiped at everything within reach. Her tools, her models—it all went crashing to the floor.

She couldn't get her conversation with Goner out of her head, his words needling her about her purpose of existence. And what was his? She knew nothing about him. All he ever did was talk about how Ia was his rival or nemesis, or both? Brinn didn't even know what the difference was.

It was like all he ever thought about was—

Suddenly, her mind cleared.

She stood up. There was something she needed to know.

* * *

Brinn found him on the flight deck, boarding one of the jets. Goner was dressed for a long journey, all of his armor fastened and his black cloak wrapped around his figure, the long hem fluttering around his ankles.

"Are you finally leaving?" Brinn asked.

"I'm on a mission," he said. "Secret."

Which annoyed her more.

He hauled his pack over his shoulder. "What do you want? To ask if we could be pen pals?"

"*She* was your reason for existence," she said.

He stared at her, angling his head as if he had no idea what she was talking about.

There was always something Brinn couldn't decipher, a small patch of Goner kept dark. His riddles, the way he deflected her questions. They were all meant to confuse her. But she had finally caught on to him.

Her gaze locked on his. "You didn't kill Ia, did you?"

Instead of making one of his witty cracks, Goner's mouth set into a grim line as he walked up the ramp. When he was at the top, he turned to her.

"Remember what I told you about ghosts..."

And he backed into the shadows, his face a shock of white against the dark.

CHAPTER 43

IA

THEY'D SPENT THE NIGHT before making a list of places to investigate. There were a few hubs in Dead Space where information brokers dwelled. Surely one of them would know where anyone who fit the description of the Half-Man was hiding. Ia packed food rations and a pair of pistols, the best weapons from Vetty's arsenal.

She smoothed out the fabric of her assist suit, testing each joint for any snags or broken circuits before she left. A malfunction would be a pain on a mission like this.

After she was satisfied with the quality check, she looked up to see Eve standing beside her.

"I think you're missing something," Eve said.

She held up Ia's helmet, the Blood Wolf's feather etched across the front.

"I already have one packed," Ia said. It was a regular red helmet with no decals or symbols. Nothing flashy, but it would keep her alive if the environmental controls broke down while she traveled.

After all the nightmares, all the visions that haunted her, she wasn't eager to don her old helmet.

Eve pushed it onto her anyway. "For when you need a spare then."

Ia took her first steps onto the flight deck in months. She had been avoiding this day, but every waking moment, she had been asking herself the same question. Would she still be able to fly?

She stopped in front of *Orca*. After many months of being stashed away, a layer of dark space dust had accumulated on top of the original burnoff that had piled up from years of use. The color was different, but the silhouette was the same. Knives had offered to polish her, but Ia had refused, preferring her jet in its current state. It covered the red feather stamped on its belly and sides, and she'd be able to travel incognito. It would be safer that way, she told herself.

Ia had never had a ladder installed on *Orca*. She used to be able to jump up the wing in one go and hop over to the cockpit opening. But today she pulled up a ladder to climb into her jet.

She took it one rung at a time instead of two, not because she wasn't strong enough, but because part of her was scared of sitting in that pilot seat. She needed the coordination to fly. She needed her precision to maneuver and quickness to evade.

And she cursed herself for being too stubborn and proud to install a fancy onboard system that could help her do all the things she used to do with ease.

Knives and Vetty were already onboard, finishing maintenance on the engine and thrusters.

Once Ia was up, Vetty approached her. "She's ready to fly."

He held up the keys. Ia clutched his hands in gratitude. The last time they were both here, she had cried. She had never done that in front of him before. Not the Blood Wolf. The Blood Wolf never cracked.

It was when you were most vulnerable that you grew the most. She knew that now.

He placed a hand on her shoulder as if he knew exactly what she was thinking. "You're always going to be the best pilot I know," he said with a wink, in true Vetty fashion.

"You know I hate it when you wink like that," she said.

He laughed. "I know."

And then he jumped off the wing.

She made her way to the cockpit and eased her way inside where Knives was calibrating the navigation and onboard systems.

The space was small. Two chairs at the front, one for the pilot and another for a passenger or crewmate if necessary.

Knives glanced up from the screens. "I don't know how you can fly in this thing."

"Hey, don't insult my child," she said with a smirk.

When he saw her expression, his face lit up, and she knew why. It felt like old times…those precious moments when they first met.

She had encountered many people in her few years as the Blood Wolf, as a cadet, as the most wanted criminal of the Olympus Commonwealth. First impressions were powerful, like threads whipping at the seeds of your memory, but she realized now that real friendships were made of a stronger type of cord. One that lasted. One that would never break.

All these people were her friends. And this boy with the cold blue eyes, perhaps he was something else. But she couldn't find out now. Time always bled away from her. There was never enough when you needed it.

He stepped toward her. "Make sure you comm us if you run into any trouble."

"Me? Run into trouble? When has that ever happened?" she joked.

"I'm serious," he said.

And then she looked up at him with a faint smile. "Thank you, Knives," she said. "For everything."

He reached for his jacket that was slung across one of the chairs and handed it to her. "Take it."

She slipped her arms into the sleeves of the jacket. It smelled like him, of musk and oranges. It hit her then, an ache in her heart. It was time to say goodbye.

"Knives, if I don't make it..."

She reached for him, so that the space between them was no longer empty. The back of her fingers grazed gently against the light stubble on his cheek. And she didn't know what he would do, after all this time. Perhaps he would turn away.

But then his eyes rested on hers, and she realized how much they'd changed. They were no longer full of ice, not when he looked at her now. No, in those eyes, she saw bright-blue skies, fields of cornflowers, and something else—a word she couldn't quite place.

He leaned in, and their lips met, a connection that was warm and safe. It was different from their first kiss. Desperate and passionate. This one had another feeling to it. Instantly, she knew what it was. That word. That mysterious and beautiful word…

Knives rested his cheek on hers, his lips whispering into her ear. "We'll see each other again." And she nodded, holding him even closer.

As they pulled away from each other and he lowered himself down to the deck, she studied his face, memorizing every detail from the scar on his chin to his unkempt blond hair and the careful blue of his eyes. Just in case.

Settling into her pilot seat, she felt the cracks of the plasti-leather conform to her body. The engines were already on and warm, primed for flight. The console had only a few displays: a navigator unit to help her find her way, a sophisticated comms unit to latch on to oncoming signals and to scramble her own, a few engine modulators to help keep track of any irregularities in the engine environment, and gauges to monitor fuel and oxygen in reserve.

Ia gripped a hand on her mid thrusters, and one on the curve of the steering wheel. Her stabilizers had long been disabled, so she felt the motion and strength of her jet a bit more. In the past, it was a good thing because her movements were more in tune, but with the condition her body was now in, her muscles began to tremble.

With all her strength, she pulled upward, trying to maintain control of the motion and direction of her jet. She took a deep breath. *Keep calm*, she told herself. *Keep steady.*

She glanced down and sighed in relief.

At least she was up in the air. That was the hardest bit. Once she was past the atmos field, it'd be easier. There'd be no air resistance. If she didn't run into any trouble, she'd be fine. No high-velocity chases, no sudden evasive maneuvers around asteroids that hurled her way.

It was all going to be just fine.

Deus, watch over me, she prayed. And she took off into the unknown.

CHAPTER 44
KNIVES

KNIVES WOKE UP in the middle of the night and walked to the chapel. The temperature controls were once again on the fritz, so he pulled his RSF flight suit over his compression shorts and sleeveless tee to keep warm. He sat in the back pew. The statue of Deus stared back at him. It was the same look that Ia had had on her face when she left Myth. Poised. Determined.

There were certain individuals who were of a totally different category. That was why people prayed to Deus. And that was why people rallied around Ia. As for Knives—well, he just wanted to exist as he was for as long as he could. At least that was what he thought he wanted.

But now he was alone. His father was gone. So were Bastian and Marnie. And now, Ia. All the most amazing people he had ever met. And he paled in comparison to them. Hell, he even paled in comparison to Vetty. Runaway son of the wealthiest, most powerful corporation of Olympus *and* a far better flyer than Knives was.

When he was gone, what would people think? Just a deserter with no goal, no mission. No friends, even.

He sighed, his breath fogging before him. It was freezing. Knives rubbed his hands together, trying to generate heat, but when that didn't work, he dug his hands into the side pockets of his flight suit. His eyebrows wrinkled as he felt something wedged at the bottom of one of them. Smooth and cool to the touch.

He pulled it out.

It was Bastian's pen.

He flipped the thin metal around in his hands. To Bastian, this was probably the most important thing in the world. A tool that represented his life all the way until the end.

Knives twisted the cap and ran his thumb against the golden nib, watching as the ink bled into the surface of his skin.

He still didn't understand why Bastian loved these things. They just made a huge mess. He unscrewed the lower half to see how much ink was left but then blinked at what he saw. There was something strange wrapped around the ink canister. It looked almost like a data coil, a thin fiber capable of storing immense amounts of information within its circuitry.

He turned the canister around, stopping when he saw the activation crystal embedded at the base.

His hands trembled at the thought of what he had just discovered. Could this be Bastian's records, the ones they never found even after turning his office upside down?

His chest tightened, the oxygen swirling heavy inside his lungs. *Could this be what they needed to stop Einn?*

He pressed down on the crystal. Holographic lights sparked

in the space before him, piercing through the dark and still air. He expected to see a simple square holoscreen linking to all the information the data coil held. Instead, a series of light pixels assembled in the space in front of him, creating a holographic image of a man, all the way from his leather oxford shoes to his white, wrinkled lab coat.

A familiar face, made of light, made of happiness and memories, stared back at him.

"Good day," the hologram said. "I'm Bastian Weathers. How can I help?"

"Hello, old friend," Knives said, blinking away the tears from his eyes.

CHAPTER 45
IA

IA WANDERED through the streets of the merchant town, the dust swirling through the alleys. She knew this location well. It was part of a desert star system with three suns, so hot that all the planets were scorched. The people who grew up here had extra sweat glands to deal with the insufferable heat. That was the only way they could survive on the surface. For others, the planet was livable if they tunneled underground.

Not a lot of people visited, and if they did, they didn't stay long. As she walked the cramped alleys that formed a maze through the underground, she noticed a refugee colony had settled here. None of their structures bore the symbols of the White Hearts, so her brother's reach hadn't come this far.

As she turned the corner, she heard a child's voice singing the Half-Man's familiar nursery rhyme. *Watch out. Watch out for the Half-Man. He lives neither here nor there. The Half-Man comes from nowhere. He'll take you and break you. Watch out, watch out. Before you disappear.*

Ia hummed along until she came upon the child playing in front of a house made of scrap. The girl's hair was pulled back in a messy twist, and there was a smudge of dirt across her right cheek. Despite this, she wore a tan jumpsuit, much like the ones the Commonwealth forced on refugee populations that they shipped around. The suit was fairly new except for a tear in the back in the shape of a shield, the Commonwealth emblem. It was obvious she and her group had escaped.

The girl stopped when she noticed Ia watching her, and she inched away.

Ia pulled down her face mask and smiled. It made the child relax just a tiny bit. Ia opened her hands, motioning for the ball. The girl's eyes brightened, and she tossed the Poddi over to her.

Ia caught it and spun it expertly in her hands. The girl's smile spread from ear to ear. Ia tossed the ball back, and the girl immediately attempted to mimic Ia's Poddi trick.

"Did you just move here?" Ia asked.

The girl nodded as she continued to fumble with the ball.

Things in Olympus must have gotten bad for anyone to seek refuge in such a remote place as this. "Where are you from?"

"Nova Grae," the little girl said.

Ia paused. That was the same planet where Brinn grew up.

"What happened there?" It was hard to mask the urgent tone of her voice.

A woman wrapped in a gray shawl leaned out of the window. She glared at Ia. "Juna, come here," she ordered.

Juna sulked off to receive her mother's scolding. Ia stood in the now empty alleyway, the little girl's words still echoing in her ears. It was no mistake. The girl had said *Nova Grae*.

Ia's thoughts jumped back to the day of the Rigel K attack. The look on Brinn's face was seared into her memory. The sadness seeping into every line on her face, holding her expression together and ripping it apart at the same time. When Ia had seen her on that rooftop before she walked off with Einn, Brinn had been despondent. Numb.

Ia cursed to herself. She knew something bad had happened.

A swirl of steaming air flooded toward her from vents jutting down from the low ceilings. Ia pulled up her face mask, remembering what she was there to do. She wandered down the alley and took a left into a narrow back passageway. The walls were made of thick cloth-like paper, its fiber strong and fire-resistant. As she passed, she saw shadows of the residents moving inside their homes. A mother rocked her baby to sleep in one. A grandmother pounded chupka flour in another house. In another, a man was counting his money.

That was where Ia stopped.

Finding the part in the center of the wall, she pulled it aside and stepped in.

A red rug was spread across the floor. From the details, she knew it was Narion-made, from an old nation known for their textile exports and the artisans who produced them.

While the walls were made of paper, the interiors were more like a cage, metal bars separating one half of the room from the next.

The man inside matched his shadow. He sat on a high stool, counting the shiny gold disks that were the currency on that planet. Gold was always easy to use for physical transactions, for buyers and sellers who absolutely wanted no digital footprint.

The man was a banker, good at keeping tabs on currency values, loans, and transactions. But bankers were also known for the information they held and the secrets they kept.

He glanced up from his pile, looked her over from her threadbare shawl to the red mask fastened around the lower half of her face, and then resumed his attention on counting his coins. She clearly wasn't worth his time, which meant he didn't recognize her.

"I don't deal in penses. You can go to a local merchant for an exchange like that," he said, assuming she had only a few cents to her name. It was quite the opposite. Her personal account was loaded with NøN, Zeroes, and even the most valuable of them all—century coin—from all her past crimes plundering the Commonwealth. She even had gold stored in an anonymous vault in the Favadine financial district, if she ever needed it. It was way more than the measly pile he was counting out in front him.

"I'm not here for an exchange," Ia said.

"Oh?" He placed the coin in his hand back down on the counter. He stared at her as if he was doubting his first impression of her. "If you're from the Albat clan, I already told your leader that I don't believe in loan forgiveness."

"No." She took a step toward him. "I heard you're good at tracking people down."

"For a price, yes." His eyes shone greedily at her from behind the bars. "Who are you trying to find? A sister lost to the White Hearts? Or maybe a deadbeat father who left you with debt?"

"I'm trying to find the Half-Man."

He burst out with laughter. "I won't charge you for that information, kid. The Half-Man doesn't exist." He propped his hands on his knees and leaned an ear toward her. "Though you're not the first person who came to ask me today."

Today? Could it be possible that her brother was just here?

"What did he look like?" she asked.

"My memory is a bit foggy."

Ia reached into her pack and tossed him a few platinum coins through the bars.

His eyes brightened at the sight. "It was a man," he said finally.

She raised an eyebrow. "That's all you're going to tell me?"

"I'm gonna need more than platinum to remember details."

She reached into the folds of her shawl for the holodeck that Eve had given her. It was an older model, but she only needed it to access her funds, and possibly contact someone on Myth if things went wrong.

She tapped on the C icon and brought up a transaction for 5,000 NøN. She sent the screen over to him. The banker drew his thin lips up into a smile.

He tapped on the screen, accepting her transaction. "Yes," he said. "I remember him now. Large fellow. Had to slouch because he was too tall in here."

That was strange. Einn was taller than she was, that was for sure, but not tall enough for his head to brush against the canvas ceiling.

"And?"

The banker sent the transaction screen back to her, and she glanced down. It was a request. For 10,000 NøN.

She didn't want to argue. Information brokers loved to

gossip about people who were out to kill them, and people who were cheap. She accepted, and then he clapped his hands together in delight.

"What did he look like?" Ia demanded.

"You've seen him before, I'm sure. A lot of people have." He waved his hand across his pointed visage. "It's hard to forget that skull on his face."

Goner. Her brother had sent Goner.

Too bad he wasn't good at actually finding things out. She was sure he was in the same boat as she was, with little to no information on the Half-Man.

"Anything else?" the banker asked.

Ia had dismissed her holoscreen when a thought popped into her head. Not just a thought. But the face of a girl who was haunting her. "Actually, yes," she said. "The Tarvers of Nova Grae. A young man named Faren and his parents. I'd like to know where they are."

The banker squinted an eye at her. "A whole family. That'll cost you."

All of the nerves inside her snapped. Her hand whipped through the thin space between the iron bars, just large enough to fish her wrist through. She was done negotiating. She clutched the man's throat before he could snake away and yanked him forward so his forehead crashed into the metal separating them. Her gaze remained on his face, watching as his eyes bulged out.

"Let go of me," he choked.

She sneered. "*That* will cost you."

He let out a final gasp before sputtering, "Fine."

Ia's fingers relaxed, and he slipped out of her hold, stretching his neck from side to side while gasping for more breath.

"Now give me the status of the Tarver family."

He pulled up a screen of an updated Citizen database, and he made a humming noise as he scrolled through the lists. Until finally he stopped. He cast a hesitant glance in her direction and then looked back at the page.

"You better not lie to me," she said, her voice low.

He swiveled in his chair to face her. "Faren Tarver, age 15," he said. "Deceased."

Her throat grew tight. This was what had caused the expression on Brinn's face, the same anguish she saw in the footage of Brinn shooting Queen Lind.

This was why she'd joined Einn, Ia realized.

"What about the rest of the family?"

He pulled up a screen of an updated Citizen database. "The two adults are"—he tapped a line of data—"alive."

Thank Deus, she thought, and she felt like she could once again breathe.

The banker passed her a screen of information with the location of a send-off camp.

"Nasty places, those are," he commented. She knew what they were. That was where the Commonwealth had sent all the refugees, even the ones who had successfully claimed citizenship. No one knew what happened at the camps, except people rarely came back from them.

Ia turned, her feet dragging back toward the tent entrance. As she pulled open the flap, the banker called out to her. "Wait. Who are you?"

Ia stopped at the tent's opening, the cyan lights from the alley slashing across the floor. "Do you want to die?"

The banker shook his head.

"Then you don't want to know." And she took off into the alley, the fabric flapping in the ventilated wind.

* * *

Back inside *Orca*, Ia placed a hand on the glass and gazed into the All Black. She had powered down her engines and enviro systems to save on fuel. The ship was adrift. She had unstrapped, her body curled up on its side, floating somewhere in between the floor and the curved top of the cockpit glass. To keep away the chill, she threw on Knives's leather jacket. Its insulation offered very little warmth, but in a way, it comforted her. It made her feel a little bit less frustrated, a little bit less alone.

The glow of the holoscreen illuminated the vicinity. She stared at it. The banker was the last on the list of names to tap. No one had any information on the Half-Man. He was nothing but a memory from their childhood, a lullaby.

Einn had always been obsessed with these things—pieces of data that seemed unimportant to everyday people, but for some reason meant everything to him. She wanted to believe there was more to the Half-Man. There were times, hopeful fleeting moments, when she thought the search was for someone real. Someone she knew. A father who'd been lost to them years ago. Perhaps he was the Half-Man, and this was all about their father after all.

Or maybe not.

The people on the list were the best information brokers

on this side of Dead Space. If they didn't have even a hint of information, then who did? There had to be some clue that they had overlooked.

Whatever she had to do, she needed to do it fast, especially with Goner on her tail. If they crossed paths, who knew what would happen. Well, one thing was for sure: she would unleash all levels of hell on him for shooting her point-blank that day. Maybe she'd get shot again, but it'd be worth it. She had to pay him back for breaking a promise and for all the damage he'd done.

Frustrated, she shoved her hands into her pockets and sulked. At the bottom of one of the pockets was a crumpled piece of paper. Odd. Paper was such a rare and useless commodity these days.

Ia fished it out, picking apart the wrinkly ball gently with her fingers. It unfolded like a kothra moth's wings after it pushed itself out of its chrysalis, the wrinkles forever there no matter how much she'd wait or even attempt to iron it out.

She let the somewhat flatter piece of paper float in front of her. Gazing lazily at it, she read over its contents. It was an old handwritten receipt from a ramen joint.

And Ia almost snorted from inside her helmet. The universe was about to end, and Knives still had found the time to feast on a 10 NøN bowl of ramen.

Her eyes zeroed in on the heading on the top, and she nearly did a backflip. The name of the restaurant—

Nowhere Ramen.

It was a long shot, but it was the only lead she had.

Ia extended a leg, kicking it against the wall so she could get back to the pilot seat. The engines started, and her voice trilled up and down as she sang.

The Half-Man comes from nowhere. Nowhere. Nowhere.

CHAPTER 46
BRINN

BRINN STOOD at the control panel, a line of Sino Corp investors staring over her shoulder, ready and waiting for her to flip the on switch. As if it was that easy.

Penance wasn't even ready. She still had to address a slew of problems, but that didn't matter when the Sino Corp ships arrived in their pocket of the galaxy.

So there she was, turning on the modulators, checking the gauges, and keeping a close eye on the power intake because that was where things got rough.

They had enough power on hand for Penance to open wormholes to other places within the galaxies, but not enough to generate a bridge to another universe. That would take an enormous amount of energy. But what worried Brinn more was the unknown. No simulation could ever predict what would be across that bridge when it opened. That was another reason she had insisted on attempting the experiment on a smaller scale, using the replica she had built in the labs. This unit was kept in a controlled and quarantined room, made of four walls of thick, reinforced glass. If the bridge opened, anything could come through, a plethora of unknown atoms and matter—things that no one in this universe had ever seen or studied, but at least it'd be contained.

"Are you ready to start?" Einn asked, his voice low.

Brinn nodded, her hand moving from one screen to the next. Typing in commands. Checking on a million things at once.

Einn turned toward the line of Sino Corp partners, all suited up in high-collared jackets with brushed silver notches, their eyes gleaming with interest. Or was it greed?

Everything was ready to go. Brinn pulled up the activation screen, her hand hovering over the start button. Whispering a quick prayer to Deus, she tapped it.

There was nothing at first. A slight humming that soon switched frequencies. Lower this time, so low and thick that it vibrated the ground underneath their feet. Her eyes flicked to the structure as the arches rotated in a blur, so fast that they no longer appeared to be there. A reaction would have produced a flash of light or illuminance, but instead the whole quarantined room was shrouded in swirling shadow.

A loud noise warbled throughout the room, and everyone gasped. Brinn turned away from the screens, looking past the thick, multipaned wall of indestructible glass, her eyes trained on what lay between the rotating arches.

It was faint, but a light-blue shimmer flared within the ring's perimeter, like a thin veil draped upon the unseen.

She heard murmurs behind her.

"Is that it?"

"Did it work?"

Einn stood so still that she thought time had stopped. It very well could have.

"Congratulations," Einn whispered so only she could hear. "I knew you would succeed."

A flitter of pride took hold of her. But then a churning rumble sounded from beyond the glass, as though something was coming toward them. Her eyes locked onto the ring, and she saw a shadow of black beyond the shimmer of blue.

"What on Ancient Earth..." she whispered.

It pushed against the glistening blue veil, that thin boundary between their universe and the next. The bridge wasn't completely open, she realized. Not yet, at least, and she watched in horror as the plane flexed before them, ready to crack.

The shadow pulled away, and Brinn let out a sigh of relief.

But too soon. The shadow returned, this time to the point where it blacked out the whole ring. It shattered through the mesh of space-time in one blow, a dark mass swirling and growing toward them.

Its dangerous tentacles invaded their space, reaching for wires, equipment, and anything else that was inside the enclosed glass room. Once it had fully burned through whatever it had latched onto, the mass grew larger, and with that, stronger. This thing completely covered everything it touched, as if it were absorbing it, *eating* it. Before long, the destructive mass would reach the heavy glass paneling separating it from the rest of the laboratory, including everyone in the observation deck. Brinn's hands flew to the control screens, trying to find a way to deactivate the bridge between the two universes.

Suddenly, the lights around her shuddered, dimming once before finally cutting completely to black. The emergency sconces activated.

"The power is out," she said. Her eyes were on the gate. The blue veil was gone, and the black mass had vanished, leaving acid burn marks in its place.

Thankfully, the ring itself didn't seem to have incurred any damage.

She turned to Einn, who was still staring at the now empty space.

"Incredible," he said.

As for Brinn, she had nothing to say.

* * *

Outside in the hallway, a crowd of Sino Corp employees surrounded her.

"Why did it stop in the middle like that?" Kilio Sinoblancas asked.

Einn looked to Brinn for the answer.

"We don't have enough power to keep the bridge open. That's why the whole thing collapsed," she said.

Kilio rubbed his chin. "What kind of power requirements are we talking about?"

"Enough to power a hundred interstellar gates," she said.

His eyebrows rose.

"Per use," she specified.

And his eyebrows rose even higher.

All the while, Einn watched the Sino Corp executives, analyzing every move and expression they made. "Will you be able to secure something for us?"

Kilio shook his head. "The Civil War has token a toll on our power sectors."

Einn adjusted the ring on his finger. "Well, it will all fall into place eventually." He extended his arm to the CEO, then went down the line, congratulating them, gripping everyone's hands. "I think you can still count this day as a success."

When he was done, Einn waved down the hallway to usher them back to the flight deck. But the CEO raised a hand, stopping everyone in their place.

"You mentioned privately before that you were able to turn the previous model on with a neural network," Kilio Sinoblancas said.

Immediately, Brinn felt her spine lock, vertebrae by vertebrae. They were talking about what Einn had done on GodsEye.

"Would it be possible to use that same concept here?"

"It is," Einn said easily. "But only for a short amount of time. A person's brain only generates so much electricity."

"But what if there were populations at your disposal?" Sinoblancas postulated.

Brinn felt her heart sink, because he could only mean one thing. The refugee camps, the ones created by the Olympus Commonwealth after the repeal of the Sanctuary Act.

Einn pursed his lips. "Then, perhaps..."

"Can I speak to you in private?" Brinn insisted, tugging at his sleeve.

Einn turned back toward the Sino Corp investors. "Would you excuse me?"

When they were out of sight in a different room, Brinn glanced over at him. "You can't be serious about all this."

"This is what you wanted, isn't it? For Penance to be up and running?"

"The people you use will die," she said. "It won't be quick, and it will be painful."

Einn's storm-gray eyes studied her, analyzing her as if she were a game of Goma. "You know, I'm a little disappointed. I thought you and I understood each other."

"It's xenocide." They would be murdering whole populations of refugees, some perhaps the last of their civilizations.

But Einn only shrugged. "You killed Lind. What's a few more?"

She stared at him in frozen silence. The truth was in his eyes. She was a murderer. But she still had loyalty to her people, all the refugees who clambered to survive like she did.

"Theoretically, this would work. Don't you agree?" he asked, his voice as calm as the lightest breeze.

"Yes," she said, "but..."

Einn's words sliced through hers. "Then that's all I need to know."

He turned to leave.

She had to stop him before he could set this all in motion. Makolians, Dvvinn, Tawnies—Brinn didn't want their blood on her hands.

"Wait!" she called out desperately. "What if I can figure out another power source?"

Einn stopped in the doorway. He didn't turn around, but she knew he was listening.

Her thoughts raced for something to grab onto. They could rig together smaller, scavenged power grids. Or they could steal... Her eyes focused as the answer became clear. Of course, it was there all along. "The uranium core on Aphelion," she said.

Einn turned with a smile, as if he hadn't just threatened to kill thousands of people, or maybe even more. "See," he said. "I knew you'd figure something out."

Einn might have represented the beauty of the unknown, but Brinn realized there was also an ugliness to it, something that was hard to face. Like a colorful snake that hid its venom. For the first time since she arrived on Nirvana, she followed him carefully, their footsteps bringing them back to the hallway.

Brinn stopped at the corner and stilled at the sight before her. The men from Sino Corp were on the floor, their bodies limp, some twitching, trying to hold on to the life that was quickly slipping away from them.

Einn shook his head. "And I thought they'd be on their ship when this happened."

She glanced at the ring on his finger, the one he had adjusted before he shook everyone's hand. "You poisoned them."

"You heard what they said. They don't have the power source we need, so I had no more use for them," he said. "Besides, I felt sick looking at them. The filth of corporations and government. I don't believe in any of it."

"Then what do you believe in?" Brinn asked.

His eyes were an endless abyss. "Chaos."

He turned, leaving the bodies where they were, but before he was out of earshot, she called after him. She could keep this to herself, but she wanted to see him falter, just a little bit. He'd done the same to her, hadn't he?

"Ia is still alive, Einn."

Brinn felt a hint of pleasure at the slight rise in his shoulders.

And now she knew—you can make even a snake squirm with the right kind of poison.

CHAPTER 47

IA

SHE LANDED *ORCA* in the dusty parking lot. Pushing open the hatch to the cockpit, Ia leaned out into the sunlight, where she was hit with a blast of dry, tepid air. The planet was called Armpit, which, based on the name, was her type of joint. She wondered why she had never heard of it before. Then she stepped out and knew why.

The place was deserted for miles on end, high cracked mesas and natural rock pillars reaching for the skies like the prisoners in old movie streams.

The ramen shack itself was built on one of these pillars, just large enough for the restaurant and a line of parked jets along its edge. Currently, there were no vehicles present, except for a sky schooner anchored nearby. Probably the owner's, and that meant no customers. Unless someone climbed or used a wind pack to get there, which Ia seriously doubted.

Well, mif. She'd hoped there would be more people there that she'd be able to question. Surely someone inside would know *something* about this Half-Man. Or maybe they'd laugh at her, like everyone else did.

If this whole thing was a bust, then at least she'd get a bowl of ramen out of it. She hoped to Deus it was good.

The outside wood on the restaurant was stripped of its ordinary luster, a dead-looking gray where it had been completely parched by the sun. She walked toward the entrance, an open doorway covered with two square pieces of fabric hanging from the top edge of the doorframe. Stitched into the fabric were two words, one on each flap. *No. Where.*

She pulled one of the flaps to the side. Ducking in, she blinked, allowing her eyes to adapt to the darkness. It took a while for her vision to adjust, especially now that her eye mod was gone. Normally she would have been able to switch onto thermal or IR view, but now she had to just rely on plain old sight.

The interiors were as sparse as the outside. One wall, she noticed, was painted red up to the middle. The owner must have given up or ran out of paint.

There was counter space in the center of the tiny room. Behind it, a small opening was left for the cooking preparations, where a tall older woman stood. Her back was toward Ia as she scrubbed at the white bowls soaking in the sink.

Ia sat down at the counter, and the woman glanced over her shoulder. Ia stared for a moment too long at the woman's tanned face, her gray hair pulled back into a loose braid. It was as if she had seen her somewhere in the past, but Ia couldn't place where. Strange, since her memory was usually impeccable.

"The shop's closed today," the woman said.

"That's a shame," Ia said. "A friend highly recommended this place."

"Which friend?"

"Blond hair. Taller than me, but not as tall as you. Kinda broody."

The woman turned, her back straightened to almost full height. Her head craned to the side to keep from bumping into the dried reeds thatched across the ceiling. She stared off slightly as if she were trying to remember. "The kid with the Kaiken?"

Ia nodded. "That's him."

The woman wiped her hands on a nearby rag. "Well, I guess it's always good to get new patrons." She nodded to a steel pot that was on the burner, steam curling upward from its silver mouth. "There's broth, but I still have to prepare the noodles."

"Don't let me get in the way," Ia said.

The woman leaned an elbow on the counter. "You are. The noodles are my specialty, and I don't make them in front of my customers."

"Oh," Ia said.

The chef jutted her chin back toward the entrance, and Ia got the hint.

She stood up. "I'll come back in half an hour."

Before Ia could head back out in the blazing heat, the chef called out to her. Ia turned to see a bottle being hurled toward her. She caught it before it could knock her in the face. The bottle was an emerald green, condensation already slicking the glass. She knew what it was. Good old archnol.

Ia gave the chef a smile.

"It's not free," the woman said gruffly. "I'm putting it on your tab."

Ia walked out into the parking lot, all the while struggling to twist open the bottle cap. After the long journey, she couldn't wait to guzzle it down. She was so focused on opening her drink that she almost didn't feel the rapid movement heading for her from behind.

An attack.

Ia dodged out of the way, feeling the air around her displace, like an invisible knife slicing down toward her. She spun to face her attacker. The ramen chef stood out in the open, now rising to full height. She was taller than any person Ia had ever encountered. The woman's fingers moved like a spider weaving a web. She plucked a long index finger in the air and tugged.

Then, somehow, Ia was on the ground, unable to move.

What on Ancient Earth was this?

Ia struggled to get up, but she was pinned down by some invisible force. The woman walked toward her.

"You're not here for the ramen," the chef said. "Are you?"

The woman's gray hair had come loose from her braids, whipping back and forth like a banner of war. As she looked at the woman's features, Ia realized why she looked so familiar in the first place. It was so hard to tell in the shadows of the ramen shack.

She didn't want to believe it. Hell, not many people would.

But it was her. Older, though. And a scar that wasn't there before was slashed across her once immaculate face. But there was no mistaking those eyes, bold and compassionate, the same eyes Ia saw every day when she was training in the chapel on Myth.

She was a woman that came from holy legends.

But here she was now. Flesh. Real. And here.

"Deus," Ia whispered, her voice laced with pure reverence.

And then her vision fell to black.

* * *

Ia woke up to the sound of sharp, relentless banging. Her eyes fluttered open, and she saw the same woman, her fists kneading at a pile of fresh dough. The loose tunic was now gone, exposing her bare back, tan and knotted with strong muscle. Sharp shoulder blades moved like engine parts as the woman cycled through her motions.

Ia's memory of what had happened shoved its way back into her brain. For a moment, she didn't even dare to move. Only to breathe.

"You're up," the woman said, her focus still turned on the dough before her. "You know, I thought you were coming here to kill me, but then I quickly realized that you're not even strong enough to do it."

Despite the woman's casual manner, Ia remained reverently silent.

The ramen chef separated the dough into smaller pieces. "All right. Let's hear it. Get it all out."

"You're Deus," Ia whispered.

"Actually, my name is Kami," the woman said. "Deus was

a title you people gave me. I've been in this realm for several star spans now, and that's just one of the names I've collected. I have a feeling you understand what that means. Blood Wolf of the Skies. Sovereign of Dead Space. The one and only Ia Cōcha."

The woman knew who she was. *Deus* knew who she was.

She was still in a cloud of shock when Kami turned to her. Ia couldn't help but stare. The front of her torso was no longer flesh, completely replaced with something Ia couldn't even explain. It was like Kami had been ripped into two and then bonded back together, with what looked like a dark pit—*a wormhole*—at her core.

With sudden clarity, she pieced it together. "*You're* the Half-Man."

Kami nodded. "Yet another name you people gave me. One person happened to see me without a shirt on, and it scared the heavies out of him."

"What happened to you?" Ia asked.

"Oh, it was over a century ago—the battle that changed it all." Kami sighed. "I thought I was unstoppable. With all my power, I could transform the mass and density of anything, tear holes from universe to universe. I was indeed greatness personified. But then all it took was one stray grenade to rip me in two. Now I use the majority of my strength to keep myself together like this."

She stood up, grabbed a piece of dough, and tossed it into the swirling emptiness inside her.

"It's a spatial tear," Kami explained. "I don't know where the dough goes. But I do know it makes great noodles." After a short moment, Kami grabbed an empty bowl and held it at an angle before her. Seconds later, the dough came hurling out of her, its shape a lot more noodle-like than when it came in. "Now you understand why I keep it secret," Kami said. "Kind of unappetizing when you think about it."

Ia laughed nervously, scratching the back of her neck. She was sitting in front of a god. A figure that many people believed in, that some even feared. She was powerful and strong—and she could defeat Einn.

"There *is* a reason I'm here," Ia said. "My brother is trying to open a bridge to another universe."

"I know. I can sense an unbalance somewhere in that mess out there," Kami grumbled. "If your brother opens a bridge that size, anything can come through. Things that don't exist in this universe. Dangerous things. It's not good, trust me."

Then that meant they needed Deus more than anything. The universe was in danger, and this woman was of the few who knew just how much. "So you'll help?"

Kami turned back to Ia and shook her head. "I've given up on getting involved in this realm's matters. I just want to live the rest of my days in comfort."

Ia felt a weight drag at her shoulders. "But I can't do this on my own. I'm not strong enough. I'm not like you."

As Ia spoke, Kami threaded her arms through the sleeves of her tunic and then braided her long, silver hair. It seemed like she wasn't listening, but finally, she stilled, her amber eyes suddenly focused on Ia. Sharp, intense, in a way that almost took Ia's breath away.

"You are like me in many ways," Kami said. "Do you know

why I thought you were here to kill me? It's because I sensed *more* in you. Your origins aren't completely from this realm. Usually, those like us have abilities."

Ia thought of the experiment footage from GodsEye. Her father was from another universe, but she had never thought about how that affected her. "What kind of abilities?"

"It's like this broth." Kami reached for the soup ladle and stirred the pot, a plethora of aromas filling the air. "There are many dimensions to it. The flavor isn't the same for everyone because not everyone has the same taste buds, you know. Your abilities are going to be different from your brother's. And different from mine," she said. "Mine are better, though, in case you haven't realized."

Ia furrowed her brow, remembering the day she fell from great heights. "I've seen my brother create wormholes with his hands."

"There are those of us who can manipulate matter, energy, gateways, sometimes even the temporal plane." Kami eyed her carefully. "But there are some who can't."

Ia understood what she was trying to say.

The woman placed a bowl of fresh ramen before her. Ia stirred the contents of the bowl, watching all the ingredients swirl together. Even if she took a bite, she wouldn't be able to taste it. There was too much on her mind. With all of this new information laid before her, Ia felt helpless and desperate. But that was why she was here to begin with. Because she was *already* desperate. And she already knew she needed help. Ia had come here to find the Half-Man, and she'd found someone even better.

She looked at Kami. "That's why we need you. We need a leader."

"I told you. This isn't my fight," Kami said, then sighed, seeing the look on Ia's face. "But maybe I can at least help even the odds."

Ia looked up from her bowl.

"I can try and open up your abilities, if you'd like."

Ia stiffened, understanding the power of such an opportunity. If she were able to do all of these things, then she would be equally matched with her brother. She could be as quick as him, as nimble. She could jump from point to point, keep on his heels. And if he tried to drop her again, she would not fall to her death. Not this time.

But something about all that seemed wrong.

"No," she said finally. "I don't need it."

"You'll lose," Kami said.

Ia pointed to the hole in the middle of Kami's chest. "Whoever did that to you was just an ordinary person." A very ordinary person who took down Deus herself.

Kami angled her head in thought. "Very well."

If this was Ia's fight, then she was going to do it her way.

The Blood Wolf of the Skies, the Hunter of the Wastelands, the Sovereign of Dead Space. All legends originated from seeds of truth. And this was her truth. In the beginning, she was just one name. She was Ia Cōcha. She had gotten this far because of her skill, her guts, her self.

Her brother had tried to kill her twice and failed. *Failed*, she had to remind herself. Now it was her turn, and she wasn't going to make the same mistake.

Ia took a big heaping spoonful of ramen and slurped it down, every noodle and ounce of broth giving her the strength she needed to face the fight.

"This is delicious," Ia said.

Kami winked at her. "Best ramen in the universe."

CHAPTER 48
KNIVES

"STILL NOTHING?" Knives asked.

"Nope," Eve said. "Not a peep."

They were all in the workers' lounge. Knives and Vetty sat at a rusty table. Security displays hovered over its center. Eve had taken up one of the shabby couches, her back leaning against one arm and both legs draped over the other. A small holoscreen hovered before her. Her finger flicked up and up, scrolling through a long list. She had spent the past week reaching out to her old Dead Space network. In order to have a shot against Einn's growing fleet, they needed to have allies. But no one was answering the call. After Lind's death, fewer and fewer patrons were visiting Myth. Knives didn't know if it was because people were scared or if they were flocking over to join Einn's cause. If it was the latter, then they definitely needed whatever help they could get.

"So far, all we've got is us. Two pilots—one above average, one decent—a knowledgeable bartender, and a dead scientist that Knives found in a pen," Vetty said.

Knives wanted to throttle Vetty until the smug look fell off his face. Decent pilot…

"Don't forget Ia," Knives said.

"If the Blood Wolf actually comes back," Eve said under her breath.

Knives glared at her.

"Hey," she said with a shrug. "I'm just being realistic. The All Black is a merciless beast if you can't hold your own against it."

They hadn't heard from Ia in a week. Knives had told her to contact them if there was an emergency, so he could only hope her lack of communication meant that even if she was getting in fights out there, she was still breathing, winning, and alive.

Suddenly, a short but sharp tone beeped from the mass of displays by the table. Eve rushed to the perimeter monitors. "We got incoming."

Knives leaned over her shoulder to take a look. He expected to see one ship on the approach, but instead, he saw much more than that.

"What the mif is all that?" Vetty asked.

Knives recognized the models of the ships just by their silhouettes.

"That's the entire Star Force fleet," Knives said. "Or what's left of it."

* * *

Knives was the first to run to the landing dock. A small shadow of caution crept into his head. He was a deserter. They could be there to arrest him, to throw him in prison.

Both Vetty and Eve had the same look of alarm stitched across their faces. A runaway heir and a Dead Space bootlegger. He was sure they didn't want the attention either.

Knives spun on his heels, taking tabs on the approaching ships. They were surrounded, with barely any gaps in the line for them to barrel through, even if they jumped into their jets to escape.

"So, Adams, tell me all about Commonwealth prisons," Vetty said. "Do they have good food?"

"Yeah, maybe for you, Sinoblancas. At least your family has the money to barter for a luxury suite."

"Really, you two?" Eve interrupted. "You're arguing now?"

They fell quiet when a lone ship broke away from the convoy. Knives looked over the details of the ship. It wasn't a Star Force jet. The golden crest was painted elegantly across the front hull. It was royal.

"I don't think they're here to fight," Knives said.

The royal jet, a white ship with a rounded massive girth to luxuriously accommodate the passenger or passengers within, pierced swiftly through Myth's atmos field. Its silver landing gear lowered, and it settled down gracefully before them.

The shimmering gold on the royal crest slowly disappeared as the entry ramp lowered, and soon they were faced with a line of royal guards in beautifully embroidered jackets. They streamed out, making a living wall between them and the woman who would soon follow.

Once they were in place, they started to shift with her footsteps. Closer and closer, until the guards in the front stepped to the side to allow her through.

They were in the presence of the former Queen Juo. Although not the same glamorous, sophisticated Juo he had seen on the screens. The Juo he saw now was still elegant, but her dark eyes were lined with red from the trials of war and the loss of loved ones. The love of her entire life. She stood before him today, her hair shaved off entirely in mourning. She was slender and tall, but her shoulders were broad and squared, accentuated by the golden armor that ran across her collarbone and down her chest to protect her heart and other vital organs in case of attack. Her arms were bare, revealing a length of toned, athletic muscle, and her dark skin was luminous even in the harsh light of the surrounding atmos field.

Her gaze focused on each of them, a face of calm as if she already knew who she was meeting with. Finally, her eyes centered on Knives. "Officer Adams."

He bowed slightly out of habit, even though she had already forsaken her title. "I am so sorry to hear of your loss," he said.

"And yours," he heard her say, even as his head was turned to the ground. "Your father always spoke highly of you."

At this, he raised his eyes. He was startled by her words. His father *never* spoke highly of him.

She saw the look of confusion on his face and then smiled gently. "He said that out of all his children, he saw himself in you the most."

What? No. It was always Marnie. Marnie was the star student. Marnie got things done.

His eyes studied the steel expression on Juo's face. It was hard to decipher. She was a royal. She was trained to curry favor with her words. But what could she ever want from him?

"Why are you here? I know it's not to exchange pleasantries on lost loved ones," he said.

"I'm sure you're aware. There is a line of order within ranks. And with your father gone..."

"If I'm not mistaken Commander Nole is his second-in-command," Knives said.

Her answer was quick. "He's dead."

Knives thought back to his father's yes men, trying to pinpoint the next in line, when Juo spoke again. "They're all gone," she said. "Both the Civil War and the battles against Einn have taken a toll. We've suffered so many losses. So many good women and men."

"Then who's in all those ships?" Knives asked.

"Cadets," she said. "From all the surviving academies. Those who choose to remain for the final fight."

Knives stilled. He knew where this was going.

Juo's eyes remained on his. "I want you to lead them."

So that was why she was here—the Civil War. He had no desire to get tangled up in that mess. "Find someone else. The Civil War is yours. Win it. Lose it. I don't care."

She held up a hand. "Please. Let me finish."

A momentary flash of desperation and uncertainty in her eyes was enough to make Knives pause.

"It's true the Civil War still rages. It will be a long time before the United Cause and the Commonwealth come to an agreement," Juo explained. "But none of that will matter if there's nothing left for us to return to. There's a larger enemy afoot. Someone who must be stopped at all costs."

Realization dawned on him. Juo was here because of Einn.

Knives turned, studying the fleet surrounding them. "How many are there?"

"Two hundred."

"Well, it looks like we've got our army," Vetty said.

Barely, Knives thought. That wasn't even close to half of Einn's forces. He had seen more than that when he crossed the wormhole that tore apart the skies of Rigel Kentaurus. Back then, there were a thousand of them, easily. And he had a feeling there were more now.

Eve's eyes zipped back and forth as if she were running through all the logistics. "That's a lot of people to house. Myth doesn't have the infrastructure to support all of them." Then she turned to Knives. "But before we even get into all that… Knives, is this something you want to do?"

Knives bit his lip, his head sinking in thought.

He looked back at Juo, the fleet shadowed in the background. All of those people would need him. All of those people could die because of him.

But then his eyes settled on the spaces between. On the shimmering stars still sparkling in the distance, planets filled with people who were still fighting to survive. This wasn't about the Star Force. It wasn't about the Academy. This wasn't about *him* anymore.

He turned to Juo. "I'm in."

And he knew the perfect place to set up base.

CHAPTER 49

IA

THAT NIGHT, Ia worked behind the counter of Nowhere Ramen, serving bowls to the rowdy crowd of regulars who'd traveled far and wide just for a spoonful.

"You look familiar," a few of them said, but all she did was shrug.

To one she had replied, "Perhaps I remind you of your first love," and watched as the man's cheeks flushed ruby red.

"Don't tease them," Kami hissed at her as she stirred the broth.

Ia flashed her a broad grin and continued with her chores.

When the last customers left for the night, Ia helped Kami with the cleanup. She had collected all the empty bowls on the counter when her head snapped to an empty seat. She stared at the chair, her eyes darting not at the outline of the chair itself, but the space before it. She shifted her balance from one foot to the other, trying to get a slightly different view. There was something about it she couldn't quite explain.

Kami passed by, a potful of unused broth in her hands. "Yeah, I know," she said. "He's been sitting there for a while."

He?

Ia immediately grabbed the pot from Kami's hands and flung it across the counter. The broth flew out, splashing every which way, and for a moment she saw a very familiar outline. Ia's arm snapped forward, reaching over the counter until her fingers clutched around thick muscle. A neck.

Hands grabbed her shoulders, flipping her across the room. Her back hit the wall with a sharp crack, and she crashed to the ground.

Blinking, she saw a mirage, a blur of an image growing sharp. A figure stood in front of her, wiping the broth from his cape. There was that skull. The skull she couldn't wait to crack.

"I gotta say," Goner said as he stared down at her. "I didn't think I would find *you* here."

Ia scrambled to her feet, staring daggers in his direction, and instantly she was brought back to the night they met at Aphelion. They had made a deal, one he had completely broken.

"Traitor," she yelled with an ear-piercing cry.

She launched herself at him, fists clenched and knuckles out. But before her hit could land, she felt someone hold her back. Her eyes snapped over to Kami, who was between them, grabbing them both by the collar.

"Stop wrecking my restaurant." Kami dragged both of them out the door. "If you have stuff to take care of, do it outside."

With more force than Ia could ever imagine, Kami hurled them out into the parking lot. It was a few seconds before Ia tumbled to a stop.

She pulled herself up to her knees and rubbed her temples, then glanced over at Goner, who had landed a couple meters farther than she had. He shook the dust out of his hair and stared at her. "Who was that woman?"

Ia narrowed her eyes at him. He was even denser than she remembered.

As she stared at him, she tensed. They could have been at each other's throats once again, but that second had already passed. She couldn't shake a notion that had been bothering her since she woke up after the accident. The last thing she remembered that day on the roof was Goner pointing a pistol right at her heart. It was a miracle that she had survived that fall, but it was even more of a miracle that she lived through that bullet.

Ia pushed herself to her feet and wiped the sand off her pants. She walked over to Goner and offered him her hand.

He stared at her, confused.

"I think we need to talk," she said.

* * *

Ia set a bowl of ramen in front of him.

He eyed her cautiously, even as he reached for his chopsticks.

"I thought we had an agreement." Ia crumpled her napkin in her fist. "You were supposed to track down Einn. Not join him, and then try to kill me."

"But I found him, didn't I?"

He was right. He did uphold his part of the deal. She stared at him, watching the white cut of cheekbone move up and down as he took his first sips of broth. If this was part of his plan all along, then perhaps he wasn't as oblique as she originally thought.

"So, my brother—" Ia started.

"Is going to destroy the universe," Goner said as he slurped up a swirl of noodles, lips pursed with the heat of the broth. "This is really good, by the way."

Goner stared off at the curtain separating the main space from the back room, where a series of wet slaps echoed out.

"What is she doing back there?" Goner asked.

"You don't want to know," Ia said.

"Shame on me for assuming she would be a man," he said, then rubbed at a bump on his head. "'Take you and break you.' At least the nursery rhyme got that part right." And Ia knew that Goner had already pieced everything together—that Kami was actually the Half-Man. But there was no way he would know how much greater than that she was. "I'm surprised you're even letting me this close to her."

Ia leaned forward on her elbows. "That's because you don't have a chance."

Goner snorted before tilting his head to look at her. "So, what's new? You're alive. I can tell that." He pointed a chopstick at her. "You did a good job hiding it, by the way. Your brother is going to be miffed when he finds out." He laughed, then choked as the food in his mouth went down the wrong windpipe.

She knew her brother would be surprised when he saw her. At the thought of him, an image seared into her and made her pause. The twisted joy on his face when he tried to kill her all those times. She grabbed a glass of archnol and took a sip, trying to wash away the phantoms.

"How's that Bug that I met? The guy with the hair."

She straightened up from her slouch, surprised to hear Goner bringing him into the conversation. "You mean Knives?"

Goner slapped his knee. "That's his name?" His voice went up a pitch.

Ia rolled her eyes. "You should talk. You have a terrible name."

He leaned in. "But I like it when you say it."

Her eyes whipped to his. A moment of surprise before she shook it off. She could never tell when he was joking.

"When did you two even meet?" Ia asked.

"I entrusted your dying body to him." He pushed an empty glass for her to fill.

Ia grabbed the bottle of archnol and poured. "And why is this the first time I'm hearing this?"

"Because I guess your Bug is good at keeping promises," Goner said before slamming back the entire drink.

She raised an eyebrow. Goner had asked Knives to lie for him? "What was the point in that?"

"I couldn't have you waking up and thinking we're friends."

Oh Deus. "Because we're rivals..."

His eyes brightened a light shade of lavender. "Well, Ia. I'm touched. That's the first time you've ever said it."

Ia leaned in. "Why didn't you kill me back then?"

He turned to her, and the roguish smirk dropped from his face in earnest. The outline of his skull darkened just a bit so she could only see a hint of his true face underneath. "Because life would be boring without you."

If they hadn't spent almost five years hating each other, she'd actually think that he cared for her. She looked away, staring at her fingers, waiting for this new but strange moment between them to pass.

"If you were on Nirvana, then you saw Brinn," she said. "How is she?"

"Other than killing the Queen?"

Ia shook her head. "The Brinn I knew would have never decided to do that on her own."

"Then you don't know your friend very well. Maybe some of it was part of your brother's machinations, but the kill—that was all her."

Brinn wasn't always like that, Ia thought sadly. But she was a fool to think things would stay the same. If it had, then she would still be the Blood Wolf of the Skies, reigning over Dead Space. Unchallenged. Unbeatable.

Goner pushed his empty bowl forward. "Thanks for the meal. Now what favor do I owe you?"

Ia snorted. "How'd you know?"

"You always like to barter."

Knowing that he was willing to work together, Ia gave him the details of her plan.

Goner tilted his head with mischief. "That's genius. I hate you for thinking of it," he joked, then stopped when he saw the hesitation in her eyes.

There was something else that had been bothering her since she'd left for Nowhere.

"Can you make a stop at Cajitore? There's a refugee camp there."

"Really? Your brother is going to unleash chaos unto the universe, and you want me to save some refugees?"

"There's one more thing," Ia said. She grabbed her helmet from her pack and handed it to him, the blood feather a rich red even in the dim. "I need you to tell them. Dead Space. The Fringe. Tell them Ia Cōcha is alive, and now's the time to choose a side."

* * *

After their talk, she walked Goner outside. He reached into his pack, took out a small black remote, and handed it to her.

"What's this?" Ia asked.

"A gift for when you reach your destination," he said with a wink. "That's all I'll say for now."

She smirked at his response. Perhaps this would be the last time she would ever see him. She hadn't forgotten their deal from months ago, and she was always good at following through.

"Your twin is on Oelophira. It's a monastery in the far corner of the Jiyon Empire."

His head tilted downward. "Are you sure?"

She pulled down her collar, revealing a scar on the tip of her shoulder. "Pretty sure."

Goner smiled. "I'm glad she gave you trouble."

"She reminds me of you in a lot of ways," she said.

"How do you know that I'm not just going to take this info and run?" he asked.

Her answer was simple. "Because I know you're better than that."

Goner snorted. He laid out his hand before her, and she clasped it. A momentary truce. She looked up at him, and from this distance, she saw the rising sun capture the lavender in his eyes. They were beautiful in a way. Just for that fleeting moment.

Ia watched Goner as he took off into the early morning sky and then went to the back room to collect her things. She put on her assist suit, zipping it up and listening to it whir as it turned on. She looked up to see Kami standing in the doorway, watching her. There was something Ia had been wondering, ever since she found out where Kami had come from.

"Do you ever want to go home?" Ia asked.

Kami chuckled, motioning to the paint peeling off the walls. "And leave this paradise?"

"You know, my father left me when I was young. I think he wanted to go back." Ia looked off in the distance. A sea of memories flooded toward her. Her father's skin, like gritty sand. The rough calluses on his hands. His old chair, with the creases and molds of his body still in the leather after he was gone.

"There was part of me that thought you'd be him," Ia admitted. Sadness curled into her like a familiar beast. It happened whenever she thought of him, of all the times he let her down. And now, it was like he'd done it all over again by not being the person Ia thought she'd find. All this time she wanted to forget him, but perhaps it was her, not Einn, who really needed to find him, who wanted answers. Who wanted to believe that he was still out there somewhere.

"Sorry to disappoint." Kami took in Ia's expression, then pressed her lips together in thought. "I'm not your father, but I've lived a long time. I've seen stars born and seen them die.

Empires rise and crumble. There are bonds that stand the test of time, and there are precious homes that turn to dust."

Ia raised a cautious eyebrow. "That sounds kinda sad, Kami."

"Not at all." A knowing smile settled on Kami's lips. "All of that is just scenery to a long and winding path. One day you'll understand." She shoved a cylindrical thermos into Ia's hands. Ia unscrewed the lid, unleashing the fragrant aroma of broth. "For the road," Kami said. "You'll need the strength." There was a separate container filled with vegetables and Kami's special wormhole noodles for Ia to add in when she was ready to feast.

"Thank you," Ia said, and she meant it.

They walked to the entrance of the restaurant. Ia ducked her head past the white flaps that hung above the doorframe. Outside, the horizon had turned pink with the oncoming dawn, while above, gray clouds lay thick in the sky.

"It looks like it's going to rain today," Kami said.

Ia turned to face the clouds. She had been preparing for the storm long enough. Her brother was as fast and unpredictable as lightning.

Bring it. Bring the storm.

She wasn't going to get struck down, not this time.

"Where are you headed?" Kami asked.

Ia's eyes simmered as the rising sun hit her cheeks. "Home."

CHAPTER 50
KNIVES

KNIVES OPENED THE COCKPIT of his Kaiken and looked up at the dark cavern that used to be Aphelion's flight deck. Eve jumped out of the copilot's seat and climbed down to the ground.

The rest of the fleet landed behind him. It was a hodge-podge of people, Queen Juo had explained, comprised of a handful of flyers who survived, whatever borg force they could reprogram for the fleet, and even guards who wanted to con-script. But the majority of the fighting force was cadets.

"Not bad," Eve said as she looked around at the flight deck.

Not bad? The place was a wasteland, even worse than he remembered.

"Totally salvageable," she explained. "I'll get to work."

He remembered that Myth was a hub made from a crum-bling space station. Aphelion was in decent hands. "Do you know where the power is?"

"I do," a voice called from behind. He heard the *tip-tap* of

footsteps, and a woman stepped close enough for him to recognize—with a very familiar borg by her side.

"Who's *she*?" Eve asked, her cheeks noticeably more flushed
than a second before.

"A friend," he said.

"Good to see you're not dead," Meneva said with a smile.

Suddenly, Eve was between them, with that same look
she'd had on her face when she and Knives had first met each
other on Myth. Lips pouted, her eyes on a target. This time
that target was Meneva.

"Hi." She leaned in flirtatiously. "I'm Eve."

Aaron, who was standing at Meneva's side, narrowed his
eyes at her.

Looks like Aaron has some competition, Knives thought.

"Sir!" a high-pitched voice called. He looked over to see
Angie Everett bounding toward him. Behind her were more
familiar faces, including Ia's old guard, Geoff, and Nero
Sinoblancas, who he had to admit he was surprised to see.

Geoff, who had proper function of both his arms now,
excitedly scanned the faces of everyone around them.
"Where's Ia?"

Knives shook his head. "I don't know."

Geoff's expression deflated. Ever the fanboy, Knives
remembered.

"But you know Ia," Knives said. "Wherever she is, she's
fighting."

Geoff beamed.

Knives hadn't realized how much he'd needed to say it. To
remind himself as well. There was still no word from her. But

Knives didn't want to think about it. There was a long list of things for them to do.

Eve disappeared with Meneva and Angie to attempt to get the power and the communications systems up, leaving Knives in the company of someone he'd never expected to patrol the grounds with.

"You don't want to catch up with your cousin?" Knives asked Vetty, giving him an easy reason to excuse himself. He knew that the Sinoblancases might have a lot to talk about. Juo had brought news of Kilio Sinoblancas's death, and Knives wasn't exactly sure how that was affecting Vetty.

"No need to," Vetty replied. "I haven't been part of the family for years now. Nor do I care about the company's current state of flux."

Knives jutted his chin over at Nero. "Seems like he doesn't either, based on the fact that he's here and not *there*."

Vetty stared at his cousin while toeing the ground awkwardly.

Knives was well acquainted with the feeling of wanting to avoid family and the quiet pain that came with grief.

"Well, come on," Knives said. "Let's check out the jets."

The models were a mix of training and combat vessels. Knives had grown up among these models. Judging by the way Vetty studied them, he had, too.

"Most of these need a tune-up," Vetty said.

"You cool with doing all that?"

Vetty wheeled over an engineering station. He grabbed a soldering tool and scorched out a Sino Corp seal hidden underneath the wing of a nearby jet. "I am now."

Knives snorted as he walked away, because he knew exactly how Vetty felt. Perhaps Eve was right. They could be friends once this war was over, he thought. That is, if they both survived.

CHAPTER 51
BRINN

NIRVANA WAS QUIETER than usual. Einn had all of his people scouring the galaxies for Ia. There was an elite team still stationed on the base in case they needed to defend themselves against an attack—or worse, to fight for their lives if Ia came for them. Which was entirely possible.

Brinn wondered how Ia had survived after that day at Rigel K. So much had changed since then. The Commonwealth was fractured. With the head executives of Sino Corp dead, the company was at a standstill and on the verge of dissolving. The universe had changed. But most of all, so had Brinn. She was far from the good model Citizen that she used to be.

And what about Ia? Was she the same as always? Brash, opinionated.

Loyal.

Compassionate.

Brinn quickened her pace, trying to do away with her questions. But no matter how fast she walked, they followed. If they met again, would Ia be disappointed in her?

She forced her heart to reharden. It didn't matter what Ia thought. Brinn's decisions were her own. That was what freedom was. *She* could choose to do whatever she wanted, to be whatever she wanted to be.

But then why did she feel like she was spiraling out of control?

Perhaps it was because she had as many questions when it came to Penance. The gate was supposed to be her steady ground, the work she did to prevent her mind from falling apart. To keep all those emotions at bay. The anger. The grief.

And now there was doubt.

Einn had already retrieved the core from Aphelion, and Brinn had a crew of engineers swapping in the new power source, but it was everything else that made her worry.

She hadn't been getting much sleep, not since the day of the peace treaty, so she was always in the lab. That night, she went straight for the isolation chamber, where the bridge had torn open several days ago. For a moment, her experiment had worked, and she'd felt her heart thunder inside her chest. It was everything she'd ever wanted.

Then that *thing* had come through.

She had no idea what it was, but she still remembered the look of it. She didn't even need a holo replay to remind her of those nightmarish tentacles reaching out from the dark depths to drag any poor soul into the abyss.

But Brinn needed to get inside the quarantined room to make sure everything was still in working order. In full sterilization gear, she opened the clear enviro seal door to the isolation chamber. All meters were on, to gauge if there was anything dangerous and potentially invasive in her close vicinity. Her sensors didn't detect any foreign pathogens. The radiation levels were low, so she flipped off her mask. A quick yet thorough investigation showed nothing left of whatever had come through. The only sign she could see was the black residue it had left behind.

Taking a metal prod from her pack, she knelt down and poked at the slimy mass. It was a gel of some sort, with thick enough viscosity to adhere to the end of the prod when she took it away. She looked at the string of goop as it elongated with the pull of gravity. As she neared, she thought she saw something glimmer on the surface. She angled her head, checking her surroundings. It could have been a reflection of the lights overhead, she convinced herself. But when she turned, it happened again.

She leaned in to get a better look. The surface of the sample wasn't smooth like she had previously thought. It was barely detectable, but at this distance, she could see it. Small, thin spines covered the gel's surface, and as she grew close, it *bristled*.

It was alive.

She gasped and pulled back, but the dark mass lashed toward her. She saw a swipe of black as it attached to her hand, quickly bleeding through the thick fabric of her glove until it hit her skin.

Brinn scrambled back against the wall, staring down at the black mass covering her hand. It pulsed and grew and ate, spreading from one finger to the next, the pain causing her vision to go red.

She had to stop it before it spread farther.

Her eyes darted around the lab until she finally saw what she needed. A laser blade, meant for clean, precise cuts.

She held it at the base of her hand and took a deep breath.

Biting the inside of her cheek, she guided the blade as it cut through flesh, then bone. She stood up within moments, her other hand now lying unattached on the ground as the black matter dissolved it like acid.

She ran out of the room, slammed the door sensor with her elbow, and activated another flush sequence to get rid of what was left of the contamination.

Steadying herself against the glass, she looked down at the bloody stump at the end of her arm, pulsing like a beacon for its lost limb. It was a piece of Brinn that would never return. Like her brother, her parents. Just like the foolish ideas and dreams that used to be a part of her. And now, she was a fragment of a person.

Because she was Tawny, she could start the healing process, but instead Brinn stared at the raw flesh, the sliced-off bone, the tattered veins and nerves.

Goner's words echoed through her ears. *I see it. A sliver of something deep inside you.*

That bright and shiny *hope*.

Brinn gritted her teeth through the pain.

Goner was wrong.

She wasn't ready to heal herself.

Not quite yet.

CHAPTER 52
KNIVES

KNIVES WAS THE LAST to turn in. He wanted to make sure everyone was safe before he could try to relax in his own bed. The following day would be a long one. They had to plan their next moves. Everyone would look to him for decisions, and even now, he wasn't certain what they would be.

He walked through the hallways, staring into the dark. The power wasn't fully up, and like before, Meneva was having problems getting the grid to stabilize. Because when they had gotten there, the core was gone. Stolen. Not an easy task for some random scavenger, he noted.

He reached into his pocket and took out Bastian's pen. He twisted off the cap and pressed down on the activation crystal. A series of lights came together before him, zigzagging until he stared at the hologram that came within. A little bit of its luminescence breached through the darkness.

"Hello, Knives," Bastian said, his voice deep and raspy like Knives remembered it. "How may I assist you?"

"Just needed a little bit of your light," Knives said.

Bastian's expression remained neutral. Blank.

Knives had to remind himself that this thing was a Monitor, a holographic AI, comprised of data Bastian programmed into it. It didn't have emotions or memories. It didn't remember the advice the real Bastian gave him, the jokes they shared.

But still, it felt nice to talk to him.

Perhaps it was because for months Knives hadn't been able to talk to anyone. About the feelings trapped inside him. The guilt he felt for leaving his squadron that day. He could have commed for someone to go after Einn's ship; he didn't have to do it himself. He replayed the moment over and over in his mind, trying to persuade himself that he couldn't have done anything to change his squadron's fate.

Every day he asked himself why he deserted them. To go after Einn, yes.

But there were other, more selfish reasons.

He wanted to live.

Yet for months, he hadn't felt like he was alive.

"Do you remember this place?" Knives asked, trying to will his thoughts in another direction.

"Aphelion Academy, founding establishment of the Royal Star Force. Notable graduates include Korr Nema, Jilo Triss, Raykonne Ang. Its current student body is overseen by Bastian Weathers, headmaster."

Knives sighed. "Not anymore."

"Then please update my data. Who is the current headmaster of Aphelion Academy?"

"Well," Knives said. "I supposed that would be me. But

trust me, it's not like I wanted it. My father made me do it."

"Why did you not want this position?"

That was simple. "Because my father wanted it for me."

"And why is that wrong?"

"No one likes having decisions made for them. Trust me, it wasn't my life goal to be headmaster of a Royal Star Force Academy."

"Then what is your life goal?"

The question made Knives pause. He rarely thought about it. Maybe because that was the exact question he was always running from. He reflected on the big decisions he had made in his life: stepping away from his first colonization campaign, retreating back through the wormhole on Calvinal.

"To protect myself…" he said.

He kept people at a distance, especially since Marnie. And Ia, well, he had never truly told her how he felt. If he said it out loud, told the universe there was someone he loved, he knew that it would take her away.

He looked up at Bastian's face, still staring blankly back at him. "That's the closest thing to an answer I could get. I'm not like you, though. I don't have a specific goal."

"And what is my goal?"

"Well, to complete that miffing bridge to another universe, GodsEye."

"I see," Bastian said. "GodsEye. That term is in my data files."

That confirmed the data coil was where Bastian had uploaded a backup of his work. After all that time spent looking for journals, Bastian had put everything where everyone would least expect him to—on a piece of tech.

"Do you know of any weak spots in the GodsEye build?" Knives asked.

A string of light flashed momentarily in the whites of Bastian's eyes as he combed through his data. "Of course. To create something, you must also know how to destroy it."

That was exactly what Knives wanted to hear.

* * *

By morning, they had gotten a string of backup and solar grids up and running, which also meant the kitchen was open. There wasn't any fresh fruit, but Knives wasn't going to turn away an orange slosh of breakfast mix on his tray. Juo had called a meeting early that morning, and as was the case for many of these meetings in the past, Knives was late.

Except this time there was no general there to yell at him. No hiss from the speakers as his father listened and judged him. No one to check him, to push him to be better than he actually was.

This time it was all on him.

So when he arrived at the door to the meeting room, he took a deep breath. This wasn't what he wanted. He wanted to pick oranges, learn from a bokhi bean master, sleep for a whole week, take Ia to the beach, and complain about how the red sand was getting everywhere.

This wasn't what he wanted, but he knew this was what he had to do.

He tapped the sensor to the door, and it slid open. Juo, Eve, Meneva, and Vetty waited inside, eyes turned to him in expectation. There were plans to be made, and there were other things to protect beyond himself.

"Let's go," he said. "We're not the only ones who should be part of this conversation."

He was responsible for everyone in this academy. What he'd hated most about being a cadet was that the decisions were made behind closed doors, in rooms just like this. It made him feel like a Goma piece, ready to be sacrificed at any moment.

It was true that the cadets were counting on him, but he needed them to know that the universe was counting on *them*.

In this whole chain of things, they mattered the most.

There was a reason their salute was a fist to the heart. A fighting fleet was nothing without its soldiers, the fingers to the fist. Take them away, and there'd be no protection.

And a heart unguarded was as good as dead.

* * *

Knives stood on the same stage that Bastian and every headmaster before him had when they welcomed the new cadets. And today, his flyers and support crews were lined up before him.

This was probably the biggest speech Knives was going to give in his life. He thought back to all of his father's tele-vised speeches, trying to figure out a way to cobble together something inspirational. Something about charging toward the horizon.

More like charging toward their deaths.

Knives looked to the others who accompanied him onstage—Juo, Meneva, Eve, and Vetty—all watching in an-ticipation while two hundred more pairs of eyes were staring up at him from the crowd.

"Chien, they're waiting," Vetty whispered beside him.

"My father was the greatest general in Commonwealth history," he whispered back.

"And mine was the richest man in the Commonwealth, but they're not here anymore, are they?" Vetty asked. He took a prolonged breath before angling his head back to face Knives. "I wouldn't be standing here if I thought you were an idiot, okay? Be yourself. That's all you gotta do."

In these halls were the remnants of the Commonwealth, of an age now gone. Of a government that drew borders and favored their own. Olympus was proud. Vain. Their fathers and forefathers were giants, watching as everything crumbled.

And now its people were lost. But they were *not* dead.

Knives took a deep breath and began. "General Erich Adams. Kilio Sinoblancas. At one point, they were just like us. Just like you. My father stood where you stand now, watching someone else give a speech about honor and valor. But I'm not going to give you that speech. We are at a point where there is no honor and valor. What we have left is desperation."

"I know you're probably asking yourself how on Ancient Earth we can survive in battle when we're outmatched and outnumbered.

"I'm not going to lie. I ask that question with every breath I take before you. And I'm scared, just as you are. But fear is an interesting thing. It means there's something left at stake. There's something worth fighting for."

His voice rung throughout the cavern. "Our future is still there. It's up to you to see it for yourself."

He made a fist and brought it up to his heart. He didn't know if they would salute him back. But one by one, row by row, they did.

And he saw it in their eyes, so open and clear. A glimpse. A future. A break of light before the dawn of a new day. Tomorrow and tomorrow and tomorrow.

CHAPTER 53

IA

IA TOOK THE SHORT WAY home, hacking whatever intergalactic gates she could find to cut down her flight time. She had the ship's scrambler systems on to get past security. Normally she had to keep her eye out for RSF sentry jets, but there were none to be found. It was something she had never seen in all her years of breaking through Commonwealth territories. The government must be so fractured, so broken, that their resources had been spent.

She thought about all the times she'd wanted the Olympus Commonwealth to collapse. It was all she'd worked for, revenge for what they'd done. The home they took. The mother they stole from her.

She dreamed about it every night. Watching Olympus's capital planet implode until all that was left was a ghost of a system. She'd laugh at the floating ashes.

And she would do it with her brother at her side. That was their calling. Their destiny.

She snorted to herself whenever she thought about that

dream. How foolish she had been.

Anger. Rage. Those existed.

But destiny? There was no such thing.

And here she was, sitting idle as the gate before her activated. The swirl of light circling around like streaks of white paint. A mirage of a new set of stars.

The Olympus Commonwealth had fallen without Ia even taking part in its demise.

And she had to laugh, because there was nothing else to dream about. But there was still a fight to win.

* * *

Ia flew nonstop, only taking a few breaks to get some rest. She needed to stay alert. Where she was going was a place not many ventured. One would even say it was dangerous. But she knew the path like the back of her hand. The dips and turns, the gravity swells and solar flares that would hit at just the right time.

She glanced around at the constellations to orient herself. She was sure she was almost there. In the distance, she saw a massive spherical void, light swirling all around it. A black hole. She eased in the jet's reverse thrusters, slowing down its velocity, and stopped close enough to the event horizon without being pulled in.

Ia flicked on a holoscreen and clicked through the small list of her contacts until her eyes stopped on a name.

A screen flashed before her, a stream tone beeping through her speakers before it connected. A face appeared. Rugged.

His blond hair was long enough to tie back, and it made her smile.

"Looks like you and Vetty have been exchanging style tips,"

she said.

Knives's expression steeled, and he reached back to pull his hair down.

"Don't," she said. "I like it."

His cheeks reddened just a touch, enough for her to notice even through the screen's bluish tint. Behind him, she saw people bustling back and forth.

"Where are you?"

"Didn't you get any of my messages?" he asked.

She clicked through her holodevice, and there they were. Four unopened messages in her inbox.

"You didn't read them," he said.

She glanced up with a shrug. "Can you just tell me the important bits?"

"Well, there's good news. I think there's a way to bring that bridge down from the inside using Bastian's own research."

"Good," Ia said. "Then there's a plan B if I fail. Give me the details."

"What do you mean 'I fail'?"

Her fingers drummed on the dashboard, something he couldn't see. She had news to tell him, and she knew he wouldn't be pleased. "The Half-Man isn't coming," she said.

"Ia—" he said, his voice taking on a desperate edge. He shook his head, as if he already knew. "Please…"

Outside, a planetoid hovered in the distance, the same one she'd found with Einn by her side all those years ago. She placed a hand on the glass. She was home.

Her eyes met his.

"I'm at Nirvana. And I'm going to take my brother down."

CHAPTER 54
KNIVES

"ARE YOU SERIOUS?" His voice rose. The cadets behind him stopped and turned.

But the girl on the screen didn't flinch. "I am."

"We need you here," he pleaded. "There are formations we need to decide, weak points to discuss."

But at this point he was rattling things off just to buy time. To keep her there for as long as he could.

"I need you," he said. "I can't do this on my own."

"You're not alone, Knives," she said, her voice softer now. "You have your own role in this, your own battlefield." Her eyes went past him to the starjets being prepped in the background. "It seems like you're already ready for it."

He'd always thought he would be fighting the big fight by her side. Shoulder to shoulder. Fists out. He'd thought he'd be there to help her. But she was right. He had his own battle to win.

Ia looked off to the side at some unknown sight, and even

from here, he could see her eyes glowing in anticipation of the oncoming fight. A determination he hadn't seen in her since they were back on Aphelion.

"I'm getting close," she said. "I should go."

"Ia, wait." He stopped her before she could sign off.

If he said it, the universe would take her away.

But the universe was going to take her away anyway.

"I love you," he said.

She blinked. And blinked again. Until finally, a smile found her lips. "I never thought you'd say it."

Her eyes came close, wide like the endless universe, and he looked into them until he saw the beginning of it all. And that was where her answer lay.

She didn't have to say anything.

He already knew.

She held her hand up to the screen, and he placed his against hers, her palm print so small that he could no longer see it.

She gave him one final look, then ended the stream.

He looked back at the flight deck, at the people he would lead to the battlefield. He knew where Ia was going because he had been there before.

"Suit up," he ordered. "In fifteen minutes, we fly."

CHAPTER 55

IA

IA'S VIEW WAS FILLED with black, an absence of light and matter. She was staring at Aokonic, the largest black hole in the Commonwealth territories. And the most dangerous.

It was hard to picture a black hole until you actually saw one. They weren't flat disks like most people thought. No, they were orbs of nothingness that sucked everything into their bellies from up, down, and all which ways. Greedy, insatiable pits of destruction. Gods of death, some people called them. And just like the gods, they had their own tendencies and habits—their own personalities. You had to understand them individually if you wanted to keep all of your matter intact.

After all his wandering, Einn had kept Nirvana near Aokonic, the only thing in the Olympus Commonwealth that he respected. He had been fixated on it when he was younger, always curious what was on the other side. No wonder he was obsessed with opening a bridge to another universe.

Ia brought her engines back up and skirted around Aokonic's event horizon. If she hovered a sliver over, she'd be pulled in instantly, the force too strong for her engines to overcome. She held her breath and concentrated, and it was as if all the cells in her body had come to a stop. Thank Deus her suit was there to steady her. To keep her arms as still as a borg.

As she crested around the edge, she caught sight of a familiar outline. The planetoid that she and her brother had claimed after the day of K-5 Neptune. She had been so withered from that battle, so ready to recharge, when it came across their paths. It had grown since then. There were more sophisticated living cubicles, modded together in blocks and built into the planetoid's existing crust. A colony now, it pulsed with life, and ideas, and danger.

Finally, she was here. She was home.

But there was a dragon waiting for her in its depths.

A dragon that couldn't wait to breathe fire.

She looked at the large archways that hovered in the beyond, dwarfing the Nirvana colony with their colossal size. It was larger than any gate she had ever seen, with so much potential to change their universe. But change this grand was never good. Technology was the same as any weapon: a hunk of finely crafted metal and parts, harmless until the wrong mind got to it.

When she saw her brother again, it would be like staring into Aokonic. A monster with his own wicked tendencies and unpredictable habits. And as she had always known about any black hole, you had to individually understand it if you wanted to keep all your limbs intact. Ia didn't fully understand her brother—he had almost killed her twice because of how little she understood him—but she was the only one who could even come close to guessing what he could do.

Before she was in plain sight, she received a message. It was from Goner. All it said was one word. Safe.

Which only meant one thing. He had been successful, and hopefully, it'd be enough to change the tide. It made her more anxious to get to Nirvana, to set everything in motion.

She flew forward, outside the protection of the event horizon, where her starjet would be easily seen. There were a few secret passages that Ia knew, ways to get in without detection. This was her home, after all.

But she headed for the main entryway to the flight deck instead.

Before she left Nowhere, she had switched jets with Goner, knowing she would need his for this exact reason. The force fields, reading the White Hearts data signature, opened as she approached.

And then she saw them. All of Einn's supporters. She had heard they were quite the collection. Refugees. Dead Spacers. Fringers. Even Commonwealth folk. She couldn't tell them apart, because they were all wearing his hearts.

She set the jet down in the center of the flight deck so everyone would see. Getting up, she lowered the ramps and took a deep breath.

She walked down, her eyes whipping back and forth to keep on guard. She had her pistols on her side, but she didn't reach for them.

"I think you know who I am," Ia said. And she raised her arms in surrender.

CHAPTER 56

BRINN

BRINN RAN AS FAST as she could. She had heard the frenzied gossip before the lab closed down for the night and approached the first group of people she saw.

"She surrendered?" Brinn asked them, incredulous when they confirmed it. That was not something Ia would do. Brinn took the long elevator ride that connected Penance with Nirvana. She had no idea where they had taken her former friend, but it didn't matter. All she had to do was follow the lengths of people lining up for a glimpse of her.

Brinn pushed through the crowds and used her clearance to get into the room of Ia's holding cell. Behind the bars and force fields, Ia paced back and forth. Her suit wasn't the sleek black one that she usually donned but a mining suit. Still, under that bulky mess, Brinn could see a gaunt sliver of Ia's neck. She looked thinner, as if she had lost muscle.

Brinn did her best to hide her injured hand, wrapped in white gauze, behind her. She wasn't forcing the regeneration process as she'd done in the past. It was still healing, but slowly.

Einn wasn't there, though she knew he'd be on his way. For now, it was her and Ia. Alone.

Ia stopped when she saw Brinn and edged close to the force field. Ia's dark hair had grown longer, and she had pulled it back into a messy ponytail that swished angrily around her neck. Yet her expression was calm, not a furious knot like Brinn had thought it'd be.

"Brinn—" Ia called.

Brinn kept her distance. She already knew what Ia was going to say. She was going to tell her what to do, how to think. She was going to tell her that what she was doing was *wrong*.

"I don't need to hear it, Ia. You can't convince me."

Ia knit her brows, a flash of something indecipherable on her face. "That's not what I wanted to say. I'm so sorry." Her voice was small and gentle. "About Faren."

At the sound of his name, memories rushed back, ones that Brinn had pushed away because they were too sharp. Reminders of a brother that was lost.

"That's enough." Brinn cut in, turning to avoid the look of pity on Ia's face.

"You're not alone, Brinn."

"Stop," she hissed as she started to walk away. Ia was wrong. She was alone. Everything had been taken from her. "If you're going to say that *you're* here for me, don't."

But Ia said something different. Unexpected.

"Your parents are alive."

Brinn stopped. That couldn't be true. Einn had told her that they were dead.

But if Ia was right...

Her heart faltered, and she shook her head, trying to wrestle away visions of a different future. One where she was reunited with her family. One where she was happy. She needed to remember why she was here in the first place. Killing Lind, making these weapons. It was her choice. Her own decision. *This* was her path.

In another life, she could take Ia's hand and they could fly out of this place, leaving all of this behind. But she had already gone too far, waded too deep into the thick. There was no turning back, not from the things she'd done.

"It doesn't matter anymore," Brinn said. "Nothing does."

The door opened behind them, and a voice drifted through. "My little sister, back from the grave." It was Einn, his long frame running the length of the doorway.

"How was your birthday?" he asked. "I missed it."

Ia sneered at him. "I wouldn't know. I was in a coma."

Brinn watched their exchange. His words were as smooth as ever, yet there was something different about Einn today. A new set of thoughts and emotions emanated off him. There was rage and anger, maybe even fear that his sister had come for him.

Perhaps the viciousness that Brinn had glimpsed would finally come out, and she didn't think it wise to be there when it did.

She inched away, but before she could make it to the exit, Einn stopped her.

"Let's show Ia what we've done."

CHAPTER 57

IA

EINN MADE HER WALK in front of him so that he could keep an eye on her. Ia knew he was watching her, observing each move. She tried as hard as she could to seem "normal." Like the Ia she was before the accident, whose body held an arsenal of modifications making her a stealthy and lethal weapon, and whose presence alone could invoke so much fear that her opponents chose to run away instead of fight.

"Is that a new suit?" Einn asked.

Ia didn't say anything. But she knew what the question implied. That he was aware of her weaknesses. That the next time he tried to kill her, he would succeed, because when she dreamed, she saw his horned face coming for her.

"Interesting strategy showing up here like that. You were always so reckless," he said. "Acting without thinking things through."

She worried about the blades he surely had hidden and ready, but she kept her back straight and her shoulders squared.

Her chin tilted high and proud. "Isn't that what you taught me? The least obvious choice will create the most disorder."

And she heard the falter in his footsteps. Perhaps it had been a while since he had encountered someone who knew his strategy, the patterns to his chaos. She wished she could see the look on his face right then, different from the face she met in her dream, that devil waiting to condemn her. In reality, he was just a man. Faulty. Flawed. Flesh.

And he was out of practice.

For so long, she had been the reckless one, as he had said, while he was the one to strategize, to plan. He made sure every move they made wreaked the most havoc possible. While she was the hand of it all. A destroyer. But she had learned from him, bit by bit, growing almost as clever.

Einn wanted the power that came with creating chaos and disorder, but her brother didn't know its true nature. If he really wanted that, she would show him what it was like.

For now, she would wait. She would listen to him. And wait.

He paraded her through the crowds. Some looked at her curiously. A glimpse of the Blood Wolf was something few would want in their lifetime. It usually meant she was coming for them, and in moments, they'd be dead.

They entered an elevator connecting Nirvana to the massive arched structure. It was just the three of them. Brinn stood behind them, trying to seal herself into the shadows. And Einn stood by Ia's side, as he had for most of her life.

She stared at the archways as the platform approached.

"Another universe awaits," he said. "A bridge to the heavens."

His words made her pause. Even Kami hadn't referred to it

that way. To her, the other universe was simply another realm. Not the *heavens*, not a place for the—

"You think you're a god," Ia whispered.

A smile rippled across his face, sharp and full of teeth. Hungry for chaos and destruction.

Not all gods were honorable. From the texts of Ancient Earth and the different mythologies she had heard from all the worlds she'd been to, she knew that the gods were as pitiful and cruel as everyone else. And they all had egos.

So, let him think he's a god. Let him think he's invincible. That didn't change why she was there.

She hadn't come as the Blood Wolf. But as Ia. A girl who had a brother. A girl who would *kill* her brother.

When the elevator reached the top, its doors slid open to an empty laboratory. From behind, she heard a gasp. Brinn pushed past them and ran up to the observation deck, her eyes wide as she stared at the archways, the rings turning. A beast rising from its sleep.

"Penance." Brinn's face paled. "It's on."

CHAPTER 58
KNIVES

KNIVES SAT READY in his Kaiken. Behind him was a fleet of two hundred, separated into their own squadrons, the squad leaders lined up in the front alongside him as they waited before the Birra Gate, the interstellar gate that connected this system to the rest of the Commonwealth territories.

"Ça va, chien?" A voice came through his speakers, perfectly pronouncing the language's nasal tinge, asking Knives how he was doing. He looked to the side where his holoscreens hovered and saw Vetty holding a fist up in solidarity.

"Ça va," he replied automatically. The direct translation was *It goes*, a very simple way of saying that all was fine.

Knives rarely used the elite language, but he'd take any words of brotherhood before they crossed over. They would all go in as allies, but when they crossed, that was when they'd be tested. Sifted into fools or cowards. The fools would be the ones who rushed into the fight. And the cowards—they'd be the ones who'd survive.

Which one would he be in this fight?

If he died today, time wouldn't stop. It would go and go and go. Everything would exist without him.

But if that bridge turned on...

Today, *ça va* wasn't good enough. Knives couldn't be just fine, just okay, just all right. He had to be more than he wanted for himself. He had to rise to the miffing occasion, just as the general had wanted.

But this time it was different.

Today, it was completely his choice.

A hiss crackled through the speakers as a new holoscreen popped up. It was Angie. She was back on Aphelion with Meneva and Eve.

"Sir, it's Professor Patel for you."

Meneva came onto the screen, her brows furrowed in complete concentration as she scanned the string of monitors on the side. For a brief second, her eyes whipped toward his. "We found Penance, right where you said it'd be. We just need Bastian to finish the rest," she said. One of the things Knives had asked Bastian was if they could patch into Penance's network, but even Knives knew from being on the GodsEye prototype that the whole thing was analog. Fortunately, with Meneva and Angie's help, they'd figured out that there had been revisions to the new model. They had located Penance in the infinite, ever-expanding All Black, and now they had two doors. Penance, and the Birra Gate. They just needed a way to tie the two together.

"Bastian," he said. "Can you rewrite the programming?"

Bastian's voice came in from the speakers. "Affirmative.

I've recalibrated Birra's pathway to match the coordinates provided."

And immediately, Knives could see it with his own eyes. The center of the gate first became awash with swirls of light before finally settling into a new view of a foreign swath of stars. And in the foreground was the same battle colony that had destroyed his own fleet only months ago. Their forces took down nearly every vessel that crossed into their territory.

The plan was to break the White Hearts' defenses and board, then load Bastian into the Penance servers so that he could infiltrate the system's code. Bastian would do what only he could do best. Unravel the knots. Undo everything that his work had done.

And then they'd be safe.

"If we fail, it's over. I hope you realize that." Meneva's voice sliced through to him, and he noticed the edge in it. It was very unlike Meneva to worry. Even she knew they had only one chance to get this right.

Outside, the gate was fully opened.

Fool or coward? It was time for Knives to make a choice.

The universe still needed its heroes. And what were heroes but just fools in disguise? He'd play the part of the heroic fool, but he wasn't going to die. Not until he got the job done.

This time, instead of turning back, Knives charged forward with a full army behind him.

CHAPTER 59

BRINN

"HOW ARE THEY getting through?" Einn asked, his voice tight and strangled. But Brinn's mind was elsewhere. Despite how much she tried to cut its cords, she was still tangled in the thought of her parents being alive. Einn had told her a different story entirely. Perhaps he was confused between one ashen corpse and the next, or maybe he hadn't even bothered to look for them after all, which was worse, because that meant he had lied—

"Brinn!" Einn interrupted her thoughts.

Brinn glanced up from her command keyboard and fixed her sights on the observation windows, which showed a string of RSF starjets flying through the gate.

Penance had other functions beyond opening the bridge. It was how they created wormholes to Rigel K, Nova Grae, and other locations that Einn had targeted. As long as they knew the coordinates, the setup allowed immediate transport to any location within their universe, and it didn't even require a receiving gate. That was the beauty of Penance. It did things that she thought existed only in the imagination. But she had never fathomed that Penance could act as a receiving gate itself.

Who was doing this? There was no one left in the Star Force who would be able to match her. She had made upgrades to the system to ensure that no one would be able to hack in. Her eyes scanned the code, pinpointing everything she didn't recognize, digital fingerprints that weren't her own. She worked on trying to close any holes that had been ripped open. Whoever had hacked in had left shrapnel in their wake, messy code that just gave her obstacles to clear. But one thing was for certain: the person who did this only had access to the in-universe jumps. It couldn't shut anything down, nor could it reprogram this whole place to turn on itself, to self-destruct. And most of all, it wouldn't have control of the bridge.

Whoever wanted in had to come for it.

CHAPTER 60
KNIVES

THERE WERE TOO MANY of them. Thousands, maybe. It was more than Knives expected. Their jets were the same ones he'd faced that day. Sleek, fast. Deadly.

It wasn't long before they took out their weapons. It was like before. Lines of light traced through the enemy jets' bodies, as if gathering a charge. Quick and relentless as a solar flare, they fired. The attacks were never-ending, raining down on his fleet.

In his periphery, Knives saw a few of their jets go down, clipped by the blasts.

Just moments in, and it seemed as if they had already lost.

Fortunately, he had experience fighting this fleet. He had noticed their movements during the attack on Rigel Kentaurus. He could see it as clearly as yesterday, those jets following Captain Nema to the force field like a swarm. Some of them were piloted—those were the erratic ones, the ones that veered from the path when they were faced with the moment of death. But most of them were automated, programmed as if they were running through a flight simulation.

And he knew *all* about those.

Maneuvering through a clearing in the enemy's path, he saw Vetty's Yari lower in next to him.

Before they set out, they had called a strategy meeting on Aphelion, discussing the best ways to confuse their enemy, going through many options before settling on the plan Knives suggested. They had to knock the first block down to get the other pieces moving, and Vetty was the hammer. Now was as good a time as any.

"You ready to lead them through the maze, Minotaur?" he asked.

"That's what I live for," Vetty replied. "You sure you'll be okay?"

"I have to do my part."

Vetty lowered his dimpled chin in a nod. "Don't do anything too heroic."

Knives let out a haughty laugh. "I'll survive, and the first thing I'm going to do is head to the Harix Corridor to beat your time."

Vetty had no words, but the grin plastered across his face was enough.

"All right, Bugs," Vetty ordered. His holoscreen was being broadcast into every RSF jet on that battlefield. "You know the plan. Follow me."

Knives raised a fist so it could be seen through the cockpit window. "See you on the other side, chien."

Vetty pulled away, and the other jets fell in line behind

him. Just as they had expected, the enemy jets followed. But Knives was headed in a different direction. Their squadrons were spread out thick like a cloud and provided enough cover for him to slip away without notice.

As he circled around, hovering near the outer archways of Penance, he watched Vetty, his Yari still the fastest starjet among them, lead their forces and the enemy back through the wormhole still open within the gate's center. Once the last jet disappeared, the gate closed.

The enemy had taken the bait. The skies of AG-9 were well-defended. All of the mines and defense systems had been reactivated, giving his fleet a fighting chance.

But for him, the main battlefield lay ahead.

Knives recalled the day he'd followed Einn back through the wormhole, leaving his squadron behind. This time, it was reversed. He was the one who'd stayed.

He was alone, left with the structures floating before him, a little less guarded than they had been a few moments before.

Now all he had to do was find a way in.

CHAPTER 61
IA

THEY WERE DISTRACTED.

And they had underestimated her. The moment the gate was activated, Brinn hurried to her troubleshooting and Einn prattled off his useless orders. Ia had no idea why anyone would follow her brother, not after seeing him like this.

She was starting to wonder why she had been scared of him in the first place, why her nightmares were haunted with his face, joyous and devious as he watched her fall to her death. She realized it wasn't him that frightened her. It was Death itself, constantly knocking down her door, forcing it open without even waiting for her to ask who was there.

Because that was Death for you. It just broke into your life like that and watched as you quaked where you stood. Until it was all over. The end.

But she was in control now, at least for a little bit. While Einn and Brinn's attention was focused on deactivating Penance, Ia had caught glimpses of Knives's Kaiken and

Vetty's Yari out there along with a sizable Star Force fleet already on the attack.

She let out a breath of relief. Their arrival was good news. It meant Knives's plan to get Bastian into Penance's system was well on its way. But even better than that, it served as the perfect diversion while Ia tried to break out of her handcuffs.

Before leaving her side, Einn had fritzed out the motor systems of her suit, so that the resistance levels were five times more than she was used to. It was a clever thing for him to do. It made her slow. It made her tired.

But there was one thing that Einn hadn't taken into account. The handcuffs were placed over the fabric of her suit, and mining suits were not molded like others. It was bulky, creating extra space to wiggle through. Ia inched to the back of the room, far from everyone's sights. From the inside of her sleeve, she pulled one wrist as hard as she could through the narrow openings of the binding. She threaded her arm up through the sleeve and pulled at the zipper on her chest. The suit fell open, and one arm was free. She used it to guide the other arm out of the cuffs.

Shedding the suit so it fell quietly to the floor, she stood vulnerable in a pair of gray leggings and a black long-sleeved shirt, meant as a base layer to protect her skin from the friction of the metal frame. When she was sure that no one had noticed her, she knelt down to the discarded heap, taking a square device from the confines of an inside pocket.

"A gift," Goner had said before he left.

He wasn't good at spying, she knew. No, where he really shined was destroying.

There was only one button in the center of the device.

She pressed it, and the ground around her shook. Through the observation windows, she had a good view. A series of explosions tore through the Nirvana colony and the lengthy glass tunnel that connected it to Penance. From the way the floor underneath her quaked, she knew Goner had also planted them within the archways. And for once, she wanted to commend that rival of hers on his work.

Outside, it was complete mayhem. Einn whipped around, the light from the explosions blooming briefly upon his face before his eyes landed on hers.

"You want chaos?" Ia's voice rose above the noise. "Well, here you go."

CHAPTER 62
KNIVES

LIGHTS FLASHED in a fury, momentarily blinding his eyes. The explosions tore through the clear tunnel connecting the colony to the archways. This wasn't just an accident.

Knives silently thanked whoever had done it. This was where he'd find his opening.

Maneuvering to avoid debris and torn metal, he flew in closer to where the tunnel separated from the archways. Anchoring the Kaiken to the side, he readied the controls on his grav suit. He needed all enviro systems on to make that jump. He hadn't anchored too far from the opening, but he'd be out in the vacuum of the All Black. If his suit tore, all odds would be against him.

Knives set down his visor and raised the hatch on the cockpit. He placed a grappling spear into his pistol and aimed it as close as he could to the jagged opening. He pulled the trigger, and the spear flew across the gap. The sharp end buried into the metal paneling. A line of wire pulled taut behind it. This time, Knives released the trigger and the wire coiled, hauling him closer and closer to the opening. When he reached the end of the line, he detached. Angling himself, Knives pushed his legs off the structure. He floated toward the paneling that had been torn open and grabbed onto an edge. As he pulled himself inside, a large shadow loomed before him.

All at once, his muscles froze, and his mind flooded with the stories of Fugue.

Of monsters and horned men lurking in the shadows.

He took a breath as the shadow passed him. It was not a monster, nor a man.

But it used to be.

A corpse floated through the opening, rotating so Knives could see the charred flesh on the man's face, his jaw torn open by the explosion. His suit and skin had been burned down through to the tissue.

As the corpse passed, a sliver of white glinted from the ash. The shape of two hearts. It didn't matter what side people chose in a battle, Knives realized. There were always going to be casualties.

When he pulled himself inside, it felt like déjà vu. Even though the word *Penance* was stamped along the hull, it was a clear replica of GodsEye, the structure he'd found his way into at Fugue. All he had to do was close his eyes, and he'd see the layouts traced in the dark canvas of his eyelids.

He needed to get to the server room, a place he knew well. Back on GodsEye, it was tiny, stuffy. And it was where he'd first met Einn.

He made his way farther in, navigating around more

bodies hovering in a ghostly ballet. There were teenagers, a few years younger than he was, among the dead. They hadn't died from the explosion, but from the cold, from the lack of oxygen, from the vacuum of space stretching their tissues and bloating their organs.

Knives avoided their eyes, because he knew he would never be able to unsee it: the fear still plastered on their faces.

He reached for his side pouch and took out Bastian's pen. Quickly unscrewing the cap and pen tip, he pressed the activation crystal and a pattern of lights assembled before him. A Monitor appeared, bearing the exact likeness of the old headmaster, the familiar look of pensiveness present on his face. It was the look Bastian gave in all his photographs. He was sure the real Bastian had just loaded in all his academy portraits and compiled them for the Monitor's visage.

"This looks familiar," Bastian's Monitor said.

"It should," Knives said as he floated onward. "It's based on your work."

Bastian walked on the metal ground, phasing through the floating corpses that passed. He looked straight ahead, but Knives knew he could see everything. A white orb floated over Bastian's image, serving as a camera Eye of sorts.

"It's a little different from what I remember."

"There *are* dead bodies everywhere," Knives said as he twisted past another one.

"But it is suitable," Bastian said, "for what I have to do."

Once Bastian was loaded up to Penance's servers, he'd be able to turn the whole thing off from the inside. It would be simple. And then Knives would be alive and well. Well enough to nosh on all the oranges he could ever want. Well enough to go back to Nowhere Ramen and eat that bowl of hope the owner talked about. Then visit his father's grave and tell him his son did well.

"Did Bastian load any info about my father into your records?" Knives asked.

"Affirmative," the Monitor replied. "Erich Adams was a dear friend. He defended Bastian several times to the Council. It was Erich who got Bastian instated as Aphelion's headmaster. He was the final vote. If it hadn't passed, Bastian would have been forced into seclusion."

"What?" Knives scrunched his eyebrows. As far as he knew, Bastian had assumed his role as headmaster willingly. He had been a better headmaster than the ones Knives had met from other academies. Knives's friends from other campuses often complained about their headmasters being brutes or focused entirely on siphoning the school budgets into the upper faculties' wallets.

"For the destruction of Fugue, Bastian alone was responsible," Bastian's monitor responded. "Yet his work lies unfinished."

Knives tensed at this statement. He wanted to ask more, but then they came upon the server room. Right now, there were more important things that needed to be done.

The server room looked the same as Knives remembered, except now there were floating corpses, and one less Einn. Knives circled around the control booth, looking for the right port, then stopped.

There.

He took one last look at Bastian's pen. Carefully, he unfastened the data coil and plugged it into the Penance servers.

"Is it working?" he asked Bastian.

"Yes, I am being copied into the system," Bastian's Monitor said. "I can see it all now."

That was easy, Knives thought. At this rate, he'd be back at Aphelion by dinner.

"The real Bastian would be proud of you for what you're doing," Knives said.

"Yes, for completing his work," the Monitor responded.

Knives's shoulders stiffened. "What?"

"You said before. Bastian's life goal was to complete GodsEye and bridge the two universes. That is why I exist."

"No," Knives said. "That's not what I meant when I said that."

All around him lights flashed on, and the machines whirred to life.

Knives grabbed the data coil from the upload port, but it was no use.

"I have already been fully copied," Bastian's Monitor said.

No, no. This wasn't how it was supposed to go.

Knives had to stop him. He was a fool. Why hadn't he seen it earlier? That Monitor was a machine. An AI that had a mission, written into the very nature of its programming.

Knives pulled himself out of the server room and pushed against the walls, increasing speed with each bounce. The bridge was going to open. He wasn't going to be able to stop it. But he had to try.

Deus be damned, he had to miffing try.

CHAPTER 63
IA

IA KEPT A FEW TABLES in between them. Einn walked slowly toward her, that warped smile stuck on his face the whole time. She knew that all he had to do was pull his magic trick, and he'd be right at her with a knife slicing through her throat.

His eyes narrowed on her. "Every time you face me, you lose," he said, trying to find holes that would make her falter. "Look at you now. Hanging back like a frightened animal. The Blood Wolf of the Skies."

The smile only grew more twisted the longer it took, and she wished she could just twist it right off his face. It was meant to throw her off-balance, to make her feel like she would soon see defeat. But he was also trying to distract her from what he was actually doing, grabbing items off tables as he passed. From that distance, she couldn't tell what they were. They looked like utility belts of some kind.

Ia forced herself to concentrate. To think faster than Einn.

That was the only way she was going to win.

Weapons in one hand, and that *thing* in the other. A spatial tear, a small wormhole that he could fully control. Just like he had at Calvinal, his fingers plucked the air as though it was an instrument until finally a small tear appeared in the center of his palm.

In a flash of movement, he threw all of the utility belts toward her.

And just like that, more spatial tears ripped through the air around her in a moment of perfectly crafted confusion. She twisted away to avoid colliding with them, and when she turned back to find Einn, he was nowhere to be seen.

Mif. She had to get out of this pit of wormholes.

Ia turned to escape, but Einn was right in front of her, stepping through the shadows of a tear.

She couldn't run, but she could fight.

Her muscles tensed as she strengthened her stance, and she attacked quickly so he wouldn't have time to think. But he dodged—right, then left. Her punches missed him every time. She hopped into a kick, but he had already stepped back, disappearing into another spatial tear, only to appear at her side, daggers flashing from his hands. Her back arched away from him, but she was too slow. She winced as the blade dipped deep into her side, the pain electric. Her brother smiled as he pulled it out of her.

Ia stumbled away, looking all around her. She didn't have any weapons; the guards had taken away her pistols at the flight deck. But she did see something useful on a table nearby. A power magnet. Ia grabbed the metal orb from the countertop and jammed her fist on the button, activating it. She lobbed it toward him.

As it arced, every loose piece of metal went with it, including Einn's daggers. They flew out of his hands, attaching firmly to the magnetic orb as it landed across the room.

He glared at her, which only made her smirk despite the gash in her side. Because now Ia wasn't the only one without weapons.

Her brother laughed. "Is that it? Is that *all* you can do?" he asked, his voice flat as if he was unimpressed. She understood what he was asking. He wanted to see if she was like him, with abilities and other unnatural tricks hiding up her sleeve.

Ia's eyes narrowed, cutting at him. But by her silence, he knew.

"How weak you are," Einn said with a playful tone. "How slow." He charged toward her, but she stood still, watching him, waiting for just the right moment. He was almost at striking distance when she skirted to the side, grabbing hold of his arm as he passed.

"No, Brother." Her gaze locked onto his, savoring the momentary confusion in his eyes. "*Now* I'm giving you everything I've got." Then, using his momentum, she swung him to the left, smashing him into one of the lab tables. When he didn't move, she let the tension in her muscles pool out of her.

But too soon.

Like a demon, he rose, and when he turned, she didn't see his bare face. Instead, he had pulled on his horned helmet. Her throat grew tight, and her lungs compressed. She blinked quickly, trying to erase the image from her vision, but it remained. Her nightmares had come for her.

Whatever strength she had left drained away.

This time when he attacked, it hit. Right in her side. Then another blow to her chin. She staggered, grasping onto the rapidly shredding strings of her consciousness.

His hand darted out, grabbing her around the neck. In one motion, he shoved her to the floor. The spatial tears created by the utility belts disappeared around them as if they had been drained of their charge. Leaving only Einn's—the most dangerous one. Einn used his spatial tears like they were his knives. He opened another one near the ground and forced Ia's head through, stopping right at the neck.

Ia's eyes widened in fear as she looked down at her own body. Her head, she realized, was now on the other side of the small wormhole, which was hovering in the space directly above them. Ia struggled, and she could see her legs kick uselessly and her arms flail in attempt to get away.

Einn's fingers curled slowly into a fist. As he did, the spatial tears narrowed, closing in on her neck.

From above, she could only see the black outline of his devil horns. But when he turned to her, his visor came up automatically, revealing the true monster inside. Her brother's lips twisted into that haunting smile, and the words came out of his mouth slowly, like smoke.

"How much fun would it be to watch yourself die..."

CHAPTER 64
BRINN

OUTSIDE, PENANCE was coming alive, but in a way Brinn had never seen before. It was hard to work fast with just one functioning hand, yet her fingers jumped furiously across the keyboard, writing and rewriting code to align things her way. But every time she did, her efforts were erased by something new. A phantom in the machine. She tried to access the admin codes, but even then, she was blocked out. A deep anger throttled her throat, because this was supposed to be her domain. Everything she tried was useless, but she still kept her eyes on the keyboard. Because if she looked up, she'd see Ia. And witness, once again, what Einn would do to her.

Long ago, Ia had told her that family was the anchor that always brought you back. Clearly, Einn didn't think that.

She was certain he hadn't felt anything when he saw his sister fall to her death. But when Brinn saw Ia in the sky that day, reaching for something, anything—it felt like Brinn was there with her, asking for help and no one was coming.

She felt helpless, unable to move. Because that was the Brinn she was back then. Weak. Useless. Recently broken by the universe that had taken everything from her.

She glanced over at Ia, her body struggling as she was forced to stare into Death's gaze once again. And just like then, Brinn was on the sidelines, watching.

But this time the universe did give her something.

Her mother was alive, Ia had said. Her father was alive. Ia's words rang through her ears. *You're not alone.* These were words that meant more than any promise of peace. It was something greater than that.

It was another chance.

Brinn took her hand off the keyboard and ran toward Einn as fast as she could, so all she could see was him. Just as it had been for the past few months. She knew what he could do. She had seen how it all worked, and how—as with any instrument, any weapon—his hands were the most important part.

She reached for her pistol, the one that had killed Lind, the one that Einn himself had given her, and she aimed.

One hand.

Bang.

And then the other.

Bang.

Crouching, Brinn pulled Ia out of the spatial tear before it closed and chopped her head off. She looked back at Einn. His fingers were shattered, strewn across the metal floor. There were gaping holes where hands should be. He had fallen to his knees, like she had when she heard Faren had been taken away from her and everything she loved was lost.

"What are you doing?" he screamed.

Einn had lied to her about her parents' deaths. Brinn knew who this man was now, so good at manipulating people to get exactly what he wanted. But there was one thing he'd taught her that she would never forget. Einn had told her that freedom was all about making a choice. She looked at him, her eyes open and her own. "I'm breaking free."

Suddenly, the machines around her whirred. Program holoscreens popped up one after the other, crowding her vision, and she read the data as fast as she could.

Her mouth hung open.

No. This shouldn't be happening. Brinn was the only one capable of running the activation sequence, but someone else had started it.

She stood up, speechless as she watched the sight unraveling outside. There was no questioning what she saw. She had already witnessed a version of it in her own laboratory. Her injured hand throbbed at her side from the memory.

In between the larger archway, a dark tear had formed. This time it didn't go to Aphelion, or Nova Grae, or Rigel K.

It went to the unknown.

Ia rose up beside her. "This isn't good, is it?"

Brinn shook her head. "No."

The bridge was open. And Brinn didn't have to see into it to know. There was something waiting on the other side.

CHAPTER 65
KNIVES

THE HALLWAY was too long to cross on his own.

Knives tapped on his holo. "Kaiken. Find me."

The jet came barreling down the tear in Penance's hull, the tips of its wings piercing through the metal paneling. It flew toward him, the cockpit still open. He bounded over to it, keeping his eyes on the distance, and timing it so that when he jumped, he was able to grab on to the frame. Maneuvering himself into the seat, Knives hit the reverse thrusters at full power, threading the path, precise as a needle.

He swerved through the jagged hole that split into Penance and flew out into the All Black. He steered clear of the swirling vortex that had appeared between the large archways. His face paled when he saw what was coming through. A mesh of matter, snakelike in form and speed, lashed about, trying to get a hold of whatever it could. For now, it was the battle colony. Its dark tentacles wrapped all around it, disintegrating everything it touched.

If this was what happened when the bridge opened back then, no wonder Fugue had been completely destroyed.

A younger Knives—a more selfish him—would have had thoughts of unquestionable escape.

But instead, Knives circled back.

A beep sounded on his holo, and a screen popped up with Ia's image. "Knives. The bridge—"

"I know," he said. "Bastian took over the mainframe, but he's just a machine. There has to be a way to stop it." He flew around, trying to find the answer. If he disabled the power source, maybe…but they needed a big blast to take down that type of core.

Ia's gaze tensed. "If you're thinking of doing something mungheaded, like sacrificing yourself, then stop right now."

"I'm not," he said. He wouldn't be sacrificing himself just yet. Because there was a better way to stop Bastian in his tracks, and he was looking right at it.

Aokonic. The largest, most dangerous black hole in all Olympus.

He looked back at Ia. "I think I have a plan."

CHAPTER 66

IA

"WHAT IS THAT?" Ia asked, staring into the spatial tear in the center of Penance, at that gaping maw from which several dark and dangerous tendrils unfurled.

"I've seen it before," Brinn said as she stepped next to Ia. "It's some sort of exotic matter, and it'll wipe us out if we get in its way."

Ia watched in horror as these dark appendages destroyed everything in their path, and they were only getting stronger. Pretty soon they would be impossible to stop.

A laugh came from the corner of the room. Einn sat on the floor, his legs tied together, his arms lying bloody and limp at his sides.

"So it's happening after all," Einn cackled.

Ia ignored him, keeping her eyes trained on Brinn.

"Is there any fail-safe?" Ia asked. "A command to turn it off."

"Bastian has locked me out of everything," Brinn said. "But even if I got in, the bridge is in an unstable state, and it's only going to grow and tear. The only way is to destroy the entire structure."

"Then Knives is right." He had detailed his plan to her, and Ia had hoped there'd be another way. Because Knives's plan was reckless. But hell, she was more than familiar with the word.

"Does this structure have a piloting system?" Ia asked Brinn as she ran to the control board.

Brinn kept up with her. "Stabilizers but not full thrusters."

"That won't be enough."

They needed to send Penance into Aokonic. Quickly. But with no piloting system, that was going to be difficult. If only they could get a push in the right direction. Her focus locked on Nirvana, which was almost completely destroyed by the black mass leaching through. Once it was done with the battle colony, it'd reach for whatever it could get next. A stray asteroid. A nearby planet. A whole galaxy. Her thoughts raced trying to figure out a way, her eyes trailing out the observation windows. She squinted.

There was something peppered in the distance, getting larger by the second. She knew that silhouette. It was *Orca*, and behind it was a long line of starjets coming their way.

Ia had told Goner to find her supporters, and he had. He'd brought legions of them.

She could see him, his obnoxious skull a shock of white through *Orca*'s cockpit windows. A beep came through her holo, and she accepted the stream.

Goner's voice was crisp and tinged with mischief. "Are we late to the party?"

CHAPTER 67
KNIVES

KNIVES GUIDED the new starjets to line up against one half of the archways. There had to be hundreds of thousands of them, one of the largest fleets he had ever seen.

Goner pulled up next to him in Ia's *Orca*. His voice came through the Kaiken's comms system.

"What have you been up to?" Goner asked casually. "Relaxing?"

"I never thought I'd be happy to see your face again." Without Goner, without that fleet of jets, they wouldn't have nearly enough power to push a structure that large.

"Are the force fields and stabilizers down?" Goner asked.

"As far as I know." It seemed like Bastian had rerouted all of Penance's existing power to opening the bridge, which was good, because they needed the force fields down for any damage to be done. And the stabilizers had to be deactivated for them to even move this gigantic thing. He hoped that this wouldn't be all for naught.

Goner's voice rasped through his speakers. "You know, on my list of things I've always wanted to do, this was high up there."

"Sending a wormhole to another universe into a black hole?" Knives said.

"Yep," Goner said. "You never thought of it?"

"Trust me. This is on top of my to do list right now," he said, then turned all the streams on so everyone would hear him. "On three, all jets forward. Full power."

"1..."

Down the line, everyone's thrusters flared, ready to go.

"2..."

Knives's hands gripped tightly on his steering wheel as he said a quick prayer to Deus.

I hope this works.

"3..."

CHAPTER 68

BRINN

THE GROUND LURCHED underneath Brinn's feet, and outside, the view shifted. "We're moving," she said.

"Then we'll be there in moments." Behind her, Ia had changed into one of the flight suits that were lying in a pile on a worktable. It was sleek and fitted with thin sheets of armor, shaded in a deep maroon against the black webbing of the suit. A utility belt and black hole grenades were around her waist.

"Did you make these?" Ia asked.

The question was innocuous enough, but Brinn looked away, a feeling of shame staining her dark. The weapons she'd invented had killed a lot of people. It was something she had known all along, but this was the first time the words had sunk in, hard like concrete.

How do you stay afloat when everything is so heavy inside you? She asked herself this question a lot. But there was something that Ia had said to her back at Aphelion so many months ago, and they were words that stayed with her, even with all the things she had done.

"Remember what you told me about right or wrong? Can you say it again?"

Ia looked at her, her black eyes sharp as they always were. "But you already know it, Brinn."

She did, but she needed to be reminded. To have that permission to open her eyes to the rising sun, to get up and breathe, and live.

"After Faren, I became familiar with the night. I couldn't sleep. I couldn't rest. And after what happened with Lind, my hands began to shake," Brinn said. "There's a part of me that wants it all to end."

She had expected Ia to scoff, to lecture her like she always did. Instead, Ia sighed.

"I stood in your exact spot," Ia said. "Where I thought I'd gone too far. Where I wanted to die because of all the things I've done. But if I did give up, then I wouldn't be here now. With you."

She took a step next to Brinn and looked out into the All Black.

"There are so many sad moments in our lives," Ia said. "But also glimmers of good ones. They may be far and few between, but they'll be there."

Ia took her hand, and Brinn felt a warmth that had been gone for so long.

Tears blurred her eyes, and she let them fall. Silent. A release she hadn't allowed herself for quite some time. She had been reaching out, waiting for someone to find her. The anger she had carried inside herself these past months was so great that she hadn't realized she was drowning.

Ia squeezed her hand, and Brinn wiped her tears briskly with her knuckles.

"We're almost there now," Ia said, nodding to the view outside. Aokonic was before them. A swirl of dark and light along its outer edge, flecks of matter and energy caught in a tide pool. And they were dangerously close to being pulled in.

"There is a possibility that this plan won't work," Brinn said.

"Don't worry," Ia said. "I'll make sure it does." And she stepped back from the observation deck. "It's time to go."

Brinn pointed to the belt wrapped around Ia's suit. "That's the last device, but it should be enough to get us somewhere safe. We just have to point ourselves in the right direction."

They walked to the other end of laboratory, to the windows that faced the endless line of jets that were pushing them toward Aokonic.

"All of these people came for you?" Brinn asked.

"Not for me." Ia shook her head. "They came because they had something worth fighting for."

Brinn looked at the faces in each jet. They were refugees from different planets, criminals who had journeyed all the way from their Dead Spacer undergrounds. There were civilian jets mixed throughout the crowd—transport vehicles, freighters, and other vessels that weren't even meant for combat. Some were even jets she recognized from Einn's own fleet.

Ia stopped in front of a specific starjet. The metal paneling was ragged with black burnout all along its undersides, but even through the grime, Brinn could detect an outline of a red feather burning through. It was Ia's jet.

When she looked through the cockpit windows, Brinn was surprised to see that Goner was piloting it. "I can't stand that guy," Brinn said.

Ia smirked. "He grows on you."

She pressed the button on the belt, and a spatial tear formed in front of them, a rip in space connecting one point with the next.

Through its center, Brinn saw the inside of Ia's jet and Goner looking back at them from the pilot seat. "Are you getting in or not?"

But there was only one extra seat.

No.

She swiveled to Ia, who immediately folded her into her arms. It was a deep hug, one that was meant to last. "Remember what I said about the good moments."

Ia's words brought to mind a memory from their first months at Aphelion, when Brinn was standing in the head-master's office watching the simulation of the teamwork test. That was when she'd realized that this girl was not what Brinn thought she was. That there was light inside all the darkness.

The tears rolled down her face, and Brinn nodded into her shoulder. Because she knew what this meant.

She let go of Ia's hand and stepped out of Penance alone.

CHAPTER 69

IA

AS THE BELT around her waist lost charge and the worm-hole connecting Penance and *Orca* began to close, Goner held up her helmet.

"This is yours," Goner said. "Are you ready for it?"

Ia opened her arms, and he tossed it to her. She rotated it in her hands, the feather burning into her eyes. It was a mark that everyone feared. In the end, she was frightened of what the Blood Wolf had become, too.

But it wasn't always like that.

She had to remember what it used to represent. When her father gave her the crimson feather all those years ago, it had only one meaning. *To rise.* Clawing through the clouds, tearing across the skies like a Blood Wolf. That was its nature. She hadn't felt that ferocity, that determination for quite some time.

She'd hidden from it.

Maybe because she knew the end would be exactly this.

There were only so many times you could look Death in the face before it started to recognize you.

Ia walked back toward her brother. He was sitting up against a lab table, staring out into the depths of Aokonic—a never-ending well of unknown possibilities or absolute destruction. It was impossible to tell. No one had ever gone into a black hole before and returned.

Outside, between the archways, the bridge was still open and growing. To a point where she could feel it in her bones. The call of the other universe. It was a part of her, as it was a part of Einn.

"Once we pass the event horizon, the bridge will collapse," she told him. "Aokonic is too strong."

Einn's gaze turned down to the raw flesh at his wrists. "Then why are you still here? To finish me off?"

She had come here to take down her brother. To kill him before he killed the universe. But instead, her fists uncurled. She stood before him with no weapons, no rage.

She had to see things through to the end.

"I wanted to see you lose," Einn said under his breath. "A crimson child. Beloved." He laughed lightly. "And who am I?"

"My brother," she whispered. "You are my brother."

"Now I see your weakness," he said.

She shook her head. "It's not a weakness."

"You believe that in the face of Death, my feelings will change?" Einn's voice was still sharp, a weapon meant to hurt her. He had used all his anger to put up walls between them, but standing this close, Ia saw how tired he was.

"I would hope that, in the face of Death, you'd feel solace that we're together," she said. "No one wants to die alone, Einn. Believe me. I know."

His gray eyes finally turned to her, no longer cast in impenetrable steel. She saw a glimpse of the brother she once knew.

Eyes open, a path now clear.

Her body ached from a life of fighting, but she ignored the wounds. She sat down, leaning back beside him. "I'm not going anywhere."

Einn studied her posture, her body carefully curled to one side, and his eyes narrowed. "You're bleeding."

She touched her side. The blood had already seeped through the fabric of the new suit. His dagger had pierced deep during their fight. Too deep, she had already known. But she bit down the pain—all the pain that her brother had brought, not just that day but so many days before.

With him by her side, she stared out into the unknown, just as they had when they discovered the planetoid they'd claimed and called Nirvana, as they had so many other times in the past. Those moments were a part of her memories. And even after everything that happened, they were still sacred.

Because it was Einn, after all.

"Do you think Dad's out there?" Ia asked.

There was a measured silence as her brother stared into the infinite, his memories a weight on his shoulders. "Yes," he said finally. "I do."

Her eyes softened as she looked at him. So there was a part of Einn who still wondered about their father after all.

They crossed into the event horizon, and she felt all her

atoms. Rattling, torn, then pulled apart. Soon, all sense of her being would be gone.

Beyond the structure, the dark tendrils from the other side were getting crushed from the force of the black hole, until one by one they were no longer. As the bridge started to collapse, she could see flashes of the other universe. It had a dark sky just like theirs, filled with infinite stars, with dreams and disasters, with brothers and sisters. And the fathers who would never leave them.

She saw a life she had never led.

Even though the universes were infinite—

Though the possibilities were infinite—

She...well, she had come to a point where her road would end. So she stopped to look back at the scenery. The way was long and hard, with twists and dead ends. There had been people who'd joined her on this road, and those who'd left. And in the end, that path was carved by her alone.

She looked down at the feather on her helmet. Even as the seconds fell away like sand, even as she faced the end, she heard the song that her father had sung to her, and she remembered what it was like to not be afraid.

CHAPTER 70

BRINN

THEY TRAVELED for weeks, stopping only for fuel. As they flew, everyone in the caravan was quiet. Even Goner, who loved to prod and poke, only spoke when he had to.

Brinn hadn't realized that their jet had pulled away from the main convoy until she saw a blue planet below them.

"Where are we?" she asked.

"Ia told me to bring you here," Goner said.

Brinn had to close her eyes at the sound of Ia's name.

"Why?" she asked.

"So you can start over." Goner smiled. "You've never seen it before, have you?"

Brinn peered down, taking a closer look. Her breath stilled in her lungs. Green valleys. Cerulean oceans as blue as her own hair. She knew in her heart where she was.

Tawnus.

He landed *Orca* in a nearby port, a bay surrounded by a curve of land. The starjet bobbed in the water as she jumped from its wing, her feet landing on the wooden pier.

It led to a rocky beach, empty except for a house with a blue door.

She walked up to it cautiously, unraveling the bandages on her injured hand. The layers fell to the ground, exposing the skin on her palm, then each of her fingers. A hand fully healed.

Her body was now whole, yet she wandered like a ghost up the path. Her footsteps still heavy with the things that had happened to her, and the things she had done to rage against them. She tried to remember, to open her hard heart and see the Brinn she used to be before the war. But she was too far gone to even recall.

When she arrived at the blue door, she didn't even have to knock. The door opened, and out flowed the warm, orange light of a fire. It jolted her back to the living, and she looked up and saw those eyes. The same deep-gray as Faren's. The same color as her own.

And instantly, it felt as though a lost piece of herself had returned. A vision of the Brinn that she used to be.

She felt her knees shake, her shoulders, her lungs. She could finally say it. After all this time, she could finally say it.

"Mom..."

CHAPTER 71
KNIVES

KNIVES TOUCHED DOWN on Aphelion a few weeks later than everyone else. When he popped open the hatch to his cockpit, Vetty was there waiting for him.

"You're back, chien," Vetty said.

Knives forced a smile. He could tell by the strained lines in Vetty's expression that his was forced as well. They had won the battle, but they both knew what they had lost.

"You should rest," Vetty suggested.

Knives shook his head and started to walk away. "I just need some air."

When he made his way down the tarmac, he saw familiar faces. Juo dictating a message to Angie and what was left of the comms team. Meneva and Eve clearing up debris that was left over from battle.

The flight deck was filled with activity and more people than he'd ever seen at Aphelion. In a way, it made him happy.

Knives walked to the end of the tarmac and looked up into

the cloudy sky. A common sight. It was as if nothing in the past few months had ever happened.

He sat down.

A woman's voice floated toward him, the sound of it laced with its own set of woes and history. "After the journey you've had, you need to eat."

He looked back to see the owner of the ramen shop standing behind him, so tall even when she hunched.

"What are you doing here, Kami?" he asked.

"I answered a call for help," she said. "Plus no one wants to eat that slop that's served in your academy kitchens."

Kami sat next to him, crossing her legs, and joined him to look up at the sky. "You know how people always say that black holes are gods of Death? They're wrong."

Knives pressed his lips together. "How do you know that?"

"Because I survived one. A long time ago." What she said made him stare. He hadn't noticed before, in the dark corners of her ramen shack. But out in the open light, he recognized her. The slender jaw, strong cheekbones, eyes sharp as blood diamonds. Only this wasn't chiseled in marble, but in flesh.

"You're—"

Before he could finish his sentence, she poured ramen from her thermos into a bowl and placed it beside him.

"There's nothing wrong with keeping hope alive, kid."

When Kami left, he closed his eyes, recalling the moments after Penance had collapsed. He was the last to leave.

He'd looked up to his communications screen to see a new message blinking in his box. The subject was a single phrase: Just in case.

He tapped it, and an image popped up. It was Ia. She must have sent it a few moments before entering Aokonic.

She looked calm, despite everything. Unwavering as always. Her eyes flashed up to the screen, a dark star in the forever night. "I'm going to keep this short," she said with her trademark smirk.

Her voice was pure music, tuned to his heart, to his soul.

"As if you didn't already know," she said. "I love you."

He didn't want to blink. He memorized her face, her words, her everything.

It would be a photograph that he carried with him forever. And for once his memory wasn't a curse, because all he had to do was close his eyes…

When he finished replaying the message in his mind, his eyelids fluttered open, and he was back at Aphelion. Only now the clouds above had parted, and the sun cast its light onto their cold, cold planet.

Knives took his first sip of broth, and savored it.

Yes.

That was hope.

ACKNOWLEDGMENTS

ECLIPSE THE SKIES was a whirlwind to write. To everyone who helped me along the way, I will be screaming my thank-yous for a lifetime. And I will start it all right here, right now.

To my editors, Eliza Swift and Christina Pulles—for fangirling over my characters and finding ways to strengthen their stories. My characters owe a big debt to both of you, and I can't thank you both enough. Thank you to Tracie, Lisa, Annette, Ellen, and the whole team at Albert Whitman for all of your amazing work and for constantly brainstorming new ideas to get this book to our readers. Thank you to Seth Fishman, Jack Gernert, and everyone at the Gernert Agency for all of your support.

To my amazing friend and writer, Anna Rabinovitch, for hanging out at cafes with me and catching up on all the K-pop gossip.

To Gabe Sachs, for constantly being a champion of my work then introducing to me to new champions, and for talking cameras with me. One day, I will get my Leica.

To my writer friends in the LA crew: Bree Barton, Bridget Morrissey, Farrah Penn, Emily Wibberley (a galaxy of gold stars for being the first person who read this book), Austin

Siegemund-Broka, Marie Cruz, Aminah Mae Safi, Robyn Schneider, Romina Garber—thank you for reading and responding to my publishing emergency texts and having tea dates with me.

And to the everywhere crew: Jo Hathaway, Kristin Dwyer, Natasha Ngan, Shea Ernshaw, Parker Peevyhouse, M.K. England, Emma Berquist, Simon Stålenhag, Josefin Peters, Kass Morgan, Jodi Meadows, Stephanie Garber—thank you so much for all of your advice and support.

Immense gratitude to Leor Ram for reading an early draft and offering your wonderful perspective. To the amazing Jessika Van, thank you again for bringing your fierceness to the cover. Thank you to Ryan MacInnes, Anna Ellison, Eric Greenburg, little Nico, Isaac Hagy, Clay Jeter, Sarah Hagan, Will Basanta, Hiro Murai, Joie and the Botkin family, the Spektor family, and to all of my friends who let me talk about writing, but then also for not letting me talk about writing because sometimes it's good to turn off for a minute.

To my family—my mom, my aunts and uncles, my cousins, nieces and nephews—thank you for supporting me and taking pictures when I sign your books. And to Thor, for your cute face!

Never-ending gratitude to all the readers, bloggers, and bookstagrammers who've been with me on this journey since it started. Thank you for loving these characters as much as I do.

And lastly to seventeen-year-old me, for letting yourself see and feel more than you wanted to. And to all the young people out there who are currently doing the same—the world is still a scary place, but we have to know that in order to survive it.

ABOUT THE AUTHOR

MAURA MILAN grew up in Chicago but now resides in Los Angeles, where she works in video production. She can be found in cafes drinking green tea lattes and writing and writing and writing. In her free time, Maura enjoys watching Korean dramas, collecting K-pop gifs, and hanging out with her dog, Thor, who she believes should become a professional comedian. She received a BA from USC's School of Cinematic Arts and has placed a number of short films in festivals all over the United States. She is the author of *Ignite the Stars*. Visit Maura online at www.mauramilan.com and on Twitter at @mauramilan and on Instagram at @mauraisdoomed.

100 Years of

Albert Whitman & Company

1919–2019

Albert Whitman & Company encompasses all ages and reading levels, including board books, picture books, early readers, chapter books, middle grade, and YA

Present

2017

The Boxcar Children celebrates i 75th anniversary and the secon Boxcar Children movie, *Surpris Island,* is scheduled to be release

The first Boxcar Children movie is released

2014

2008

John Quattrocchi and employe Pat McPartland buy Albert Whitman & Company, continui the tradition of keeping it independently owned and opera

Losing Uncle Tim, a book about the AIDS crisis, wins the first-ever Lambda Literary Award in the Children's/YA category

1989

1970

The first Albert Whitman issues book, *How Do I Feel?* b Norma Simon, is published

Three states boycott the company after it publishes *Fun for Chris,* a book about integration

1956

1942

The Boxcar Children is published

Pecos Bill: The Greatest Cowboy of All Time wins a Newbery Honor Award

1938

1919

Albert Whitman & Company is started

Albert Whitman begins his career in publishing

Early 1900s

Celebrate with us in 2019!
Find out more at www.albertwhitman.com.